Magic America

Coming of Age in an Altered State

D0778352

C.E. Medford

For Keith and Mac
Hope manifests

Acknowledgements

Thanks are necessary to friends from then and now: Kat Robinson Antinoro, Sean Baker, Julia Bell, Marcia Bishop, Karen Bonstein, Donna Baker Delgado, Dean Dillon, Katie Fine, Louise Hadley, Russell Celyn Jones, Liz Kusmierczyk, Jon Langley, David Leedom, Greg Lichtenberg, Paul and Kathy Lichtenstein, Toby Litt, JoAnn Lupo, Phil Luthert, Pat Manning, Nancy Kolanski Naulty, Martin Paulsson, Rudy Perrine, Patti Rosta Riggi, Sandra Turnbull and Luisa Vasquez

Special thanks to Larry Kniskern, who always has a quick and thorough answer to a dark and technical question

To my parents, Betty and Werner Vosskaemper and Jonathan and Nancy Medford, who taught me to get up and fight, to laugh, to learn, to survive, to love, to read, to write, and to never, never give up

To Omie, Vickie, Steph and Chris: Thanks for being yourselves.

To the Unwriteables: Thea Bennett, Martha Close, Pippa Griffin, Anna Hope, Keith Jarret, Olja Knezevic, Philip Makatrewicz, Josh Raymond, David Savill, Matthew Weait, Ginevra White. I shudder to think of what the writing life would be like without you. And I spend a lot of time thinking of scary things.

And to Keith and Mac Wilson, for taking so many walks in all kinds of weather. And for believing.

6

Last night my soul flew over Trenton.
It was winter, but only up in the sky.
Down below it was every season.
It was every time of my life.

The Tree of Heaven

The summer I was seven, a blue tree of heaven sprouted out of a crack in the crumbling wall of the old barrel yard and grew a foot a day. When the drainage pipes were laid between the canal and the new factory, my mother told me not to play down behind the park anymore. But a knot of tadpoles had hatched in the dredging pools, and I needed to keep an eye on them. A glance over my shoulder told me no one was watching and I slipped through the weeds to check the largest puddle. Mom didn't understand that somebody had to watch. She didn't get that if I took my eyes off that canal for even a single day, the barrel man could do anything he wanted.

I arrived to find the puddle empty. Disappointed, I patted the oily rainbows on the surface. The tadpoles were gone but one startled frog somersaulted into the mud on the far side. Its hop was quick but crooked and I pelted after it. It threw itself toward the canal with lopsided somersaults that sent it in an arc behind a tower of old tires. I caught up in time to see it smack into the trunk of the tree of heaven and fall dead, its soft green underbelly facing the stinking flowers. On the right side, above his big back leg, two front legs branched off the same joint. That frog was the barrel man's doing. I knew his signature. One more entry for my hidden toxic warrior diary.

I was trying to figure out whether it was the right thing to pray for a five-legged frog when a breeze came up the canal, bothering the plants along the way. The shivering reeds snapped me out of my thoughts and I noticed how far behind the park I was. A creaking groan came from the barrel yard and every hair on me stood on end. I tried to peer through the ivy-tangled fences to see if anyone was there, but all I could see were the big drums stacked beyond.

When a second groan rose up I took off, tearing a path through the weeds until I burst onto the field below the playground. Two boys were throwing a Frisbee to a brown dog wearing a bandana. Not wanting to appear chicken, I walked along the edge of the field picking hitchhikers off my shorts like I didn't have a care in the world. But I was listening to the weeds.

Our yellow house sat at the top of the park with a red mailbox at the curb and a wishing well on the lawn. I looked up at the windows, hoping my mother was still watching *The Price is Right*. I checked myself for evidence. There was a tick on my leg and I crushed it. I fished the dandelion seeds out of my hair.

I was about to cross the street when the pain wrapped around my skull like an angry claw. I hunched down on the grass and held my head, trying to stop my skull from bursting open. But the world started closing in on me all the same. I squeezed my eyes shut. The sound of the boys, a plane overhead, traffic, the barking dog, compressed inward like my brain was an old TV someone shut off. In a few minutes the outside world was no more than a pinhole in a dark static of hurt.

It was my third migraine that week.

Father Benno straightened his robes as he stood, giving me his final directive as he covered me with the sign of the cross. "Try to use your pain to understand the suffering Jesus endured to save us from damnation."

My eyes were closed. Though I nodded in agreement, I couldn't picture Jesus in his crown of thorns forgiving anyone. All I could think of was the men who'd forced it onto his head. Hate seemed like the only right thing to feel. Since Jesus couldn't hate for himself, I decided I could do the hating for him, in exchange for his dying for me. So while my mother sat on the side of my bed and read me *Little House on the Prairie* I focused my hate on the barrel man: a tree of heaven should be green, not blue, a five-legged frog was never going to make it to the canal, and I only got headaches when I played behind the park.

Every so often Mom would rest the book on her knees and look out the window at the bright purple smoke churning out of the LoboChem factory. When the phone rang she left to answer it. Then she dialled. I heard her voice down the hall. Daddy had passed his probationary term. We could now visit the in-house clinic at LoboChem for free. For that one thing Mom would cross the picket line. For me.

The drapes were drawn but through the window I could hear the groan of the drums in the barrel yard. "There's a man in the barrels." I said when Mom came back in.

"No baby, it's just by-products from making chemicals. When it's hot out the drums expand. When it's cold, they get smaller. There's no man."

Well, if she wanted to lie to herself, there was no stopping her. But I knew better. There were ghosts guarding those containers. Dead wolves that howled inside the metal.

I shut my eyes again to stop a parade of sparking can-can skirts from dancing across my vision and watched them shimmy down my eyelids instead. Finally I slept, and my dreams were full of lightning, but the lightning passed my house and swept away to disappear down the Delaware, and when I opened my eyes in the morning, there was a puppy on my bed.

"I said I didn't buy it!" Mom insisted.

"Where'd she get it from?"

At the sound of my father's voice down the hall I lay still and listened. He and Mom were like ammonia and Clorox together. She blamed it on his going to work for a man like Gordon Lobo. He gripped his fists whenever the subject came up. Work boots thumped toward my room. I pulled the puppy under the quilt but Daddy shot past my door without looking in. His new uniform was a blue jumpsuit with a yellow wolf's head on the chest pocket. The wolf glowed. I knew better than to touch its face. It would eat us all, given half the chance.

Mom followed with the slip slapping of flip-flops, pouring her words over the banister like she was bailing out a ship. "It looks like those dogs they used to breed in the field behind the old barrel factory. Somebody must have stuck it over the fence, trying to get rid of it. As long as it keeps her quiet, what do you care?" Mom stood outside my room, shouting down the stairs.

"Ain't no barrel factory no more. You just remember LoboChem is why you got a roof over your head. Shit! I'm late for my shift. Just keep that mutt out of my way or I'll drown it like the owner should have." Daddy shouted up the stairs.

The front door slammed and I got out of bed. I put the puppy on the floor and watched her tumbling investigation of my room.

Mom came and leaned against the doorframe, a wrinkle in her brow. "I don't know if we can keep her, Hope. People used to say those dogs were part wolf."

You had to be careful with the word 'please' in our house. Like a gun, it could win a battle, or start one. I sat cross-legged and held the puppy up so that her white belly and big dark eyes faced my mother. Mom never gave up the chance to pet a puppy if we saw one. The ice cream man drove toward our house and away again, the tinkling song like a ticking bomb to me while I waited for her decision. I'd wanted a dog for as long as I could remember.

Mom took a breath. The verdict shivered in the air. "What are you going to name her?"

"Sticky." I announced in triumph.

Mom laughed. Her dark hair slipped down her shoulder as she leaned down to scratch the puppy's chin. "That's kind of a funny name for a dog."

"But we're going to stick together no matter what."

Sharp tiny teeth gnawed on Mom's hand. "Why not name her after something sticky, like 'Honey'?"

I turned the puppy upright. Her coat was golden brown and silver except for her black ears and blaze and the tip of her tail. "Toffee."

"Toffee it is." Mom kneeled and looked Toffee in the eyes. "Just so long as she watches over my little girl."

"She'll come with me when I go across America. We'll climb down into the Grand Canyon. And in Alaska, she can pull my sled."

"Well she might be big enough to," Mom wiggled Toffee's paw. "Look at the size of these feet."

We went to the clinic at LoboChem. In the parking lot, the men in the picket line moved aside to let my mother and me pass. I heard her apologize as we went through. The doctor, when we finally saw him, had hair in his ears and smelled of pickles. He scanned the list Mom handed him, detailing the length and frequency of my migraines, then dropped it on a table. I looked at the curly black antennae in his ear while he shined a bright light in my eye. Mom negotiated the terms of my bravery with me; one Marino's cherry ice, in exchange for a needle jabbed into my arm to take blood. Then, without looking at me, the bug-doctor told my mother that there were no signs of a tumour and I was probably reacting to stress in the household. He handed her an appointment card and walked us to the door. "Let's go with eye exams and blood tests every three months, shall we?"

In the elevator, Mom said, "Stress? He can eat me." I reached for her hand and she gripped mine tight.

I woke in the night on the beat of an argument. Toffee made her way over the lumpy covers and curled up against my chest. I felt a headache starting and buried my face in her fur.

Angels on Hogs

Bryant Park sprawled the distance between our house and the Delaware-Raritan canal path. When Mom took us over at the start of the following summer a row of motorcycles was parked near the entrance. Between the blinding chrome the bikes glittered scarlet, lime green, orange, gold. The tanks had pictures painted on them, of flames and dragons, eagles and angels. As we neared them I reached to touch a midnight blue tank with a Kodiak bear growling out of it.

"Uh-uh," Mom pulled me back. "Not without permission. Bikers don't want fingerprints all over their paint. Not even little ones like yours."

I wondered if some kind of circus had come to town. A tent had been set up on the playing field. People wearing hats with stars and stripes were handing fliers out. Some of the women had angel wings strapped around their shoulders.

It was a short walk down a slope into the sunny field. "It's the union," she said, shading her eyes.

"What's that?" I tripped as Toffee ran around our legs, tangling them with her leash.

Mom stopped. "It's the people who used to work for Bantam Barrels before the chemical company bought it. They're trying to make the factory safer."

"Is it dangerous?" I thought of Daddy.

Mom got hold of Toffee but Toffee tumbled free. "The old barrel factory workers believe it is. The company says it isn't. Daddy thinks everything's fine as long as he's getting $8.50 an hour."

Excited by the commotion, Toffee bolted forward, tightening her leash around us again. We fell into shadow as Mom tried again to untangle us. I looked up to see a big man looking down at my mother. "Angela?"

Mom stared, disbelieving for a minute. Then her face brightened into a grin. "Well, Rooster Pete

Stumpenauer! Aren't you a sight for tired eyes?" She unfastened Toffee's collar. Toffee raced around us in a circle.

The man hugged my mother and she bent like a willow branch in his thick, tattooed arms. Rooster. I eyed him. He looked more like that Kodiak with his arms around my mother. "And this must be Hope," he turned to me with a smile, his arm still clamped around her shoulders.

"He met you when you were a baby." Mom stroked my ponytail as I tried to grab Toffee, who was cavorting just out of reach.

"Call me Rooster."

"Can somebody catch my dog?"

Toffee scampered over as Rooster bent down. He stroked her head while she encircled his wrist with her front paws and chewed on his thumb. "You bring her to a vet yet?" He looked her over carefully while he took the leash I held out and clipped it on. Mom didn't answer him.

"She's gonna be one big dog. Waist high at least." Rooster shot another look at Mom but she was watching the activity on the field. If there was a person who was always looking right when something important was happening on the left, it was Mom.

Rooster stood up. I knew when Mom was avoiding answering and it looked like he did too. "I bet you three would like some hot dogs." He said.

He seemed more clued in than most, and I nodded.

The paper tablecloths inside the tent were printed with fluttering American flags. I looked around while I waited for my lunch. Beside the food counter was an information stand where people stood filling out forms and signing petitions. Behind that was a booth with couple of chairs and medical carts. *Free Blood Test* was posted over the entryway. There were posters with photos of skin rashes and people's eyes – the irises an electric green. A list of symptoms read: skin infections, ocular changes, respiratory problems, hair loss, severe migraine headaches.

Rooster had asked what I wanted on my hot dog instead of just piling stuff on like Daddy did, so when he delivered it with just a thin stripe of mustard, I grinned. It was my opinion that sauerkraut burned and relish looked like whale snot, but Daddy threw it on no matter what I said, telling me he'd paid for it so I better eat it.

I told Father Benno once that I wanted a different father. He told me I already had one and pointed at the ceiling. Father Benno didn't seem to understand that while God might always be there to talk to, he didn't make my hotdogs.

Mom and Rooster talked about pollution and people getting sick. Thought I was pretty absorbed in my hot dog, I saw an opportunity. "Mom, look it says headaches."

Rooster was in the middle of a sentence but he turned as my mother looked at the symptom sign. She clenched her jaw as her eyes ran top to bottom reading it and reading it again. When she looked back at Rooster he took her hand and squeezed it.

The people in the tent were mostly dressed like Rooster, in jeans and black Harley-Davidson T shirts, the fabric alive with silk-screened forests and winding roads. They looked like a gathering of wizards, with their beards and their inked up bodies. I started to count the different types of tattoos. Angels were the most popular. Near our table stood a tall man with wild black hair. Down the length of his arm lounged a blonde angel which I was studying when Rooster called out to him.

"Hey, Eddie, bring that petition over here!"

Eddie turned and caught me staring. He strode over, nodded hello to Mom and me and sat down, dropping a clipboard on the table. His eyes were electric green, like traffic lights.

Rooster clapped him on the shoulder. "Angela, Hope, this is Freak Eddie."

"Are those your eyes?" I pointed to the booth with the health warnings.

Eddie glanced at Rooster. Rooster shook his head and Mom reached for the petition. When she passed it back, Eddie pulled a thin book from below the stack of signing sheets and gave it to me. "In case you like to color." He winked.

"Thanks." I felt my face go red.

He nodded and strode back out of the tent. He walked like his legs were longer than they were. Like he didn't need knees.

The book was titled *Safer is Smarter*. Inside were outlines of angels, kids and animals playing together in the park where we were sitting, the LoboChem factory in the background.

When Rooster hugged my mother goodbye the two of them held on to each other so long I started counting the passing tattoos again. Then he shook my hand and stroked the top of my head. "You look like your mama, lucky girl."

Mom laughed and slapped his arm.

"How's Lee?"

"Same as always." Mom squinted, "Maybe a little worse." She turned toward our house. "Come on Hope, let's go."

A heavy hand rested on my shoulder. I looked up and Rooster tightened his fingers the tiniest bit. "If you ever need anything, just let me know."

Toffee was sitting on his boot and I gave her a tug. "I might need a map," I considered, "for when I go across America."

Rooster crossed his arms, "A map, huh? Well, we can't have you going without anything as important as that."

"How do you know him?" I asked when we reached the playground. Mom was an unknown being at that moment, bubbly and laughing in a way I rarely saw her.

She tied Toffee to a bench. I scooted onto a swing. As she pushed me, it was like her voice cut loose an anchor somewhere. A story rushed out of her and I sailed along with it. "Rooster started up Bantam Barrels, right down by the canal. I used to work there. God, he had ideas." Her fingernails clicked against the seat as I swooped into the air. "He cared about the environment, wanted to give customers a good product for a good price without cheating his employees. He really looked after us. He used to organize runs and we'd all go out to Washington Crossing Park or down to Cape May." She laughed. "Rooster and I were...well...there's a reason the company logo became an angel."

It was the first time I really thought about my mother as Angela, rather than Mom, and it made her feel far away. The pushing slowed and the arc of my swinging died down. When she spoke again, she sounded like her regular self. "Remember what he said to you, Hope. If Rooster tells someone he'll help them, he will."

After we had dinner, Mom left the radio on while she and Daddy went into the living room to watch T.V. I was sitting at the table coloring in an angel who was helping a little girl plant flowers. I dug in the pack for my yellow crayon, deciding on blonde hair so that she would look like Eddie's tattoo. It was the best picture I'd ever done and I decided with the final stroke of my pink crayon that she was my guardian angel.

Mom kept the radio tuned to a station that played *The Best of the 50's, 60's and 70's da da da*. I knew the words to *Love the One You're With* and sang along as I added a sparkling necklace to the picture. I was just starting to draw the stem of a rose in the hand of my angel when a huge crash came from behind me.

I jumped so fast that I toppled out of my chair and stepped on Toffee's paw. She yelped and I knelt and held her to me. Daddy was standing by the stove, holding two pot lids that he had smashed together. "That's for your angels." He was standing, tight and ready to spring.

"Please!" I said, before I could think not to. He lunged. I thought he was going to grab Toffee and I folded myself over her. The pot lids flew over us into the sink and broke a glass.

When he was gone, Toffee lowered her head and growled. Though I didn't dare say it I thought, *Good Girl.*

Their shouting sawed through my dreams and I opened my eyes in the dark. Toffee inched up from the foot of the bed and laid her snout on my shoulder.

"You signed it? You dumb bitch! You know what happens if management sees my last name on that form? I'll get fuckin' fired is what!" I heard the sound of a slap, then another. Then, Mom crying. My breath caught in my throat.

Toffee nudged me under the chin. I held her, squeezing my eyes shut. When I opened them again there was a lady in a pink dress sitting on the side of my bed. Her fingers stroked my head. Her skin felt like a cool cloth on sunburn. "Chemical make you sick," she said in an accent that reminded me of Dracula in the movies. "I leave puppy for you. She protect little girl from wolves."

Toffee thumped her tail.

"Are you an angel?"

She put her hand to her chest. She had a pink diamond ring the size of a golf ball. "I am Madam Ivka Repinka. Not angel, *Ivka*. I have something else for you too." In her other hand was a long green metal stem. I thought it was the rose stem but when she handed it to me I saw it was a maglite with a colored filter over the lens. I turned it on and an American flag appeared on the wall. When I shut it off, she was gone.

In the morning Mom had a cut on her lip. Daddy was on early shift so when she put my cereal on the table I asked what happened.

With her back to me she finished washing a stack of dishes before she answered. "Nothing, honey. Be a good girl and play in the back yard with Toffee today, ok?"

I was looking for Toffee's ball under the old lawnmower when a motorcycle pulled up. The rumble and blatt was so loud Toffee looked like one of those souped up cars that bounce instead of a dog barking.

The rider rolled to a stop and cut the engine. "Good morning to you, little lady," he said, climbing off the bike. He brought a bag over to the fence, held it out for me to take.

Because Daddy said people who didn't answer when you spoke to them had a stick up their ass I said hello back, but I kept my hands behind the fence. It was only when the rider took off his sunglasses and helmet that I recognized Rooster. Then I smiled and reached out for the bag and he laughed. My eyes darted from the tattoos to the bag to the bike which was shining black and blinding in the sun.

"If your Mom's in, and it's ok with her, I'll let you sit on the bike. Sound good?"

Mom was folding a sheet when I told her Rooster was outside. She looked at me, arms midair, and then dropped the linen on the bed and ran to the mirror where she whipped her barrette out, whacked at her hair with a brush and put it back up exactly the way it was. A lip gloss swiped across her mouth as she slipped her feet into a pair of sandals she usually only wore for going out to eat.

I looked in the bag. *Road Atlas of the United States* was printed in giant letters over a picture of Mount Rushmore. I bolted outside to thank Rooster. His huge hand fell on my shoulder. "Now you got maps of all the highways in America so you can go from Maine to California if you want."

I didn't know how to thank him. "I bet you have more tattoos than anyone else in Trenton." I said.

"Maybe so," he said easily.

The atlas was heavy so I opened it on the picnic table by the front fence. I was about to ask Rooster how to find the Gulf of Mexico when Mom came out with a pitcher of lemonade. Rooster looked at her a long time and his look froze her in place like a photograph. I sat with my finger in the middle of Arkansas while he studied her face, took in the cut on her lip. He stared for so long it was like nobody in the world existed except the two of them. I started to feel jumpy, like if I didn't make some noise I might really not be there anymore. My fear of disappearing got the better of me and I went over and tugged the edge of Mom's shorts. "Is Kansas part of Arkansas?"

Rooster looked at me first. "How about having a seat on the bike then?" He swung me up high and I landed lightly on the seat. My feet could not quite reach the pedals and my legs swung at the sides, chafing the warm black leather.

"Watch the pipes," Rooster warned, pointing to the thick chrome running along the bottom and out to the back of the bike. "The pipes are always hot."

I leaned forward and took hold of the handlebars. A warm breeze came down through the poplars and blew my hair back. The bike felt so solid and heavy, like nothing in the world could stop it. Not Daddy, or the dead wolves howling in the barrels, or the orange eels in the canal. I let go of the handle bars and held my arms out to the sides. "I can fly!"

26

Rooster chuckled. "Seems like she got more than your looks, Angela." His voice reminded me of barbeque sauce. Mom stood by the front of the bike, smiling down at me.

Rooster's hand rested on my back. "There's two kinds of people in the world Hope. Ones who've got wings in their souls and ones who don't. Ain't that right Ange?"

Mom met his eyes and I looked back at the bike. I knew one day I'd travel across America. I made up my mind just then that I was going to do it on a motorcycle of my own.

Toffee put her paws on my face and I woke. The door of my room was open and Mom and Daddy stood, mid-scene, at the top of the stairs.

"You think you can make a fool out of me, don't you?"

"What are you talking about Lee?"

Mom's eyes flew wide as he slapped his hand around her throat. Tears ran into her open mouth as she gasped for air. He grabbed her hair and I crept out of bed. Toffee followed me to the window seat where I'd hidden the flashlight from Ivka Repinka. My heart was pounding. Daddy spanked me if he caught me out of bed. I switched on the American flag light and placed it in the window pointing out over the park towards LoboChem, which was lit up like the Emerald City for the night shift.

I snuck to my door and watched from the shadows. Mom was fastened tight to the wobbling banister while Daddy tried to wrench her from it. She was crying, choking. "Lee, stop! Lee, you're going to kill me."

With a yank her hands came off the rail and for a minute she was suspended in his arms, her feet clinging to the top step. Daddy shook her as easily as Toffee shook her raggedy-dog. The closing-in feeling that warned of a headache came over me. Our house was inside a black halo, thin as a soap bubble. Everything was squeezing in on us and everything was about to burst. The house. My head.

"Leave her alone!" I screamed from the darkness.

Mom went soft in Daddy's arms and I thought, on the crest of my late intervention, that he killed her. My body was cold and still while my brain sparked electric black knives at my eyes; instituting a whole new level of panic from any I'd yet known. Father Benno said the devil only stuck around long enough to lever a soul away from God. When the devil slips away you notice the way your soul used to sing, because it's silent. My father was overcome in quiet and I listened to the emptiness in him, as if he were a seashell.

Then a rumble sounded way off in the distance. Daddy and I looked in the direction of the noise. And as it grew, Mom began to stir. She grabbed the banister and got her balance. Daddy cocked his head and listened toward the noise. It sounded like dozens of bikes, hundreds maybe. The growling got louder until the windows rattled and the house began to shake.

Daddy shoved Mom onto the landing. Her shoulder crashed against the bookcase, sending a pile of magazines sliding to the floor. She held onto the shelf, breathing heavily, watching him.

The motorcycles revved higher and louder. It was like a street full of dog-bikes snarling at our house through chrome teeth.

Daddy jammed his hand against Mom's cheek and knocked her head into a picture on the wall. "They ain't gettin' me," he shouted, catapulting down the stairs. The slam of the back door carried up through the house.

Mom rubbed her arm and her head. She was about to go downstairs when she saw me. Her face, which had been white with fright, suddenly looked very sad. "Oh, we woke you, baby."

I ran to her and wrapped my arms around her waist. She loosened them and hunched down to clutch me in a hug.

As quickly as it started, the sound of the motorcycles died down. Mom and I searched each other's faces for a moment and then dashed to the windows in my bedroom. The rumbling was still the sound of many, but we saw only a single tail light trailing off up the street.

A Case of Silver Bullets

It was clear to me that my witness had played a role in saving my mother's life and I became compelled to watch my parents whenever possible. While pretending to do homework or chores I studied them until I got a feel for what their plans might be. I grew to sense when a fight was brewing, could predict when Daddy was going to come home drunk and developed a feel for when werewolves were heading through the park, toting trouble up to our door, which happened more often than I cared for.

I began to see how Mom was clocking up every slap and kick and insult like it was kindling, and that she had a great big fire in mind.

I had my worries, but I was on top of the situation. Every day I practiced my special Channel 11 super judo moves. I took out library books about werewolves and exorcisms. I bought a St. Gerard medal and secretly touched my mother with it at least once a day.

Two years after that night on the stairs when the devil pocketed my Daddy's immortal soul Sister Adelaide told us that fifth grade wasn't too early to start thinking about what we wanted to be someday. A man named Officer McCool came to our class to talk about being a police officer. I raised my hand as soon as he said we could ask questions.

"What do we do if we think someone wants to be a murderer?"

He had a blue hat with a badge on it and he took it off and handed it to me. "Well, you can't arrest someone for thinking about a crime, but you can arrest them if you can prove that they are planning one."

I started to ask about the evidence I had collected but Sister Adelaide cut me off the way she always did when I was allowed to ask the questions I really needed the answers to. I listened carefully to everything Officer McCool said and ran straight home after school to tell Toffee. The most important thing, I recapped, was to remain calm and get the facts straight. She jumped in a circle and stopped, facing me. We were ready.

Toffee and I were training to be detectives. Old Mr. Wieczniewski next door had given us a magnifying glass that he used for crossword puzzles back when he could see, and Sister Adelaide showed me how to make a specimen container from an egg carton. She meant it to be used for acorns and other objects gathered from nature but I knew from T.V. how important evidence was in court. In the egg carton I had collected important items from all over the house, though most of it was derived from my parents' bedroom drawers and the garbage pails. There was a matchbook from Tony-O's bar, a torn receipt from Two-Lips florist and some condoms that I mistook for rolled up balloons but counted as suspicious due to the sexy girl on the front of the package. I also cut out three of the carton dividers to make room for Ivka's magic penlight. I hid it in the bookshelf on top of my toxic warrior diary.

This was a special assignment for Toffee and me because instead of trying to uncover a crime, we were getting ready to hide one. I had the contents of my house memorized so if something moved I wouldn't be caught off guard. My highest priority was to look out for a letter or anything else where Mom confessed she wanted to kill Daddy.

I probably couldn't stop my parents from killing each another, but I might be able to stop the police taking my mother away if it came to it.

Daddy had come back three days after the motorcycles scared him off, and he brought friends. At first it was only two, but then more and more werewolves started hanging out in the front yard, and he began to act just like them, shouting and laughing and cursing.

Sometimes they even peed in the wishing well. His hair went wild like theirs, big and curly with a beard and moustache. The werewolves worked at LoboChem and when they weren't at work there was an incessant schedule to their demands. They came over after the day shift and wanted Mom to barbeque. After the late shift they sat out front and drank beer and howled until three o'clock in the morning. Toffee liked them at first, when Daddy brought her out to show off how big she'd gotten, but then she barked when they came around after midnight and they threw beer bottles at her. After that I kept her in the house with me any time they were around.

One night Mom had enough and asked them to be quiet. Daddy told her to shut up and when she wouldn't I went to the window. As she was walking back to the house one of the werewolves threw a tarp over her head. He was calling her the Virgin Mary and had his arms around her and his hands on her backside. His eerie green eyes glowed in the dark. She struggled but they all just laughed, including Daddy.

After that, if she went out there someone always grabbed at her while Daddy called her a whore. She would get free and come in the house and cry. During those times I was unable to use my secret penlight to call for help because the werewolves might have seen it. Mom was strict in her directive that she didn't want them to see me, ever, that I should hide when they were around.

The only real break we got was when we went to the park or to Rooster's house. He had a car as well as his Harleys and he let me pretend-drive while he and Mom would sit on his porch and talk. Once in a while Mom would tell me that I had to get out of the car and go play in the backyard with Toffee while she and Rooster went inside for a while. I never minded; Rooster's backyard was like having my own playground. There was a tire swing in the oak tree and he painted his shed pink and yellow for me so I'd have a clubhouse.

Mom stressed that we should make the best of things at home so I was careful to keep at least one window or door closed between myself and anyone but her. Then that summer came and it was too hot to sleep with the windows shut.

Mom was reading to me when a werewolf threw a twelve ounce can at the window screen, splashing beer on us and the bed. Mom's fingernails dug into the book cover and she thumped the book down and marched out. I heard her call someone a dickhead and then the werewolves began to howl and jeer. When she came back in her shirt was torn and there were claw marks on her neck. I met her at the top of the stairs. Her nostrils were flaring and she was breathing hard.

"I won't live with this anymore. Neither will he." She crossed herself, "I swear on Jesus' soul."

My intestines wrenched themselves into a roller coaster. There were no *backsies* when you swore on Jesus. Mom had signed all of heaven into a contract on Daddy's head. Since Daddy had no soul, who would intervene on his part and prevent her going to jail?

I closed my window and went to sleep in the hard, heavy heat.

During summer break, Toffee and I were allowed to stay up and watch Charlie's Angels on the portable T.V. in the kitchen. The next night, after the Angels found the evidence to convict a killer, Toffee and I ran into the living room for an impromptu clue check.

"Ouch!" Something stabbed me and I snatched my hand from the magazine pocket on the side of the couch. Toffee sniffed the spot of blood on my finger. Her shoulder came up to my waist by then, her legs long but skinny. I pulled the pocket open. Sewing scissors. Mom was precise about the care of her sewing supplies and her scissors were always sharpened and tucked into a velour pouch in her sewing table. Glinting there between the *T.V. Guides* was the blatant placement of a weapon.

Continuing our search, we next found Daddy's hammer in the hallway bench with the gloves and scarves. Nobody was meant to touch his tools, and he never went in that bench because hats and gloves were for women and pussies.

We moved to the landing at the top of the stairs. On the bookshelf, behind the magazines, was a kitchen knife that hadn't been there the last time we checked.

Toffee cocked her ears and then stood on her hind legs with her paws against my arm. Then I heard it too, a bed creaking. Daddy was waking up for night shift. We snuck like mice into my room and closed the door without a sound.

From the relative safety of my bed we reviewed the Big Cleanup plan. We would keep track of every bit of evidence, and then if Mom killed Daddy we would get rid of it all before the police came. We knew from *Rockford Files* that pre-meditation was the point on which a murder rap hinged, so our job was to make sure nothing in the whole house looked like she meant to do it. A hand-paw slap sealed the deal.

I knew we were going to need some character witnesses. I was pretty sure no one thought Mom would kill anyone, but there was no sense leaving it to the last minute. Since I was never able to talk to Rooster without Mom around I went and had a conversation with Sister Adelaide.

"You know my Mom right?"

"Yes, Hope, I've met your mother several times. "

"And you know she's a nice lady."

"Well, yes, she has always been very nice to me."

"So you know she wouldn't kill anyone?"

35

Sister Adelaide sat back in her chair and looked at me very seriously.

A letter from school arrived on a Saturday. Daddy grabbed the mail and tore it open.

"Looks like you're no more use in school than you are here," he told me after reading a few lines. "Seems old Sister Purity is afraid you might be exposed to too many violent images. We'll see about that." He ripped the letter and flung the scraps at me then charged up the stairs and thumped in the direction of my room.

"Nancy Drew!" he shouted as books crashed to the floor. "Hobbits, Wild Things! Is that what's making you so twisted? How come I can't have a normal kid?" There was a pause in the crashing and he said more quietly, "Now, what's this?"

I felt a pricking at the back of my neck. Toffee paced in front of me in guard position.

Down the stairs Daddy flew two at a time with my egg carton clutched in his hands. I heard him dump it out on the kitchen table. When I snuck over to the doorway I saw him snatch up one of the condom-balloons and throw it in Mom's face. "What's that for? Where'd she get it?"

Mom glared at it on the floor. "I could ask the same question." She crossed her arms just before Daddy backhanded her and stormed out the door.

Eager to erase trouble, I tiptoed into the kitchen to gather up my collection. Mom shook her head at me and looked it over carefully before sweeping everything into the garbage pail, including my penlight. "Don't nose around," she said, lifting her eyes to my face, "Please, honey. Don't look into anything."

She might as well have told the barrels to stop groaning. Like me, they did what they did because of what they were forced to contain. Toffee and I went to my room and watched from the screen. Daddy was out front sitting

36

alone at the picnic table. He was more hairy than ever and his front teeth were becoming pointed. He even smelled worse. He used to smell of Old Spice and soap. Now he stank like Toffee when she got caught in the rain and the air that blew out of the vent in front of Tony O's bar. With his elbows resting on his knees he looked like he was waiting for a bus or for something to come on T.V. But I knew that near midnight the werewolves would pad through the park and up to our yard, sweaty and thirsty. He was waiting for them.

In the grocery store I ran past the Budweiser and loaded a case of Silver Bullet beer into the cart, counting on Mom not noticing. She didn't.

Mom didn't smile when she kissed me goodnight. There was a determination in the way she tucked me in, stretching the blankets so taut that I couldn't bend my toes. Before she left my room she knelt and whispered, "I want you to stay in here no matter what, ok? You hide under the bed if you hear anyone coming."

I didn't sleep but waited in the dark until a thumping noise from my parents' room seeped through the walls. I thought about Mom's instructions to stay put, but the noise became more frantic and I took a deep breath and remembered what Officer McCool said about bravery.

Toffee and I felt our way down the hall and after listening for a moment outside my parents' bedroom, pushed the door open.

The room was lit by a bluish glow from the streetlights in the alley behind the house. There was an outline against the window; Daddy crouched on his knees, his wiry arms pushing down against a pillow. The pillow was over my mother's face. A kitchen knife glinted on the rug near her hand. The thumping noise came from her heels as she kicked against the floor. I ran at him and threw a super Judo kick with my wild eagle death cry.

37

Daddy stood. His arms were bowed out and his knees bent as he took a sloppy step over Mom and lurched at me. "Little bitch…" he hissed, and grabbed my hair. Toffee snarled and pounced at his legs, sinking her teeth into his thigh. A rolling growl churned in her throat and spit flew from her jaws. Mom shoved the pillow from her face and struggled to her hands and knees. Her arms shook but she started to pull herself towards me. I scratched at Daddy's wrist as he yanked my head back and forth and tried to kick Toffee away.

With a shove he threw me into the night table which broke, sending the clock flying. Mom wobbled on all fours; her back hunched and head slumped forward while she gasped for air. Daddy kicked Toffee so hard she yelped and cowered in a corner. He took a step towards her and kicked her again. I untangled myself from the broken table. My body thumped with hot pain as I make my way over to my dog and threw myself on top of her before Daddy could kick her again. I felt her shaking under me and she licked my cheek. "We're gonna make it Toffee," I whispered. "I don't know how but we have to hang on."

Daddy's foot crashed into my side and knocked the wind out of me. Toffee groaned as I fell on her. Pushing myself up as hard as I could I rolled to her side to shield her from Daddy's feet.

Daddy kicked me again and my leg went numb. I wondered where Rooster was. I wished for my secret penlight that made the bikes come and save us.

A ringing thud came from the middle of the room. I peeked around and saw Daddy's head drop forward before he crumbled, landing on his face and shoulders. Mom was standing behind him, holding the base of the telephone. "Run," she ordered hoarsely. Daddy began to scrabble on the floor like a crab. I tried to get up but my arms and legs had little strength and my side was pounding where he kicked me. I lifted my head and took a breath. On my knees, I pulled at Toffee's ribs and she snapped at my hand.

"Leave the dog," Mom wheezed. "Go to your room and shut the door. Put the bookcase in front of it. Put everything you can in front of it."

Mom's fingers were spidery on my back while she tried to help me up. Toffee was curled in a ball, whimpering, patting her tail against the floor in apology. I was taking her with me, even if she bit. I gripped her collar and dragged her across the floor until she found her feet. We limped off to my room. On the way I heard the ringing bang of the phone again, once, twice.

I shut my bedroom door. I tried to move the bookcase but pushing against it made the bruises on my body throb. Even through the glass I could hear the werewolves howling as they sloped through the park. I threw the window open with one arm, discovering I couldn't move the other. "Look what you did!" I screamed after them into the trees. It was then I saw Ivka Repinka sitting on the small roof of the portico.

"Why you lock window?" she demanded. Then she was in the room and with a gentle push, glided first the bookcase in front of the door, and then the bureau too. "One more?" she asked. I nodded and she positioned the bed to reinforce the barricade. After a short struggle Toffee climbed in beside me and licked my tears. Ivka turned off the light and sat on top of the bookcase, her long pale legs crossed in the moonlight.

"You don't usually wear sneakers," I murmured, touching the pink swoosh with my finger.

"Don't usually have to climb on roof for hour waiting for window because little girl forgets her Ivka. Never lock window. You so busy reading werewolf book you know nothing about your Ivka."

Toffee lay her head down with a soft whine and patted her tail.

The next morning Mom was sitting at the kitchen table. The sewing scissors, hammer, kitchen knife and a crowbar we must have missed in our investigations were all spread out in front of her.

"Be a good girl and get your own breakfast, ok?" The whites of her eyes were splattered with burst blood vessels. Dark bruises ringed her neck and arms. I clenched my hurt arm to my side while I prepared my cereal one-handed. All through my breakfast Mom sat with her hands spread out flat on either side of the weapons. Then she stood up and declared hollowly, "It's all going to be ok," and walked out of the kitchen.

I looked at Toffee. "Ready for the Big Cleanup?"

She pressed her head into my leg gently, which meant, yes, whatever.

Toffee and I walked up the canal path away from LoboChem until we were behind the barrel yard. I didn't want to drop everything in the same place so, one by one, I drew my evidence box, my toxic warrior diary and the weapons from my backpack and tossed them into the water where they sank into the silt. I was passing behind a large stand of jimsonweed when I pulled out the crowbar. Just on the other side of it I flung the tool, too late to see that it would land with a splash in the center of a floating island of bloated catfish that stretched all the way across the canal. Goosebumps rose up all over me as I looked at the expanse of dead bodies and I turned away and ran with Toffee at my side. Though the dead are limited in their fighting skills, they are watchful. Corpses are like cameras for karma.

We were in the park when a police cruiser drew up to the curb in front of my house. Panting, we ran in the back door. In the kitchen a tall policeman was taking a seat while Mom made coffee. It was Officer McCool. When he saw me he smiled and put his hat on my head, missing the bruise behind my bangs.

40

Mom served him coffee and cake and he spied her bruises and the finger marks on her neck and then looked at me with my arm clutched to my side. "The city needs brave officers. Are you still thinking about joining the force?"

Mom glanced at me like I was someone new she just noticed in the room.

I considered the question and met his gaze when I answered. "Toffee might have changed her mind. I think we're going to stick with our original plans to travel."

The doors of the emergency room opened with a whoosh and ushered Mom and me back out into the sun. For a minute I could not see the police car but then Mom pointed to where it was parked under the awning at admissions. I held my good hand over my eyes and made out two silhouettes: Officer McCool waving and Toffee in the front seat beside him, sitting tall.

Move Over Cool Dogs

My collarbone healed with a notch, and we were told the
doctor would have to break it again. The new bandages
were even tighter than the last and the sling sawed at the
side of my neck.

When my mother wanted to comfort me, we talked
about redecorating my room. We would sit on the bed and
look at every corner of it, talking about how to make it fit
for a princess. It had become a longstanding promise that
just as soon as we could, we would put up a wallpaper
border, new curtains and sheets, all in rainbow patterns.
The deal she dished out quickly while she opened a special
delivery letter from the postman was that we would do this
in our new house. First we were going on a vacation with
Rooster, to travel across America like I always wanted to.
After that we would get a place with him, outside Trenton
somewhere. Away from it all. Daddy was gone, but Mom
said we couldn't stay in our house, that we couldn't afford
it by ourselves.

The letter said the bank was coming for the keys at
noon the following day.

I sat on my bed waiting for Rooster to pick us up. His
Barracuda was bright orange, easy to spot when it turned
the corner onto our street. Not all my clothes would fit in
my school backpack and the bags Mom pulled out of the
attic but Mom assured me we would buy new ones. I would
have to leave most of my toys though. Apparently Daddy
did Christmas on credit.

Motorcycles grumbled into our driveway. I craned
to see who it was but remained seated in deference to
Mom's new fury about obeying rules. One of the bikes was
a huge dresser with a sidecar. I had only ever seen it in
Rooster's garage. The other was a Low Rider with an angel
on the tank whose wings were formed from waves of her

long blonde hair. Rooster and Freak Eddie climbed off the bikes and my heart sped up. I guessed Eddie was coming to see America with us.

The screen door slapped shut below. "What's this?" Mom demanded, dropping her bags on the grass and throwing her hands up at the bikes.

"Starter blew on the 'Cuda." Rooster bent to kiss her. She was talking too fast though and he straightened back up and smiled at her.

"How are we getting anywhere on those? What about our bags? We'll have to leave the dog."

At that I jumped off the bed and stood in the window. Rooster waved. "That's what the sidecar is for." He ran his hands down her arms, pulled her in to him. She resisted at first but then I heard him say, "Nothing to hide anymore, girl."

Eddie crossed the lawn. He bounded up the stairs and knocked on my open door. "You ready?" I turned and his eyes fell on my sling.

Eddie took one more step into the room and Toffee leapt to her feet and growled. He paused, held his hands up. "This your bag?"

I nodded.

"Yo, Angela," he called out the window, "You better come get this dog. She ain't lettin' me near her, let alone Hope."

"Dirty son-of-a-bitch!" I thought Mom was swearing at Eddie but then saw a new copper Cadillac had slid up to the curb. She pulled a bunch of keys from the pocket of her jeans. Rooster caught her as she marched at the car. She threw the keys at the man who got out and stomped back toward the house.

Upstairs, my mother attached Toffee's harness to a leash. Toffee had never walked with anyone but me and rounded herself in protest with her feet jutting out into the rug. But Mom was nobody to tangle with just then. She got her knees on either side of the dog and won the struggle.

"Can you walk ok?" Eddie frowned but his voice was soft.

I took a last look around my room as I headed to the door. Eddie smiled but it was the sad sort of smile people had been shining on me since my father disappeared. I had to fight the reflex to look sad back. I only felt sad about the man my Daddy used to be. Him I cried for. The LoboChem Daddy was a predator and I was all about staying alive. I just wanted to go somewhere new. I wanted to see the alligators in Florida and the bears in Yellowstone Park.

Rooster had rigged up a restraint for Toffee so she could ride in the sidecar with Mom's bags on the floor. My backpack went in Eddie's saddlebag with just enough room for a few books on the other side.

Mom shook her head at the bikes. "How is Hope going to hold on with one hand?"

"I got the backrest set for my nephew, so she should fit in snug." Eddie answered as he boarded. Rooster lifted me up behind him and then took a long strip of cloth out of his saddlebag and tied it around me and the bike.

The bank man had been standing quietly by our picnic table, waiting to lock up the house. Around his waist he wore a live rattlesnake for a belt. Behind it, his stomach was a black hole of hunger. A bank can swallow a factory whole, and that's a fact. He jumped a little when the engines started.

"I hope you're proud of yourself," Mom shouted at him as she got on Rooster's bike, but I could barely hear her so I imagine the bank man went unaffected. Toffee offered her paw. Mom tried to put it back but Toffee reached again, so when Rooster rolled down the drive to the street, Mom was behind him, holding hands with a big dog in a sidecar.

At the end of the street we rumbled onto the highway. Wind whipped into my clothes and wandered over my skin. The engines roared and choked under the late spring sun. I was finally on a Harley for real, and with Eddie. Toffee's coat was blowing so wildly she reminded me of a dandelion. I thought at any moment her fur would fluff off into a million tiny seeds. Beside her, Mom looked like an Indian princess wearing an old fringed jacket she'd dug out of the attic, along with the boots that matched. We were going to see America. Mountains. Ranchers. Rodeo.

I'd learn to ride a horse. Eddie's hair fluttered like a mane and I pretended the seat beneath me was a saddle. I was a pony girl, hanging on with one arm as we flew over bumps down the road. My injuries were from my last show. I had nearly been trampled by a horse, but I got into crash position when he threw me and his hooves missed me with every stamp. The crowd were on their feet, cheering and jumping over the barricades to help the clowns catch the bucking horse before it killed me.

I was celebrating my victory comeback when we rumbled to a stop in front of Rooster's house. "Rooster'll untie you in a minute," Eddie said over his shoulder.

Rooster met my utter surprise with his own questioning look. "Aren't we going across America?" I realized I was shouting because my ears were ringing so loudly. Whether it was because of this or because of my question I was not sure, but everyone laughed. My face went red.

My mother unclipped her helmet, shook out her hair. "Honey, we're not going *right now*. I just mean soon, maybe in the summer." She looked at Rooster.

He nodded. "Sure, if you want to, we'll go see the Grand Canyon. Maybe jump one of the bikes across it." He made a big slow arc with his hand and winked. "Anyway, let's show you your new room. That sound good?"

There were a few bikes in the driveway just behind the Barracuda. Toffee and I followed Mom across the lawn while Rooster and Eddie carried the bags. The smoke trees in the front yard burst into bloom as I walked under them and I stopped a second, thinking this might not be so bad. Rooster's house was painted two shades of blue and the shutters had quarter moon cut-outs.

Rooster and Eddie's boots thumped through the door. Voices carried in from the backyard. Mom frowned.

"Right this way," Rooster held out his arm and I followed his lead upstairs. At the end of the hall was a door with an old glass knob. He opened it and my heart sank. There was a twin bed, a rag rug and a desk with crayon marks on it. Wire hangers dangled in a door-less closet. The walls were stark white.

"We'll buy you some new things soon honey," Mom promised. Then she went off down the hallway and I was alone, looking out at the driveway that ran under my window. I thought we would at least get to Philadelphia that day, to the Liberty Bell. Instead I leaned on the window frame, watching the distant smog over LoboChem, channelled from a small purple cyclone drilling into the sky. I could not hear the barrels moaning from where I was. So there was that, at least.

It was a shorter walk to school from Rooster's and the streets were tree-lined and shady and after a week my cast came off so I was able to use my tire swing again. A lady from the Division of Youth and Family Services came to see us weekly and then once a month. I'd developed supersonic hearing by that point so when she stepped a few paces away to say something confidential, I heard every word.

"So long as there are no more incidents, we can remain convinced that this is a satisfactory home for Hope."

She dropped her voice lower. "We won't need to proceed with any plans for foster care at the moment."

Toffee's hearing was better than mine and she began to pace in front of me.

I soon grew bored of the few books I had in my room. One Friday night I made my way down the hall to the top of the stairs. The front room that Rooster used as an office had a T.V. Maybe he'd let me watch it.

There were usually people around Rooster's house, especially in the evening. They drank beer and laughed a lot so when I first got my cast off I started practicing my super judo right away, but after a while I could see that they weren't werewolves. They grilled their own burgers instead of shouting at Mom to do it. There were women as well as men. No one pawed anyone.

Harley shirts, bandanas, jeans and boots milled in and out of the living room, kitchen and den. There were several people in Rooster's office, and a man pushed the door closed when he saw me so I thought T.V. might be out of the question.

"Hey little bit!" A woman took a soft hold of my elbow. "What you lookin' for sweetheart: Your mama down here?"

"I, um, I was looking for Rooster."

"You must be Angela's girl. My name's Janie." She laced her fingers through mine as she guided me through the crowd. "Spades is my last name. On account of getting married for four weeks when I was seventeen. Which, by the way, I don't recommend. Just in case you're thinkin' on it." She winked.

Janie was pretty, with long red hair. A chunky crystal hung from one of her necklaces. When we entered the kitchen she stood on her tiptoes. "Anybody seen Rooster?"

"You're blockin' my view," a deep voice rumbled. There was a burst of laughter and Janie wagged her finger

48

up at a shape in the doorframe. "I'm still too much woman for you, Dutchman."

A man with a shaved head ducked the doorframe as he stepped into the yellow room.

"Likely so, Janie. Who's the little miss?" Before she could answer he stuck out a hand bigger than my Daddy's feet were. Had been. The bad Daddy. Good Daddy had reasonable hands and feet. This man's palms were bright pink against his brown skin. "I'm Dutchman, and I don't think I've had the pleasure."

I tried to shake his hand but I couldn't get the length of mine across the width of his.

"I think your mama might be outside. Janie, you got the paint for those picket signs?"

"In the jeep. Here, take the keys." Janie tossed a key ring at him

"Have you been across America?" I asked, dodging belt buckles and leather vests as I squeezed through the throng behind Janie.

"From the time I left Bobby Spades until just last year I did nothing but travel. Been to every state in the union except Hawaii. Every last place in America you could get to on a bike."

"Really? That's what I want to do. This summer we're going to see the Louisiana bayou and eat crayfish. They have paddle boats and airboats that run along with a big fan for a motor."

"There he is!" Janie skipped down the back steps and tapped Rooster on the shoulder.

He turned and wrapped her in a big hug. "Little Janie Spades! Prettiest thing on the East Coast! How're those signs comin' along?"

"Dutchman's getting the paint now. I brought you someone."

"She as pretty as you?" Rooster put his hands on her hips.

Janie pushed against his chest, "No, here, I've got her here."

Rooster let go of Janie and straightened up when he saw me. "You all right honey? We makin' too much noise?"

"No, I just.…"

"Your Mom's in the bathroom. She oughta be back in a minute."

Somebody backed up and stepped on my foot. Rooster held out an arm to stop him tumbling over me. "Here," Rooster led me over to the bench outside my clubhouse. It was the right size for me but Rooster looked like he was sitting on doll furniture. "Now tell me what's on your mind. You can say whatever you like. I'm never gonna shout at you or get mad."

"Well, I'm glad for my new room and all, but…"

He picked up my sentence, "Not what you had in mind, huh?"

I shook my head. "I've read all my books, so there's not much to do."

Rooster put his arm around me. "I want you to make a deal with me."

"What's that?"

"That you'll always tell me what's wrong, no matter how big or small it is. 'Cos I can't fix somethin' if I don't know it's broken." He held out his pinkie finger.

I linked my pinkie with his. "Deal."

As I was getting up to go he tugged the end of my braid lightly, "You gettin' any more of those headaches?"

I stopped and shook my head. "No. The doctor said they were from tension. It's not tense here I guess."

Rooster smiled. "You mind if I ask you somethin'?"

I liked it that he always spoke to me the same way he spoke to adults.

50

"Did you get those headaches mostly when you were playin' down by the canal?" When I hesitated he linked pinkies with me again.

I looked down at the little agreement our hands made. "I wasn't supposed to play down there. Please don't tell my Mom."

He jangled our locked fingers. "I won't, but you have to promise me one more thing. See, your Mom told you not to go down there because it's isolated and there's lots of rusty old car parts sitting in the weeds. I'm asking you not to go down there because that pipe is pouring chemicals into the canal and they're the kind of chemicals that can give you lots worse things than headaches."

"No more canal," I agreed, making the sign of the cross on myself, "Swear to God, hope to die."

"Don't hope that baby girl. Never that."

My mother was setting up the T.V. in my room when I got back upstairs. "I was about to send out a search party." She said. "I've got something to tell you."

My stomach sank although I don't know why I should have been anxious at that point.

"I got a job!" she squeezed me as she smiled.

Try as I might I couldn't really smile. "But what about after school, and summer? Am I going to be all alone?"

Her arm fell away. "Hope, I was really lucky to get this job. DYFS want to see some proof that I can look after you on my own and I haven't worked since before you were born. There wasn't much in the bank account, and then the medical bills…" she trailed off. Her fingers curled and she pressed them to her lips while she stared at the black window for a minute. "Rooster's given us a place to live and food but we can't ask him to do everything." She turned back to me. "Besides, I want more for you. I'm not going to do factory work because there's no future in it. I want you to go to college and see the world. Don't you want that?"

The pressure of the endorsement she was seeking was like a weight on my chest. "Yes," I agreed, but what mattered to me was really just that I wanted to see America. There was one other question plaguing me and I thought I would take advantage of her presence to ask it. "Mom?"

"Yeah?"

"Why didn't you marry Rooster in the first place?"

She pressed her lips together and stood up in her *no answer* posture. "DYFS want me to stay in the state for now honey, but maybe we can go on vacation towards the end of summer, after I make some money." She kissed me on the cheek and then winked as she shut the door behind her.

The insurance company that hired Mom as a receptionist was not far from the house, but the job still meant she was gone from 8:30 in the morning until 6:00 in the evening every day.

After school I walked up the drive, picking my way through stray tools and men hunkered beside motorcycles. Janie said the best way to make friends was to act natural and remember names, so as I steered around a dismantled Shovelhead I called out, "Hi Dutchman! Hi Coker! Hi Billy!"

They waved or grunted as was their manner, arms war-painted in oil and ink and streaks of bright paint.

Toffee was in the yard, standing with her paws on top of the fence. She was getting much better about men, provided no one came at me too fast. We ran upstairs together, stopping when we saw my door open.

The outline of a rainbow had been sketched across the side wall from floor to ceiling and Janie Spades was working near the end, filling in the bands with glittering paint.

52

"What are you doing?" I asked in wonder.

She stood and wiped her forehead with the back of her hand. "A little birdie told me somebody around here wanted a rainbow. And I didn't go to art school just to spend my life driving a forklift. I hope it's what you wanted. "Also," she turned her face to the ceiling, "I took a few liberties up there."

All across what had been a flat white square that morning was a mural of the heavens that began with a sun-lit day and blended into a starry moon-hung sky.

Amazed, I flopped down on the bed to take in the view. "How did you do all this?"

Janie shrugged while she tickled Toffee's ears. "I got some help from the boys with the broad brush stuff. And then, Dutchman's an artist himself. Paints the tanks on most of their bikes. With four of us it went quickly."

She showed me how to refill her palette and that became my job for the afternoon.

"Do you really drive a forklift?"

Janie dabbed red at the end of the rainbow. "I did. Up until I lost my job Monday." She refilled her brush from the palette. "But they can stuff their job. I found a hairdressing school I can finish in just two months. Rooster's lending me the money. He's a good man that one."

Janie left just before my mother was due home. I ran downstairs with her to thank the others.

I stood at the end of the driveway as they rolled away, waiting for my mother to come home. At 7:00pm Rooster stepped out onto the porch. "You want some supper kid? Got franks and beans." I shook my head and kept my feet stuck to the asphalt. I heard the screen door slap shut and guessed Rooster had gone back into his office until I heard his heavy footfalls in the grass. He stood beside me, a dishtowel slung in the back pocket of his jeans. I waited, thinking he would try to make me eat dinner or do my homework, but he just stood, and waited with me, and didn't say anything at all.

A few weeks later I came home to find Dutchman scrubbing turpentine off his fingers. On my ceiling, soaring between fireworks and fairies, were a collection of angels. Mom, Rooster, Dutchman, Janie, Toffee and I were all painted on winged Harley-Davidsons. He'd painted the Barracuda as well, with a blonde lady in the driver's seat. On closer look, I saw it was Ivka Repinka, leaning back against the headrest and smoking a cigarette.

Dutchman had just swung his leg over his bike when I caught him in the driveway. He grinned while I rattled off all the new things he had put into the mural.

"And how did you know about Ivka Repinka?" I jabbered.

He scratched his sideburn.

"In the car," I said, "The blonde lady in the car."

"There ain't nobody in the car yet Hope. Plenty of people on the bikes."

He couldn't see Ivka. I darted to another topic. "Did you used to make barrels with Rooster?"

Dutchman had a way of drawing in a breath that let you know he cared about the question and answer process. He paused with his helmet resting on the tank of his bike. "Long time ago, we made barrels for couple of vineyards in Brandywine. Good times then. But we got undercut and moved over to storage containers. Fifty gallon drums. LoboChem was our biggest client, but they were too cheap to pay for the new container design and next thing you know everybody's workin' for Gordon Lobo." He fastened his helmet. "Not much market anymore for old style barrels, unless you're tradin' with bootleggers or rodeo clowns."

As his bike dipped into the street he held his left arm up, bent at the elbow with his fist in the air.

Back in my room, Ivka still rested in the car. Her cigarette was gone and her stole had slipped off her shoulder and trailed out the window behind her as if caught in the breeze. I waved at her but she remained a flat drawing and did not move.

Throughout the summer extra items began to appear in my room. Carpet, a bean bag chair, curtains, throw pillows, a bed set with white clouds in a blue sky and a closet door all cropped up at random. I thought Janie was responsible but she seemed as surprised as I was. After a few weeks of my waiting at the curb when my mother was late Rooster made a suggestion and I took to sitting in the big chair in his office where I could see out the window. I became familiar with his charts and papers and when he wasn't working he would explain to me his idea for a type of plastic drum that would be better suited to store the waste from the chemicals LoboChem was producing.

"Money," Rooster said one day when I asked why it was they wouldn't pay for his safe-barrel, as he called it. "They were interested in containers to store their manufactured products, not the junk leftover."

"So they put the junk in the same containers?"

"Some of it," he crossed his arms, studied his drawing. "But they're makin' too much to deal with just by pilin' it up in my old yard. And I got plenty of people on the inside and nobody's seen anythin' shipped off to landfill or treatment. They like to tell new employees that they use a purification system. It's not on the main site though and there aren't any trucks leavin' with by-product."

There was a thick pile of papers with names and addresses sitting on the edge of his desk.

"What's that?"

Rooster looked over. "LoboChem employees. LoboChem's got a legal requirement to let the union know names and addresses of everybody in the factory, but we still haven't been able to contact most of them. Addresses are incomplete, no zip codes and apartment numbers. Don't say street or avenue on most of them."

When I finished my homework, I started going through the list with the phone book beside me, then took the step of calling houses to find out who lived where. I wrote the addresses in next to the incomplete ones. Rooster saw what I was up to and bought me two new pens for the job, purple ink for definite contacts and green for not so sure.

I became used to the rhythm of the house. The arrival of bikes was like a tidal pattern, sweeping in and away again. Sometimes people drove up in cars and Rooster would meet with them in his office and send me back with Toffee. It was the one thing he wasn't forthright about, those people, and I imagined Rooster as one of the Superfriends, fighting evil in secret from his office lair.

Rooster found a library summer program for kids, so that occupied me for a few hours a day and meant I had a fresh supply of books all the time. One day the library supervisor had gotten a stomach bug and they'd sent us home early. I was in my room looking through a magazine of fairy tattoos when the sound of a bike drew me to the window. Billy Regret crawled his chopper up to the fence, looped a plastic bag over the ornamental swirl at the top, and rolled back down the driveway. A minute later Rooster moseyed out. He had been in his office all morning looking at floor plans from his old barrel business.

He caught me at the window, chuckled. "Well, come on down then. Ain't gonna be a surprise now."

Standing in the driveway I asked, "Is Billy the one who brings everything for my room?" Out of the bag had appeared a soft white unicorn with a gold horn. Toffee checked it in with an identifying sniff.

"Everybody's bringing the stuff for your room." Rooster stroked Toffee's head. "Once Janie got her yap goin' there was no stoppin' them."

My mouth fell open. Rooster chucked me lightly under the chin. "Don't want flies for lunch, do ya'? Now come on and have a sandwich. You ain't eaten since breakfast."

While we ate bologna and cheese he read me the new edition of the union newsletter that he was working on. If I was able to understand it, he said, everybody working in the factory should be able to.

Rooster let me keep the T.V. in my room and I turned it on that night, waiting for Mom. She said she would watch *The Incredible Hulk* with me but by the time I heard her high heels in the hallway David Banner was rambling down another long highway in tattered clothes. Mom swept into my room with a big smile. "My god, you're getting taller by the day." She rocked me back and forth in a hug and then held me for a while. "Hope...Are you happy here?"

I meant it when I told her I was. "I was afraid they were like the werewolves at first, but everybody's really nice."

"Werewolves?"

"Daddy's friends."

She stopped rocking for a minute. "Werewolves...yes, that's what they were." She stroked my hair and then held me at arms' length. My mother's eyes were always like an animal's - jet black and full of feeling. "You remember what they're like, baby. The world's got plenty of werewolves in it and it's best for a girl to stay away from them."

Her seriousness was enough to make me take heed, but then she looked over at the library book on my night table and smiled. "I tell you what. On Saturday we'll go to the mall and buy you some new books. How's that sound?"

It was a treat getting books I could keep. At the register my mother paid for *Anne of Green Gables, Charlotte's Web* and *Tiger Eyes*. And for herself, *Accounting Made Easy* and *How to Win Friends and Influence People*.

On the way out we passed the travel section. A thick spiral cover jumped out at me, *America's Roads, From Superhighways to Country Lanes.* My atlas was one of the things I had to leave behind in the old house.

"Can we get that?"

"What for?" Mom was already prying open the cover of her accounting text.

I stopped short. "Won't we need it for our trip?"

A look of bewilderment passed quickly over her face. "Oh, oh right. Well, maybe we should pick one up closer to the time. Roads…change."

Walking through the mall I felt light-headed from the recycled air. "We're still going, aren't we?" I asked, pressing the back of her hand to my cheek.

"What?,…Yes, of course honey. But for now, we'll study. Then we'll have even more fun when we go. I tell you what – if you can finish all those books by the time I get paid again we'll come back here and get some stories about pioneer girls. That way you can learn more about the places we're going to see."

When we got outside I skipped over to the Barracuda and dove behind Rooster as he leaned his seat forward. A beach towel was spread on out on the hot vinyl seats. I opened *Charlotte's Web* and did not notice when the car stopped until someone called my name.

Gypsies, Tramps & Thieves

In the summer before ninth grade my mother told me I would not be going to Sacred Heart with the rest of my class at Our Lady Queen of Angels. If she was going to pay tuition, she would pay for me to go to Lawrence Junior High where I would be better prepared for college, in her opinion.

Two months into the school year Mom was organizing herself for a job interview. She and Rooster had been fighting about it for weeks. Whenever Rooster noticed me listening the fight would stop so I didn't know exactly what the issue was. My best guess was that it had to do with her wanting more money and more opportunities and being willing to work twenty-four hours a day to get them.

The walk home was long, but made longer by the pack of boys who were following me. I'd been trying to ignore them since we left school. They were jocks - a couple were in my honors classes. One of them, Rick Rayetayah, lived in the same direction I did. I tried to stay away from them whenever I could. Humiliating people seemed to be their pastime of choice. Gym class was when they were at their most awful. During field hockey drills they tripped people with their sticks and made fat jokes about one of the girls until she cried. A boy told them to knock it off and they tackled him in the locker room and stuffed soap in his mouth. The gym teacher, Mr. Fishman, did nothing about it. I'd heard that he played golf at the local country club with their dads. No matter how much I thought about it, I could not tell if it was money or sports that turned people into assholes.

I talked to Janie about the situation at school, told her some of the girls in my English class were making fun of my clothes. She said the world was full of assholes and the key was not to let them get you down. According to Janie it was not sports or money that made people treat each

other badly, it was immaturity. When I asked about Mr.
Fishman, she said rich people just got to stay immature
longer. *And sports?* I asked. Same thing, she said. "Think
about it, sports are just kids' games played by grown-ups
for lots of money." I could see there was some sense to her
line of thinking. But of course, the bikers weren't a sporty
bunch.

Mom had not let up on the book buying. It was great
at first but then, like everything else, it became an exercise
in control. At parent-teacher night she grilled my teachers
for suggestions. At that moment I was reading *Of Mice and
Men* on the recommendation of my history teacher. As a
result I'd added California wine country to the list of places
I wanted to see when I took my trip across America. This
despite my opinion that Curly was an asshole, just like the
jocks behind me.

We were several blocks from school and the few
other kids who shared the beginning of the route had peeled
off and disappeared home. I walked the side streets so that I
could read as I went, and not worry about traffic so much.
Also, the route ran between Mother Hubbard's discount
parts supply place and home, so sometimes I could get a
ride if one of Rooster's buddies was going by.

Lenny had just killed his puppy. I was sorry for him,
and sunk deep in the horror of it.

"Get your motor runnin'!" One of the guys sang out.

"You think her mom rides a motorcycle to the
grocery store?"

"Yeah, that's probably where she works."

"Bet her mom's an easy rider."

"An easy ride." They burst into laughter.

I knew that walking faster would only let them
know they were bothering me. There were no uniforms at
Lawrence, so what you wore was who you were. Guess or
Levi's. Forenza or Timberland. And there was me, in faded
jeans and Harley shirts with a bandana on my head.

60

"I heard her dad's in jail."

"I thought her parents were dead and she was found by a pack of bikers."

"Pack of scumbags more like it. All low-lifes and criminals."

There were no religion classes at Lawrence, which I was glad of because Father Benno had gotten into the habit of singling me out when he talked about martyrs. He told me once that the reason I was beaten as a child was so that I could lead other sinners out of their living punishment. I asked Rooster if that was true and he said I was beaten because my father was a dickless bastard, excuse his French, and that I didn't owe one goddamn debt to anyone else who chose to be one too. That was kind of how it went when I tried to move information between school and home. In Lawrence, maybe because of the lack of uniforms and nuns, I thought school would be more like home. I thought I would fit in.

"Hey scumbag girl!"

Nope.

"Aw, man, leave her," I heard one of them say. Rick, it sounded like.

"Nah, I want to see if scumbag girl knows how to talk. Here scumbag!" There was a sharp whistle like when you call a dog.

Rooster told me never to take shit, but he also said sometimes you had to wait for the right moment to fight back. Mom stood firmly against fighting at all. I was trying to decide which bit of advice to take when something hit my back. I stopped and turned around. One of the boys, a tall freckled guy on the basketball team, was holding a handful of crab apples. He threw another one, which left a welt in my arm.

"Cut it out!" I said.

"Ooooh, she speaks!" The one named Donny sniggered.

"Why do you dress like that? You think everybody's gonna be scared of you because your daddy's a big fat biker?"

"Her daddy's dead."

"Guys," Rick stepped away from them, up onto a lawn. "Leave her be, let's go."

I tucked *Of Mice and Men* into my bag with my schoolbooks, looking the freckled one straight in the eyes. "You don't know one goddamn thing about my Daddy or you fuckin' well wouldn't be standing here talking about him. So maybe you pussies should just get back to the shower and soap each other off again. I can smell your stink from here."

They all stared at me for a minute. Rick raised his eyebrows and smiled. Then one by one they recovered from their shock. "Whore!" said the blond one.

"Cunt."

"Bitch."

"You callin' us faggots?"

I faced them straight on. "I don't remember saying that, but it sounds like it's worrying you. And it probably should be if you're more interested in making girls cry than talking to them."

"Why would we want to talk to you? Biker scum."

"Get in a little practice maybe, so you don't have to take each other to the prom. Although," I checked their jacket for names, "Wayne's got a fair pair of boobs there Donny, so you might discover you like him in something with a little cleavage. Hell if it's dark enough you probably wouldn't even notice the difference. Any port in a storm, huh?"

Donny chucked his books and stepped forward. Rick grabbed his shoulders. My heart pounded. Rick held Donny back while the rest of them went on shouting insults. From the corner of my eye I saw a woman in a bright pink sweat suit coming around the side of the nearest house. I

62

recognized her just as the roar of pipes hit my ears. There was a Hog coming, a loud one. At the sound, Ivka Repinka stopped and leaned against the house, obscuring herself slightly behind an ornamental shrub.

Growling up the road was a rider whose half-helmet gleamed through the ape hangers. Billy Regret.

I waved.

Billy pulled over, took a look at the struggling boys and dismounted. Billy worked the vats at LoboChem and he was tall. He stepped onto the side walk and crossed his arms, which looked about as big as most of the boys' legs. Under his helmet he had a white bandana like mine over his long blond braid. Black sunglasses hid his eyes.

The boys grew quiet but none of them seemed to want to look like a sissy in front of the rest. Donny still had his chest puffed out, though he stopped resisting Rick.

Billy stood, silent. The boys shifted, darting glances at each other. Finally Billy gestured to me with his chin, his voice deep and rich with his southern drawl. "This is Hope. If she comes home even a little bit upset because of you or anyone you know, I'll make sure you're too broken to ever hold a football again. Understand?"

"Yes."

"Yes."

"Yes sir."

"Good. I'm looking forward to never hearing a word about you again." Billy turned his back to them and got on his bike. He nodded at the seat and I swung on behind him. The boys had all fallen back, except Rick Rayetayah. And except for him, they were looking at the ground. I caught his eyes. His skin was red-brown and his face was proud, like a grown man's. He smiled. I wondered why he hung out with the others. But then, I reasoned, I would've been happy to have nearly anyone to hang out with in school. I was sick of eating lunch alone.

The bike thundered off and I turned away, away from school, and from Lawrence in general, unable to wait for the day when I'd take off forever. Under the tires the asphalt melted into old black water and I saw the skies of Mississippi reflected below my feet. We were in Trenton when we reached a traffic light and Billy turned his head. Over the engine he shouted, "By the way, Happy Birthday kid!"

That morning, up in my room, Mom told me Rooster would take us for pizza to celebrate and that the next day we'd go to Washington Crossing Park. Downstairs she and Rooster exchanged words. "Aren't you going to wish me luck?" she snapped. There was no answer. I heard the scrape as she snatched her briefcase off the boot bench. The door slammed and the house went quiet. My father's shouting made me nervous. Rooster's quiet made me nervous. I was a little sick of feeling like my nervous system was hooked up to a power grid.

When Billy pulled up to the house the driveway was crammed with bikes. I got off the chopper and raised my eyebrows. "Go on, girl. It's your party. Rooster told me you went home by the circle. Don't know what made me come down that road you was on."

I wondered if Ivka could date a real live human. She and Billy always seemed to arrive when I needed them most. I kissed him on his stubbly cheek and hurried into the backyard. The barbeque was lit and Chipmunk and Janie were taking the foil off a small herd of covered dishes. Cakes were gathered on a table next to a pile of presents. Janie threw her arms around me and a shout went up that I'd arrived and Rooster better get his ass off the phone.

A new shirt lay on my bed. It had a decal of a girl rabbit on a chopper. I'd seen it a few days before when I went with Rooster to pick up oil filters. I pulled it on just as Janie came in to fix my hair. "I don't know why I thought hairdressing would be healthier than working at LoboChem." She laughed as we choked on Aqua Net.

Roxanne, Kimmie and Ditsy Marie stood back by my clubhouse, which Rooster had updated. Janie covered my eyes while someone threw the door open and walked me inside. *"Ta-da!* " Janie removed her hands and I was looking up at another one of her masterpieces. The mural stretched over two walls, from heaven to hell with a stairway connecting them. A girl was walking up it. "That's you." Janie pointed, clearly pleased with the result. Just above me, reaching down a helping hand, was Ivka Repinka in a pink medieval gown and a pair of pink Doc Martins.

"Wicked," a boy's voice said from behind me.

I turned and saw a guy, tall with blond hair. He was wearing an Ozzy shirt and faded jeans. "You the birthday girl?"

It felt like a whole pack of sparklers had been set off inside of me. Roxanne giggled and Ditsy Marie nudged her in the ribs to shut her up. "Yeah, I'm Hope." I said.

"Kurt Thomas, but everyone calls me Kurt. I came with my Uncle Eddie."

"You mean Freak Eddie?" As soon as it was out of my mouth I wished I hadn't said it and shoved my hands in my pockets.

Kurt laughed, showing crooked teeth. "Yeah that's him."

"I'm sorry, I…"

A shrill whistle came from outside. We stepped out and saw Eddie was standing beside Coker who'd brought speakers and turntables.

"I've gotta go help set up," Kurt said, "Nice meeting you."

The girls huddled into the clubhouse and we talked about the boys at the party until the music drew us outside. *Eyes Without a Face, Jump, Dancing in the Dark, Middle of the Road, On the Dark Side, Legs, Pride (In the Name of Love).* "We should dance," Ditsy Marie said wistfully.

"What for? Boys never dance anyway," Kimmie flicked a dead lighter, sending sparks out over her hand.

A song began, full of flutes and other strange instruments. "Janie sure can dance though," Ditsy Marie nodded.

Janie's red hair flashed as a circle formed around her. In a moment she was on one of the empty picnic tables. The song was an old one by Cher. It used to play on our kitchen radio when I was a kid. Janie was whirling to the music, hands raised and jewellery jangling. She saw me and held out her hands, beckoning. A thrill went up my spine. I was scared but something in me wanted to dance too badly to say no.

Dutchman lifted me up onto the table. I started to follow what Janie was doing, spinning in circles and stomping my feet and singing. I whirled myself away from the boys at school and into a travelling show. I had bangles on my ankles and coins on my skirt and hoops jangling in my ears. My life was the road. I was free.

The song ended and a cheer went up. Janie told me to take a bow. I was about to when I saw my mother, standing by the back gate, hands on the hips of her a navy blue suit, her hair pulled tight in a bun.

Janie touched my arm. "You better go."

I stepped off the table to raucous applause which seemed to jack up my mother's temper: her mood lately was always visible, like heat mirage on a highway. She didn't speak until I was two feet away from her.

"What were you doing up on that table?"

"Dancing."

"I don't want you dancing on tables. Maybe some people here think that's an acceptable way for a woman to make a living, but I don't."

Rooster came over and put his hand on my shoulder. He had a beer in the other and leaned in to kiss my mother but she fixed him with a glare. It held him like spider silk and they disappeared into the house together.

Someone touched my elbow. "Kurt's looking for you," Ditsy Marie whispered in my ear. I turned to find him right behind us, armed with two slices of sheet cake. He'd managed to get the wheels and handlebars of the vintage Harley icing decoration.

"Where do you go to school?"

"Do you live around here?"

We spoke at the same time, then laughed. We were sitting on giant beanbag chairs in my clubhouse, cake balanced uneaten in our hands.

"You first," I said.

"You're really pretty."

A flush crept up my neck, making my ears hot. "Thanks." I glanced up at Janie's painting, trying to think of what to say next. When I looked back Kurt put the cake down and tried to get out of his beanbag, making like he'd been swallowed by some giant creature and was fighting his way out. Nervous as I was, he made me laugh.

He wound up on his knees in front of me, and reached for my hand. I let him hold it. He pressed my knuckles with his fingertips. We sat like that, sparkling with nerves for a minute or two. He was balanced awkwardly, trying not to show it and I laughed. I sat up and tried to move over, so he could sit on the side of my beanbag. Bad idea. Two minutes later my cake was on the floor, we'd kneed and elbowed each other a dozen times, I'd head-butted Kurt in the eye by accident and the two of us were laughing so hard we flopped back in the chair, legs and arms splayed out to the sides like we were making snow angels. We'd just caught our breath when he put his hand on my cheek and turned my face to his. He kissed me quickly, on the mouth.

"Hope?" My mother's call came from the other side of the door. Her voice brought me back to reality and I struggled to sit upright. Kurt was trying to help, which had us even more entangled when my mother threw the clubhouse door open, blinding us with the crimson setting sun. I shielded my eyes. Her body was a black outline in the doorway. I couldn't see her face, but her stance said everything.

"Come and join the rest of the kids," she said stiffly. "We're making s'mores on the fire." And just like that, she'd ripped me off the ladder of adolescence and thrown me back into childhood. My face hot with embarrassment, I rolled out of the chair to the side and tried to stand up without looking like a total idiot. I knew she didn't want Kurt to come along. He must have known it too, because he stayed where he was when I followed her.

I took a quick look back at the clubhouse. He was in the door, watching me walk away. When I turned he mimed with his hands like he was writing something, and mouthed "Number," with a hopeful look.

Ditsy Marie caught me writing out my phone number in the kitchen. "Do you think I should ask for his back?" I asked.

"Definitely give him yours, but…" she bit her lip. "Kurt doesn't have a phone. It's kind of a secret everybody knows – that he and his dad are pretty close to losing their house."

I held the scribbled note in my fingertips. Kurt was waiting outside the kitchen door when I stepped out. Behind him, Eddie stood by the gate, slapping his wrist watch. A group of bikes were warming up in the driveway. "How about it?" Kurt whispered.

I handed him the slip of paper. He grinned. Then Eddie shouted and he jogged off across the lawn. I could

68

have gone up to my room and spent the rest of the night reliving what had just happened. My first kiss. But Noelle arrived just then and we went inside to get a drink. The conversation dwindled as we headed for the fridge. A few people looked away from me and I wondered if it had anything to do with Kurt.

Mother Hubbard, who got her nickname because she and her husband had seven kids, broke the silence as Noelle fished root beers from the vegetable drawer. "How you girls doing? How's your folks? Anybody got any trips planned?"

"We bought a summer house in Seaside," Noelle piped up. "We're going down next week to start work on it. Soon as Mom gets her next dose."

"How is she on it?"

"Tired a lot. Dad's gonna winterize the new place and then Mom'll stay there with her Home Health Aid. We'll go down on weekends. Sea air's meant to help. She loves the shore."

"We're going to travel across the United States." I burst in, misjudging what I thought was an appropriate gap in the conversation. "To see Mount Rushmore and Niagara falls and Yosemite Park - just as soon as my mom gets vacation time on her new job."

I was met with hard looks. Noelle started fiddling with her Wigwams, trying not to look at anyone.

"Your mom wants to see the land of the free, huh?" A man with a grey beard shifted his weight. "Well she's gonna hafta go pretty far from here to see something like that, considerin' who she's workin' for."

It was as if the room had been plunged into liquid nitrogen. We stood, brittle and absolute.

"C'mon now, Smoke. Kids can't help what their parents get up to," Dirty Mike grumbled.

"Can damn well help braggin' about makin' money off other people's cancer." Smoke growled back.

Glances lighted on Noelle but Smoke stared straight at me.

"That's enough, Smoke. Rooster'll throw you out on your ass if he hears you talking to her like that." Janie pushed in next to me, put her arm around me and tried to lead me away.

But I couldn't get my feet to move. "You don't know what you're talking about!" I shouted. "My mom's been training as an accountant so we could have a better life."

Smoke took a step toward me. "Your mom took a job in management at LoboChem. So when she takes you on vacation you can just remember your friend Noelle's mom, and how LoboChem makes the money to pay those big management salaries." He threw his arm up. "Like it ain't enough we risk ourselves all day long and now we're gettin' in deeper."

"Didn't see you volunteering to get in deep enough to go along." Dirty Mike pointed with the top of his beer.

"Hush your mouths!" Mother Hubbard snapped. "Janie, take her out of here."

"No!" I screamed. "It's not true! She wouldn't do that!" No one outside paid me much mind and I made it to my clubhouse and shut myself inside. I dropped into my beanbag chair, held a pillow over my mouth and screamed. Then I just cried.

There was a soft knock at the door. I opened it to find Ivka Repinka standing in a pink denim jacket and pink jeans, a pink bandana around her head. "Come for walk," she said.

Under the streetlights, a breeze tangled the shadows of naked trees, making a spider web of the sidewalk.

"Ivka take little girl for coffee at Seven-11. Little girl should be glad Ivka is big eavesdropper." She went on speaking as I buttoned the jacket she put around me. "You know bikers always work for Rooster. They make barrels, then they make chemicals, but still they work for Rooster, trying to control the chemical men, trying to make safe."

"Janie told me they were old hippies. They didn't want LoboChem next to a park. They fought the sale, but LoboChem paid off the tax office. So Rooster formed a union."

Ivka lit a cigarette off her finger and began to exhale pink smoke. "Then people get sick. Bad pain, can't breathe. Free doctor give blood test. Say everything normal. But some get suspicious, go to hospital. By then cancer so bad they die in one month."

One of Rooster's favourite topics was how hard it was to get stable blue collar work in Trenton anymore. Most of the factories were gone. When the jobs dried up, property values went down. People couldn't afford their mortgages, and couldn't get out of them. "That's what happened to Kurt's dad? Noelle's mom?" I stopped short. "I've got to apologize to her."

Ivka held both hands up. "Little blonde friend is gone. Not mad at you. You see her other time. Come now and get coffee. Ivka freezing in skimpy biker clothes."

"Can't you make yourself another jacket?"

As soon as I said it, she was wearing a pink leather jacket, so I mentioned some pink earmuffs too and she nodded her thanks.

Seven-11 was like a neon pod in the middle of the dark night. Inside, Ivka flipped through several magazines – some of them upside down - read the labels of the candy bars, flirted with the boy behind the counter. He didn't pay her any mind, but she seemed to be enjoying herself.

"I really should get back," I tried.

But Ivka kept on, inspecting ice cream and automotive supplies, air fresheners and the cigarette display. Finally she took two coffees and walked out with them while the boy at the counter was fixing the microwave she had used to burst a container of Jiffy Pop into pink flames.

When we got back near the house Ivka stopped and grabbed my arm. I could see the rear end of a police car in Rooster's driveway. With a blare of sirens three more appeared, flipping their lights on as they sped toward the house. I ran up the street with Ivka at my heels shouting, "Little girl, no!"

The front door was standing open. As I ran onto the lawn I saw two police cars in the driveway. More were pulling up to the curb. The front yard was lurid with spotlights and dancing cherry tops. "Stop right there!" a megaphone barked. I looked toward the sound and saw two men in the back of each car. I could not see all of them, but I made out Billy Regret and Smoke. They were leaning forward, their arms pinned behind them.

The sound of police radios carried out the front door. I stepped forward but the megaphone went off again, "Do not move from where you are standing or officers will be required to take action!" Ivka hugged me from behind as four policemen ran up the grass and through the door, their hands steadying belts lumbered with clubs and cuffs and guns. A moment later three men made their way out to the porch. Rooster was sandwiched between two cops, his hands cuffed behind his back.

"Rooster!" I started toward him, but Ivka held me tight. I'd forgotten how strong she was.

He met my eyes. "Go in the house Hope, It's all right."

Two more officers appeared, holding Freak Eddie. They put him in a patrol car beside Rooster.

"No!" I started to cry. Then another shadow appeared in the doorway. "Come inside Hope." My mother said.

Ivka let me go and I ran to the police car that held Rooster and put my hands on the back window. He shouted something at me and then the cop in the front seat rolled down the window. "Step away from the car, miss."

"Hope, get in this house right now!" Mom hollered.

The past days flew through my mind, Rooster's office door shut so often, phone calls at all hours. It wasn't just my mother who'd been busy. It was just that her busyness hurt the most and so I noticed it more. I stepped back from the car and looked around, stunned and angry. Ivka Repinka had gone and Janie Spades was running through the gate from the backyard.

"What's going on Janie?" I demanded.

She hugged me but a moment later her arms were yanked away. "Don't touch my daughter," my mother hissed. "I might lose my job over this shit! You hippie bastards. Real nice thing to do at a kid's birthday party. Sneak off for a little B&E with Rooster holding the fort. You think one stupid break-in by a bunch of bikers is going to shut down LoboChem?"

Janie met my mother's gaze in a way I could not recall anyone having done in a long time. "This one might."

I looked from one to the other. My mother's lips tightened against her teeth. "You people don't contribute one goddamn thing to that company or this neighbourhood or anything else. If it wasn't for the union every useless one of them could be gotten rid of and replaced for half the salary just like they did to you."

"Mom!!" I felt sick to my stomach but there was no stopping them.

"And you'd probably get a bonus for volunteering to fire them, you heartless bitch."

"At least I understand industry. I'm not the one wasting my life hitchhiking around the country while everybody else is living up to their responsibilities. The only reason you have your new haircutting job and you people have a flophouse at all is because Rooster started a company of his own. If he'd only played ball he'd be living in a palace right now. The longer he held out the less they had to give him for that stupid barrel business."

Janie's arms swung out as she leaned into the argument. "You're one to talk about hippie flophouse! What the hell are you going to do now if Rooster stays in jail and it's your turn to pay the rent? What would you have done without us hippies when your house was repossessed? You like the idea of putting other single mothers in that position?"

There was a terrible quiet.

"Get in the house!" My mother shrieked at me. I turned and fled up to my room. In a minute I heard the front door slam and lock.

Toffee jumped up and put her paws on my shoulders. Someone had clipped a new tag onto her collar, a plastic star that snapped open when you needed to change the information inside. I thought I would ask Rooster about it and then a sick thud hit my stomach as I realized I didn't know when I'd see him again. Would they allow minors to visit the jail? Was he going to jail?

Toffee dropped down and ran in circles, barking. Two suitcases had been packed and sat by the closet. All of my clothes were inside except for my Harley shirts, which were piled on the bureau. Quickly, I stuffed as many of them as I could into the outside pockets of the cases. I got into my pyjamas and turned the light out quickly in the hope my mother wouldn't try to come in and talk.

Some premonition told me what I was going to see when I shut off the light, but still, I closed my eyes for a minute trying to postpone the vision. When I got the courage to open them, the orange Barracuda had driven itself to the far end of the painted sky overhead and sat idling with the passenger door open. It was time to hit the road, but not on my bike. Not yet.

We left the next morning in Mom's new Toyota, and headed up Lawrence Road. After a couple of miles and a few turns I didn't know where we were. At the end of a road that wound beside the highway we pulled into a small complex. Meadowland Garden apartments.

At the fifth identical brick building we rolled into a parking space beside a dumpster. Toffee sniffed out the new territory as I followed my mother, carrying my suitcases. Apart from ruining my life she was a management rat and I didn't want to look at her. Inside the apartment there were gold shag carpets and the smell of new paint. My room, as well as every other, was completely white.

For seven days she ranted about how family services might find out that she'd had me living in a house with a man who was planning a felony. I found myself waiting out the storm of her temper, which was, I realized, what Rooster always did.

But for all her yelling, when my mother made up her mind to take action, she never resorted to half measures. The following week she showed me a restraining order she'd put on Rooster, barring him from contacting either her or me. It would prove to the court, if required, that she was prepared to protect me.

The winding old farm road that lazed away from the apartment did not have any other kids walking on it, just new housing developments laid out according to crop circle patterns below the gently zapping high tension wires that bisected I-95.

My new walk from school was long, but made longer by knowing it no longer led home.

Babysitting at the Comet Motel

In a gully beside Bakers Basin Road, The Comet Motel
wrung a profit out of Route 1, aided poorly by a sign that
buzzed from time to time as fluorescent bulbs died behind
a panel that read *IN-ROOM MOVIES*. I cut through a bed
of crabgrass beneath the flickering message as Kurt and his
friend Marco jogged across the highway and jumped the
barrier. Marco was carrying a boom box, and the Beastie
Boys pounded the air around him like a rubber
sledgehammer. I waited until the traffic drowned out the
sound before I snuck across the parking lot.

     I was moving along unnoticed when I skidded on a
bottle cap just beside the office. Immaculata looked like she
was about to start hollering but she was waiting on a thick-
bodied trucker at the registration desk and only glared at
me. I flicked my cigarette at the window ledge where she
was standing, sending a spray of orange sparks up over the
screen.

     Immaculata was not of the opinion that kids
belonged in a motel like the Comet and I was inclined to
agree, but after-school jobs were scarce. Though they
denied it had anything to do with Rooster, at the end of my
mother's first contract, LoboChem laid her off. Her new job
didn't pay nearly as much and she had to cut off my
allowance. KFC hired me but I was forced to quit after a
few weeks when I failed to produce ID. At the time I wasn't
sixteen yet. They told me to come back when I was, but
leaving freed me from my recurrent nightmares of falling
into the fryer, so even though my birthday had just passed I
wasn't eager to go back. Kurt got me the only other job
around at the time, babysitting for Maxine's four kids.

     Maxine was a prostitute. She lived in the last
building of The Comet, the one Immaculata was too cheap
to redecorate. It sat where the property backed onto the
woods of Bakers Basin. The Basin was some of the only

farmland left around Trenton, dotted with a handful of worn clapboard houses. There was a single main road and no streetlights so it was country-dark out over the trees and fields. None of the short-term guests were lodged in the back building apart from on New Year's Eve when the motel was booked solid. Maxine and her four kids were crammed into what The Comet called a 'double'; one large room with two queen sized beds and a bathroom.

Wages were $15.00 for three hours to allow Maxine to waitress for the happy hour crowd at the Howl & Pussycat, a strip club on Olden Avenue. Kurt was the only person from my life at Rooster's that I had any contact with. Since I couldn't help Rooster's union in the fight against LoboChem, the only thing I looked forward to was getting out of high school and, as always, travelling. I used a little of my money for cigarettes and tapes but most of my earnings to date were stashed away for my trip across America. I had $213 tucked in my bookshelf, tucked inside *To Kill a Mockingbird* where Boo was on duty, keeping it safe.

When I knocked, Delilah, the older of Maxine's two girls, flung the door open. I stood on the battered welcome mat faced with an eight-year-old girl who was wearing nothing but a pair of boys' Aquaman underwear. Maxine was just behind her, her massive tits jiggling in a cut up T shirt while she crimped her hair. "Did that 'ho up in the office give you a hard time?" Maxine's boobs were famed throughout Trenton, each one the size of a basketball.

"No, I got by her."

Rico, the ten-year-old, leapt off the bed, knocking his sister into the door. He was pointing a toy AK-47 at me. "Die, you fucking chink!" he shrieked. Rico was a solid boy, big for his age, one of those kids who made you believe what they said about the steroids in fast food.

Maxine turned, tripped over a Fischer Price school bus and then kicked it under the bed. "I swear!" she said,

"Don't know where all this shit comes from." She waved her mascara brush at Rico, "Don't let me catch you rootin' round in people's garbage. Yeah, I thought so," she added as he sucked his teeth at her.

I stepped past Rico and helped Delilah to her feet. "Don't you want to put a shirt on honey?"

"Why?" She thrust her chest out proudly. "They're just a part of nature."

Maxine was leaning into the mirror above the bureau. It was late fall and the last of the daylight was fading from the sky. "Turn on that light, will you Hope?"

I reached for the switch by the wall. A bulb overhead flickered and then cast a yellow tinge across everything in the room. All four kids were lined up on the foot of one of the beds. The covers were crumpled on the floor. The four terrors sat on the uber-bleached motel sheet in age order, Rico at ten with his gun, Delilah, eight, in her brother's underwear, Timmy, at five, with his arm in a sling, and Lavender, three years old, fiddling with a pink kitten sticker that was had been stuck to her leg brace. They were watching a movie on TV. From a glance it looked like Rambo.

"Tonight should be a good money night, Thanksgiving weekend and all. Makes up for paying you," Maxine winked. "Tried leaving these devils alone twice last week, 'cos I couldn't afford a sitter. They decided to scream out the windows for help, just to see if anyone would come and save them." Her lighter sputtered under the packed end of a Newport. "What were y'all yelling? Fire! Robber! Once that little tease even yelled Rape." She tossed her head toward Delilah. "On the bright side, people did come to help. That Immaculata 'ho didn't see it that way though. When Delilah screamed *rape* some trucker kicked the door in to save her. Broke the lock and all. Immaculata said if it happened again, she'd throw us out. Gave every one of the kids nightmares. But just so you

79

know, that lock ain't workin' great. Sometimes it don't lock at all, other times it jams."

Behind us, on the TV, a machine gun had been going off for something like five minutes. Rico was holding his gun and Delilah was waving her hand over it. Her lips were moving like she was telling herself a story, singing a little song that no one else could hear.

I lit up a cigarette with Maxine's lighter. She was leaning in to the mirror, layering on another coat of eyeliner. She looked like Tammy Faye Baker with all she had caked on, but didn't show signs of stopping there. Sometimes you can look beyond age or weight or scars and see the pretty person that used to live in a body. But after the colossal tits, I couldn't really see what was attractive about her. Pot belly, thinning hair, wrinkled skin. As if she'd read my mind she suddenly turned to me and said, "Can you believe I'm only twenty-eight?"

No, I really couldn't. I vowed that if I looked like that at twenty-eight I would jump right off the *Trenton Makes* Bridge. I'd wear a bag over my head all the way down into that cold river. And the Delaware would wash me away. Plenty of bad things disappeared into the Delaware. Rooster used to tell me about it when Mom wasn't around. As soon as I caught myself thinking about him I stopped, before I could get sad.

"Holy shit!" Maxine checked her watch, and then threw the last of her cosmetics into a gold-fringed pleather handbag. "Just one thing quick before I do. One of my customers has been getting kinda weird. He followed me home a few times. If he comes around, don't open the door. He gets mouthy but then he goes away after a few minutes." She hoisted her bag over her shoulder. "Someone is picking you up at ten?"

"Kurt's going to walk me home," I answered, leaving out the part about my mother taking off that morning for an all-weekend date with a mutual funds

80

manager in Saddle River. It was only my objection that stopped him being at Thanksgiving dinner the night before.

"Good. I was gonna say you better not let your parents see in here. You got a nice house probably." She worked a handful of earrings into a number of holes. "Oh, and Delilah has been picking up superstitions. Just ignore her." Twirling her finger around beside her temple she stepped out on the sidewalk, then yanked the door three or four times to get it to close. From the far side she yelled, "Lock it."

The push-button popped out a few times, but finally I managed to get it to stay flush with the doorknob. I looked around the room. Most of the floor space was taken up by the two beds against the left-hand wall. Murky panelling, beaten carpet and the water marked ceiling were all coated in tobacco tar. I made my way to the sunken couch that sat under the window at the back, moving a few Hefty bags of laundry around, but gave up trying to neaten anything. As soon as my cigarette was finished I noticed the smell of grimy children and dirty clothes and pushed the window open, letting some cold air blow through the dusty screen between us and the blue-black sky.

Moving a pile of sheets, I sat on the unoccupied bed. Timmy and Lavender came over right away, though she took longer, holding on to her siblings while she limped on her brace. Timmy sat and leaned against me with his good arm. Maxine told me he broke it climbing out of a dumpster with Rico. Lavender was another matter. She was born with her one little leg smaller and weaker than the other. I felt bad for Timmy but worse for Lavender. It seemed like you ought to at least make it into the world before the odds started stacking up against you.

Lavender touched my knees and smiled.

"What are we watching?" I asked, lifting her up beside me. Her brace smacked me in the shin.

"First Blood Part II" Rico hollered. "Where Rambo kills every cocksucker in his path."

"Does your mother let you curse like that?" I asked, half-heartedly. My teachers said there was no such thing as a stupid question, but there was. It was the one you asked to make a point to people who didn't care about your point and wouldn't be affected by it at all. I know that was what I was doing, but couldn't seem to stop myself all the same.

Lavender began to slide off the bed and I pulled her back up. Her brace was awkward and heavy and it was a strain to move her around. When she was in place she pointed a dimpled smile up and then settled against my side. I brushed her hair back behind her ears.

We watched Rambo. Timmy fetched an ashtray for me. Delilah ripped open a box of Apple Jacks and the kids ate handfuls of what I guessed was their dinner.

"I want Raviolis," Rico shouted.

"Did your mother leave some?" I asked.

Rico's eyes did not move from the T.V. "No, but they got some in a machine in the office. You could go get 'em."

"You know I can't leave you alone in here. And I don't have a key, so even if I could get you all up there, carrying Lavender, I can't lock the door. Eat your Apple Jacks. I'm sorry."

"I hate you!" Rico shouted.

"No you don't!" Delilah hissed. She waved her hand around next to his temple and he grabbed his head and rolled over on the bed, howling. It sounded artificial and I stayed where I was. He was flipping around like a fish and kicked the phone off the bureau.

"What's wrong with you?" I demanded, gathering up the cradle and handset from the floor. I listened. There was no dial tone. I wondered if I was going to be in trouble for the damage. "Rico! Cut it out."

"He has attention deficit hyperactivity disorder," Delilah told me neatly.

"She put a curse on me," Rico moaned.

I looked at Delilah who was proudly surveying her fingernails. "Did you put a curse on him?" I asked, out of interest.

"Yes."

"Can you take it off please?"

"Only when he says he doesn't hate you."

"I don't hate her. I don't hate her! I want to marry her! I love her!" he shouted.

Delilah waved her hands over his head but he had his eyes closed and kept howling. "It's off dummy!" She declared.

"Oh." He sat up and grabbed for his gun once more. "You made this real, right?" He asked her, looking up the barrel like a telescope."

"Yeah, but only if someone tries to get you. You can't just go looking for trouble with it or it won't work."

He pointed the gun at me. "Can I see your tits?"

"No, Rico. And that's disgusting to ask someone you aren't going out with."

"Go out with me."

"You're ten."

Back in front of the movie, the woman Rambo was falling for came into a village dressed as a prostitute. "Hope?" Timmy asked, "Where's Mommy gone?"

"To work, sweetie."

"Work where?"

"At the restaurant. She's a waitress."

"Where?"

I hunted out a clean spot on his head, and finding one, kissed it. "I don't know where it is, baby. North Trenton somewhere."

"Why is she a waitress?" Lavender asked.

"Is that lady a waitress?" Rico pointed at the T.V., mischief in his voice.

"She's an actress," I answered. I was afraid of where the conversation was going when someone knocked on the door. My heart leapt as both children beside me jumped at the sound. "It's OK," I said automatically.

"Who is it?" I called.

"Domino's." A man called back.

"Pizza! Pizza! Pizza!" Rico and Timmy started chanting.

"That's not for us." I tried to quash their excitement on the way to the door. Through the peephole I saw a tall man in his forties with a head of wild black hair, his complexion potholed with acne scars. He was looking at the ground. He didn't look like any pizza delivery guy I'd ever seen. Too old, too tall, and also, there was no hat. Domino's guys always wore hats.

"We didn't order a pizza," I called through the door.

"You sure?"

"Yeah, I'm sure."

"Well, can I borrow your phone to call my dispatch?"

"Try the office." I answered, and returned to my seat on the bed.

Lavender got busy braiding the worn fringe on my jeans and in a minute I was back into the movie.

There was another knock at the door.

"Yeah?" I shouted. Nothing. I stood up.

It was quiet for a minute and then the knock came again, so hard the door shook in the frame. "Maxine? Maxine you fuckin' whore, let me in. I got money.

I tiptoed to the door. I looked through the peephole again. It was the same guy, and this time I realized why his appearance was so disturbing as he put his bright green eye up to the peephole. I jerked back. A werewolf.

84

Timmy was clutching my leg. I looked down at the lock, praying it was secure. "Maxine isn't here. You have the wrong room."

"Don't lie to me you fucking whore. I know she's in there."

He kicked the door and I jumped back, nearly toppling Timmy. I caught him and then reached for the other children. Delilah took my hand. Lavender crawled into a pile of blankets. I left her there. If that asshole kicked the door in, I hoped she would stay hidden. Timmy started to cry. I checked for Rico. He was standing in the middle of the bed, his AK-47 pointed at the door.

"OK, the phone, the phone." I said, my voice shaking. I lifted it up out of some crazy wish it was no longer broken, but of course it was. Were the hell was Immaculata? The guy was making plenty of noise.

I was in the middle of the room with the children around me when everything went quiet again. So quiet I remembered the quiet of the soulless. We clung to each other in that little pack, listening to our breathing slow down.

Shaking her shoulder, I ordered Delilah to put some clothes on. She scurried to one of the toppling towers of laundry and whipped on a shirt and jeans. The clock said 7:15. Kurt and Maxine should be along in about forty-five minutes. I thought of the trucker in the office, of Immaculata.

I perched on the edge of the bed. The children gathered in close. I tried to watch the movie but all I kept saying was "It's all right. It's all right." Trying to contain my panic had me seeing explosions of stars around the edges of my vision. I hadn't had a migraine in years, but this sure felt like one.

There was a scratch at the window screen. A shadow moved behind it. "It's not fuckin' all right you little fuckin' cunt. Where's Maxine?"

I jumped up, looking for something to defend us with. All I found was the plastic school bus. Hands scrabbled at the edge of the window. I screamed and flung it at the screen as hard as I could. It only deterred him as long as it took to duck but in that time I ran to the window, grabbing at the bar to release the frame. The mechanism was tricky and I dug my fingers into it, trying to get it to close. The dim shape of the man's face hovered just outside, churning out clouds of his breath in the cold. Shaggy beard, hard, strange green eyes. His neck was as thick as his head. With a smack of his hand half the screen popped out of the frame. In a second I wouldn't be able to get the window shut.

Then two other hands were working the latch. Rico freed it and together we slammed the window into the frame where it locked in place. Just beyond it, thick yellowed fingernails pried up the edge of the loose screen and yanked it fully out of the frame. A meaty palm pounded on the glass. I stumbled backward off the couch, twisting my ankle as the glass bowed under the man's hand.

"He's gonna break it!" Rico yelled.

I pulled him off the couch and then spun to see Delilah waving her fingers at the window. Her eyes were shut and she was mumbling to herself. A crash came from outside. "Mother fucker!" The man yelled.

I turned to Rico.

"He fell off the trashcans."

We looked at Delilah.

I knew I was going to have to try to get out the door, then, while the man was still behind the building. I figured I'd carry Lavender and Rico could make sure Timmy could make it with his bad arm. Delilah could run. We would try for the office, but even if we didn't get there, at least we would be outside. Someone would hear us. Someone would help us. "Get your shoes on!" I ordered.

86

The kids flew, pulling on sneakers, slippers, whatever they found. It was amazing how kids would listen when they were terrified. I remembered myself.

I scooped Lavender up. She wrapped her arms around my shoulders and pressed her face into my neck. Her leg brace gouged me in the stomach as she clung on. "OK, we're going to run straight to the office," I said. "If anybody grabs you I want you to scream your heads off."

One, two, I counted to myself. I grabbed the doorknob on three and yanked. Nothing happened. "It's stuck!" I twisted and pulled but the knob only spun in my hand. I fought off tears, telling myself I had to be brave for the kids. Giving up on the door I backed into the room. "We're going to have to yell for help," I said. I thought the kids were already scared but a new look of terror came into their huge eyes.

"No, no!" Rico cried, and to my amazement, welled up. "We'll get kicked out. We'll be on the street again."

I wanted to reason with him, to tell him no one would punish them for a genuine emergency, but he threw himself to the floor, arms and legs flailing. "I'm not living in the car again," he shrieked, his face bright red. He started to hyperventilate and I knelt beside him, awkward with Lavender clinging to me like a chimpanzee. "OK, OK, we won't scream. We can bang on the walls though, can't we?"

Rico began to rock and put his fist halfway into his mouth, his eyes wide and unfocused. I was patting heads and shushing kids when I heard a scratching noise coming from the far end of the room. In a sickening moment I realized the man had moved the trashcan down and was prying at the window of the dark bathroom. I struggled to stand with Lavender, meaning to run and slam the last window shut, when I heard the screen clatter into the bathtub.

I wanted to scream but nothing came out. I clutched Lavender. Rico was on his feet, his fists clenched. It broke my heart seeing his young arms posed to fight. This is it, I thought, this is how we die. There was a clamour from the bathroom as heavy feet landed in the tub. I heard the shower curtain rip from its metal rings.

The man appeared in the bathroom doorway dressed in blue coveralls with a wolf emblem on the pocket. He was huge, over six feet and built across the shoulders. His eerie eyes ran over us and settled on me. "If that dirty whore ain't here, one of you gonna stand in for her 'til you get her here. I know she ain't leave you without a way to reach her."

Delilah moved quickly but I was so worried about the man that I barely noticed as she dragged the toy gun from the floor and thrust it into Rico's hands.

The man stepped into the room and I pulled Delilah behind me. "You're not going to hurt these kids," I managed to get out.

"I'm gonna hurt you though," he said evenly.

"Don't come any closer," Rico warned, taking aim. I didn't have a free hand or I would have pulled him behind me too.

The man laughed and it sent a wave of electric nausea through me. The room exploded with the clack clack clack of gunfire. In the confusion I thought it was the T.V. again except that there was smoke in the room and my ears were ringing. Rico fell backwards. The kids screamed and clutched me, their little nails digging into my flesh. A smell of burnt oil crept over the odour of dirty clothes.

On the floor, his face hidden in the dark of the bathroom, the intruder lay sprawled and torn. The soles of his steel cap boots faced us, the rubber stained with the same fluorescent green as his eyes. Blood was splattered from floor to ceiling. As I looked at him the pocket of his uniform flapped back against his shattered chest. *LC Disposals* it read.

In wonder, I stared at Rico. He slid his hand from the gun and rubbed his fingers. His face was sickly white and beaded with sweat. Timmy was bawling, his face pressed into my thigh.

Only Delilah looked calm.

As the smoke began to clear I heard a key in the lock. In a moment Immaculata was standing in the doorway, her passkey stretched from her belt. I braced myself for a tirade, the children still stuck to me. She remained quiet though, only scanned her eyes across the room and looked each of us up and down. She shut the door and stepped toward the man on the floor. For a log moment she studied his boots and then waved the sign of the cross over herself and each of us. "Go wait in the office for Maxine," she said, handing me a set of keys. "There's some Handi Wipes under the desk. And open the vending machine so the kids can get something to eat."

In the motel office I unlocked the vending machine but the kids just piled onto the plastic chairs and held onto each other and to me. When Maxine appeared I wondered how the kids would handle it. Struck dumb myself, when they said goodbye and shuffled out the door to their mother, I stayed where I was and listened through the window. One of the maids stopped Maxine and started telling her something about the ceiling having collapsed in her room. None of the kids interrupted. They showed nothing, not fear, not change. Their faces amazed me, blank and alert in the way of convicts, eyes down, ears up. The maid was tall and blonde and not at all like the petite Hispanic women who usually took the carts of towels and soap around. She looked up at me, straightening the collar of her pink uniform. It was Ivka Repinka. With a quick wink she made me think twice about saying anything to Maxine.

I decided to do as the children did, to show nothing. All the way home I thought about LoboChem. I hadn't seen a werewolf since my father disappeared and I guess I had gotten around to thinking they didn't really exist. I thought about telling Rooster but I knew he would probably rush right over and insist on watching me until my Mom got home. I didn't want to put him at that risk. So for a while I just kept quiet and tried to figure out a plan.

It was only when Kurt had walked me all the way home and I was safe in the house with Toffee next to me on my bed that I told him what had happened. I thought he might want to call the police, but instead, after we debated it awhile, he called his uncle, dialling a list of payphones he kept in his wallet until Freak Eddie answered.

Whatever Happened to Christmas?

Things only got tougher for my Mom in her new job. She said the pay would go up eventually but LoboChem had refused to give her references, which had lost her a chance at two industry posts. She was working for the State of New Jersey, Department of Health. At home she became vigilant about shutting off lights and water and shopping for bargain brands. We ate pasta nearly every night, and argued over it. Only the night before I had blown up at her for nagging me about leaving the water running while I washed the dishes. "If you'd just married Rooster in the first place we wouldn't have these problems", I'd shouted. As usual, when I brought up that sore subject, she shot thorns into me with her eyes and retreated to her bedroom for the rest of the evening.

We argued a lot but I still did not like seeing her so tired and worried. Secretly I came to understand why she had taken the job with LoboChem in the first place, but my vengeful feelings toward the company were growing all the time. The werewolf at the Comet had driven the point home to me that the danger of the factory was spreading beyond pollution of the canal. But it was what happened to Noelle the night Eddie told Kurt and me to meet him at the Moorings Bar that showed me just how bad things were getting.

A Trenton love story can't be understood from the outside, so I've always remembered this the way Noelle told it.

Noelle had finished a four hour shift at the Howl & Pussycat early in the evening. Dancing always made her hungry and while she was welcome to a free plate of wings at the bar, that meant talking to customers. She didn't mind when there were friendly faces around but that night there weren't, which would only leave her fending off annoying questions. Did she have a boyfriend? Were those her real tits? No, Yes. She couldn't face a whole night of it. She wanted food, not conversation. She had P.M.S. and she'd spent four tiring hours longing to climb into a big sweatshirt and leggings and go somewhere that she did not have to hold her stomach in. Without her makeup, she barely looked her eighteen years. She was glad of it as she knotted her hair up in ponytails and pulled on her Keds.

Cars honked as she walked up Olden Avenue, her white-blonde hair bouncing beside her ears. Her boobs were killing her. Going topless just before her period was agony. They were covered up with a cotton bra and zipped inside her sweatshirt, but still, buried as they were, had guys shouting out the windows of their cars. Men flew by with howls like sirens. Wayhaaaaay. Aaaalllaaalllaaaaahooo. Yoyoyoyoyo. She had a cartoonish fantasy that one of them would turn away from her just in time to smack his face into a mailbox. But, car by car, they only wailed off into the night as she kept walking.

A short cut took her away from the traffic. The evenings were getting darker and Noelle stuffed her hands into her pockets, cozy and warm against the crisp air. Tired, she walked a little slower than usual, and found herself looking into the windows of the row houses she passed. Families framed in slung Christmas lights, eating, talking, gelled together in the gentle blue flicker of the TV; the sight of them made her wistful.

Walking along, her hunger returned and she knew she'd better eat something soon or she'd start to get dizzy. On a back road she spied a neon sign for a place she always passed by without stopping – a place between work and home and somehow too far from either to bother going in. The name on the sign opened like a neon fan: *The Moorings Bar-n-Grill*. Hot food, it said. Cold drinks.

Inside, heads turned, eyes started sucking on her. Grey men on barstools, identical and infinite. What was left when Trenton chewed up and crapped out the young men, she thought, wondering if she had a Midol in her purse. It wasn't like her to be mean about people.

The Moorings was divided into tavern and restaurant and she headed away from the dark bar and over to the brighter dining section where she sat at a wobbly table beneath a red foil garland. A waitress brought a menu. Noelle didn't want to risk getting carded and so ordered Diet Coke, a cheeseburger and fries. Marion looked down at her as she scribbled. "Where you gonna put all that? Tiny thing like you?"

Noelle shrugged. "Haven't eaten all day."

"All right, well, we'll get somethin' in ya'." Marion drummed her fingers lightly on Noelle's shoulder, then tucked her pencil behind her ear and hustled off to shout the order through a swinging door. In a moment, her tangerine uniform returned with the drink and a little bundle of cutlery, which Noelle unwound from its napkin in anticipation, even though she had ordered pick-it-up-and-eat-it food.

With the waitress gone, the room felt large and crowded with loud strangers. There were some women in the restaurant, almost none in the bar. Noelle tugged her sweatshirt forward, unzipping it a little to compensate for the warm air coming from the kitchen. She leaned her elbows on the table. That's when she saw Kurt and me playing pool while we waited for Eddie. She hadn't seen us in a while and waved but our backs were turned and just as she was about to stand, her food came, steaming in a paper-lined basket. Marion patted her hand and Noelle felt happy to hole up in a homey place for a little while instead of going back to the empty house that she still hadn't cleared of her parents' things. She knew Kurt and I would have to pass her to leave, and so she tucked in, knowing she could catch us on the way out.

Meat juice dripped onto her wax paper as she picked up her burger. Heaven was made of hot food on a lonesome night. Sinking into the meal she took a deep breath and closed her eyes while she chewed. Her dad had made the best burgers in New Jersey. Maybe all of America. The strain in her shoulders began to fade as she swallowed. Rolling her ankles, she pointed and flexed her feet under the table, glad to be out of her platform heels.

Reaching for another bite she opened her eyes to find a man sitting across from her. He was licking the corner of his mouth and he had the kind of bug-out eyes that made it look like something was squeezing his neck. "Looks like you like meat." He tweaked his nose a few times, rubbed his hands on the legs of his blue coveralls. The patch on his chest read *LC Disposals*, arched above the logo of a wolf's head.

Noelle, who was normally prepared for commentary, had gotten a bit lost in the memory of barbeque and could not think of what to say. From the corner of her eye she saw a few women starting to glance over, a sure sign that a guy had a nasty reputation. She glanced at Kurt and me again but we were involved in our game.

"Can I just ask you one question and I'll leave you alone?" He jiggled his legs under the table so hard it made her Coke shimmy.

"Listen mister, I just got off work, I'm tired and I only want to eat my food, OK?" Noelle's fingers were sinking into her burger bun but she did not seem able to lift it to her mouth. The man had put a cap on her appetite.

He leaned across the table at her, so close she could smell the beer on his breath. "Just one question missy. Don't get your panties tangled. See, you a little skinny girl but you got them big beautiful titties. Alls I want to know," he said, looking hungrily at her chest, "is whether them nice titties of yours is real, or if you gone and stuffed your bra just trying to give us all boners."

94

Noelle looked around, met my eyes. Fear showed on her face and I gave Kurt's arm a push. He laid his cue on the table.

"Mister, I just want to eat my dinner." Noelle looked back at the man in coveralls, and saw he was holding her fork. The floor was greasy and her toe slid out from under her as she tried to push her chair back.

"Just want to settle a bet, missy."

Wildly, she looked back toward the pool table. When she did, the jumpsuit man lunged across the table and plunged the fork into her left breast.

Noelle screamed and snapped back in her chair just as Kurt grabbed the man by his shoulders and yanked him from his seat. The man's chair was caught in his legs and it toppled and skidded across the aisle hitting Marion in her shins. The men wrestled but Kurt was winning and managed to drag her attacker towards the door. Noelle looked down, her head tingling, saw the fork sticking out of her chest. There was a throbbing pain in her breast and all at once she was nauseous, numb and terrified.

She saw me making my way through the crowd. Her face was pale, shocked, angry. The scene was so bizarre, seeing the fork rising and sinking with her breath. Everything seemed quiet except a rushing in her ears.

"Better pull that out," a customer from the next table advised. Tidy and pudgy with a curl set that hadn't been combed, the woman frowned with concern as she gestured at the injury. Noelle nodded, took hold of the fork, and with a deep breath, yanked it free. It tinkled against the floor as she fainted.

Noelle came to in the parking lot. *The Moorings* sign blinked across the street.

"We had to take you outside. The manager in there doesn't like fights. She never cares who started it, she kicks everyone out." I told her, taking hold of her hand. "You remember Kurt's cousin, Freak Eddie? He can take you to the emergency room if you want to go."

Noelle sat up on the hood of the car where we put her and examined us. Kurt and me she recognized immediately, but Freak Eddie took a moment. He was tall and dark and his eyes were such a vibrant green that she had to turn away to keep from staring. An ache in her chest drew her attention. There was a set of four puncture marks rimmed with crimson on her skin and she remembered what happened and started to cry.

Two arms slid underneath her and she was lifted from the car. She put her arms around Eddie's neck. Kurt and I stayed in the parking lot while he walked off under the streetlights carrying Noelle, the light turning her hair a ghostly blue. Above them, the violet cone of smoke from LoboChem wound against the dark sky.

"Where do you live?" he asked. His voice was metallic, and put her in mind of a wooden spoon hitting a heavy old copper pot. As he walked with her, she imagined he was a machine man, an invincible guardian with bike chains for vocal chords.

She told him the way, and though it was nearly a mile to her house, he carried her home. There was a tattoo on his neck, a mermaid. Another tattoo on his cheekbone, a cross. There were other tattoos, on his hands and probably all over him, she thought. His strength, as he carried her, calmed her. At her door she gave him the key from her handbag and he brought her into the house her mother had decorated in cornflower blue.

When Noelle was on her bed Eddie removed her sneakers and socks. She pulled off her sweatshirt and sat in her bra looking at the damage done her. The bathroom cabinet was open and she heard Eddie rummaging. In a moment he returned to dab peroxide on the wound. Her teeth gritted involuntarily and she closed her eyes at the sting and white fizzle. Then his big hands were in her own

96

and she squeezed until the pain stopped. Together, their fingers explored gently, defining the edges of the blooming bruise.

When Noelle woke in the morning she went downstairs to find Eddie sleeping in her father's armchair, the chair propped against the door of the house. On guard duty. At the sound of her step he woke and she asked him what he wanted for breakfast.

When Noelle figured she was ready to put some makeup over her injury and go back to work Freak Eddie rode to the Howl & Pussycat. He came on his Harley and sat with the other bikers. There were no soppy bouquets, no boxes of cellulite-producing chocolate, like admirers gave to the bouncers to deliver. Every day, Eddie waited until the end of Noelle's shift and took her to the Colonial Diner on Route 1. He bought her whatever she wanted to eat and he ate a well-done steak and baked potato. He took her home and slept in the chair. After two weeks of this she asked him if he would like to sleep in her bed.

"Show me some ID." Eddie said. Noelle laughed in surprise but he was not laughing at all and she went off to find her driver's licence.

Eddie's tall body was longer than the bed. His dark hair was wild against the blue gingham pillows.

"What would you have done if I'd been sixteen?" she asked, emboldened by the feel of his large dry hands on her hips.

"Gone home, and put my balls on ice for two years."

She bit her lip, "How old are you?"

His thumb found the small assault, gently pried her lip from her teeth. "Thirty-three."

"You're nearly old enough to be my daddy."

He pulled her on top of him, ran his hands up and down her back, across her white marshmallow skin and brushed her hair from her face. "Very nearly," he said, and kissed her forehead and held her tight in his tattooed arms.

Noelle cooked breakfast. Pancakes, eggs, bacon. Eddie started to come over at other times, not just after Noelle's shift was done. She borrowed a tarp off her neighbour so she could cover Eddie's Low Rider when he stayed over. She bought steaks. She baked potatoes. In an old box her dad left her, she dug through and found a recipe written in lime green ink for Shoe-Fly Pie. He'd thought it would be the two of them left when her mother died of her cancer. That's what they'd been expecting. They hadn't been expecting that he would get it too, in his brain. There'd only been a month to get used to the idea, and then he was gone. One of the last things he asked his wife to do was write down her recipes. "Your Mom got funny about ink near the end," Noelle's dad told her, "wouldn't write in anything but bright green." He died that night. Noelle made that pie once a week and never before would she give anybody in the world a piece of it, but she fed it to Eddie bite by bite from her own fork. That fork like a divining rod between them. Like a compass point. This is north. This is water. This is life.

Eddie. Eddie on the street at night. Eddie in her bed. Eddie at the club, making her whole world safe. She expected there was steel just under his skin, going by the sculpted feel of him, that he was bullet-proof. Only his lips, his eyes, his heart were soft.

On stage, she was dancing for Eddie, watching him, no matter who was wagging dollars in front of her. The manager noticed and told her off in the dressing room after her shift. Noelle thought about her parents' house. It was small, only four rooms in all, but it was what they'd left her

– the part they'd been able to pay for. The rest was up to her to cover. More than she could swing for a month of waiting tables or working in a store. She went to Eddie with a pact. She would act like she was dancing for other men but he was to take it as if she was dancing for him.

"If I thought otherwise I wouldn't be here," he answered, stroking her pony tail.

And she knew they were one.

Over the weeks, Eddie kissed the four little puncture marks until they and the blood-purple bruise were gone.

One night, the man in the LC Disposals coveralls showed up at the Howl & Pussycat. He sat in front of the stage and when he saw Noelle in her red and white sequins, he did not recognize her. Noelle danced her ass off to Bon Jovi and did not notice him. Eddie noticed him.

In the parking lot Eddie only stopped kicking when he heard a loud crack. It was a rib, that crack, he knew.

They were in bed, Eddie and Noelle. She was so small, and yet, when they lay down, they seemed the same size, except that her feet tickled his shin bones. Eddie was six-foot-one to her five-foot-two. He was plastered with tattoos of angels and animals and symbols of sacrifice. Noelle tripped her fingers through the black hairs of his chest, across the blue white skin until she found an angel with golden hair that ran the length of his arm.

"Me," she announced.

"You like that one?" he asked.

When she nodded, her pony tails tickled his arm. The next time he came home he lifted his sleeve and showed her the raised red skin of his newest ink, just under the angel. *Marry me*, it read.

Noelle was telling her fiancé that she wanted Kurt and me to come to the wedding, since it was because of us that they

99

met. Then, because that triggered a question, she asked, "I didn't see you in the bar the night I was stabbed. Where'd they find you?"

"They called me at work."

Noelle looked so astonished that Eddie laughed. "You knew I had a job, right?"

The truth was, she had not really thought of it. He paid for everything when they were together. Things just seemed taken care of, somehow.

"Do you want to know what I do?"

By then she was not sure she did and only continued to gaze up at him with surprised blue eyes.

"I collect money, and I look into things. When I'm working you can get me on a couple of payphones. Kurt just called around 'til he found me. He knew I'd want to know what happened."

Noelle let it sink in, what Eddie did for money. When it did, she kissed his knuckles. Pressed her lips to the little white scars, the rough red scabs, the knitted bones.

Eddie had not been to confession in twenty years so they went to Hamilton where they could be married by the mayor in a park gazebo. Noelle wore a beaded camisole, a long white chiffon skirt. Eddie wore his leather vest, his new black jeans. (I had secretly hoped that Rooster and some of the others would be at the ceremony but Eddie said only that there were too many people snapping pictures in the park and Kurt and I were told on the spot we were to be the best man and maid of honor.)

On the way home from the ceremony Eddie and Noelle argued. It was a small spat about work he needed to do later that night. Noelle did not want him to go but stopped short of saying so. We were driving back to Trenton in Rooster's Barracuda. He'd loaned to Eddie for the occasion. After Noelle and Eddie made up their minds to kiss and forget the argument, they decided we should go to the Moorings where it all began. That was how Eddie put it, *where it all began*. And Noelle liked this because it made it feel like she was in a comic book and that the world could be divided into episodes of strain and episodes of safety, just by turning a page.

Noelle made bacon and eggs. She made pancakes. She baked her special Shoe-Fly pie. Steaks, steaks, steaks. Fried chicken once in a while. Eddie sat in front of the T.V., sometimes with his hands in bowls of ice. Noelle told him about her night at the Howl & Pussycat. The last few times that he had missed her performance was because he had work to do. This time, he did not. He was only tired. He had taken on an extra job for a boss in Chambersburg.

"I don't like you being so tired," Noelle said as she rubbed Deep Heat in to his shoulders. "We have what we need. Why do you want to work so hard?"

"I don't want to talk about it."

But Noelle wasn't having it. "And where's all this extra money going? You ain't in my club, so how do I know you ain't in somebody else's? Takes a lot of money to hang out in strip clubs. Maybe that's why you're working so much. How do I know…?"

Eddie lifted a soaking limb from the icy water, grabbed her tiny hand, pulled her around the side of the chair, toppled her into his lap.

"I want to pay off the mortgage," he said. "I want to work hard so you don't have to work at all. I want us to have a kid."

When he asked her to stop taking the pill she did. She missed a period but then got it three weeks late. She missed another, but got that a month later. She missed again and paid no attention. The manager at the Howl & Pussycat told her she could pick up some shifts at his other club, The Jackal. She and Eddie were working seven nights a week, saving all they could and trying like crazy at making a baby in between. Tired of waiting, Noelle used her wages to redecorate the small bedroom, her old bedroom, into a nursery. She and Eddie had since moved into the big bedroom, the one that used to be her parents'. Eddie was on the mortgage, helping to pay it down.

Her period did not come and Noelle was feeling very tired and very sick. Suddenly something occurred to her and she ran off to the CVS. Back at home, a four dollar pregnancy test came out positive. Noelle called every payphone on her list. No answer. She ran to see Kurt and me, the closest thing she had to family. Together we called, we walked the streets, asked questions.

Two days went by. Eddie could not be found. Alone on the evening of the third day, Noelle began to call hospitals, police stations. While she was at this task a heavy knock came at the door. In her kitchen Billy Regret gave her an envelope, an apology. Eddie had been found that afternoon in the woods behind the LoboChem factory, on his back, strangled, a fork stuck in his eye. Noelle was told the police were not planning to investigate.

With her parents and Eddie gone, Noelle found most of her day spent imagining diving into the black Delaware, imagining that down in that dark cold she might find them again. She lived in a storybook hope that Eddie might reach up out of the darkness for her one more time and carry her away to safety.

If not for the pregnancy she would have leapt from the *Trenton Makes* Bridge. She knew that. The baby kept her going, first the idea, then the kicking. The sympathy envelope held enough money to pay off the mortgage, and a couple of years living expenses if she signed up for benefits and was very careful. One day at the doctor's office she saw the baby moving on a T.V screen and decided to stop crying before she drowned him in grief. For Eddie she would do this.

The following winter, when the baby was born, Noelle named him Angel before she even saw him, before she even knew he was a boy. At first glance, he had her blonde hair and his daddy's green eyes. The nurse put him in Noelle's arms and she looked him all over, fighting off the sleep of exhaustion, counting his fingers and toes through a love that pointed in upon her like an inverted sun. She inspected his arms and legs with wonder. At his shoulder she stopped. Her head was nodding and her eyes were crossing and the nurse came to take the baby from her arms. There was a birthmark on his shoulder, a bluish black smudge that, as she forced herself to focus, became an angel.

 Her sleep was deep, dark, like a canal she swam down that only lightened as she approached the surface. She woke calling for her baby just as he was crying for her. Propped on pillows, after the nurse got her set up for the first feeding, Noelle told her she would rather be alone. When she was, she uncovered his shoulder, looked for the mark. It was there, as she remembered it, only larger.

 Days went by, weeks, and every morning she looked at the birthmark – a dark-haired angel that grew with her son, making tiny changes with the passing days. The head defined, the wings lengthened, and finally a ribbon of letters formed at his feet, just where Eddie's proposal to her had appeared on his arm. Noelle turned the bedside lamp toward her baby's shoulder and leaned in close to decipher the tiny print. After a moment she sat back, smiling.

 Daddy's watching, it said.

Junkyard Cats

Congenital tattoos were just the sort of wonder you could expect in Trenton. We were covered in little miracles to carry us through the tragedies, like each of us had a bejewelled flak jacket tailored right to us. Toffee and I had walked with the boys over to Noelle's for a cookout and I imagined we were like knights, called to prove ourselves time and again in order to strengthen our armour made of marvel.

Marco scraped chop meat from the grill. He had spent the whole morning with Kurt and me talking about how to get Noelle to see things clearly. When he tried to talk to her directly she became defensive, so he busied himself with the hamburgers, and kept his reactions to the occasional frown. Eddie was one of the few men Marco could admit to respecting, but his feelings for Noelle were running fast in the direction of hopeless, stupid, death-defying, sacrificial, do-not-pass-go-and-fuck-you-and-your-$200, love.

It was summer. There was a pink sky over Trenton, dotted with sardines making their way to the Delaware for spawning. I was sitting at the picnic table, waiting for a burger, watching Marco watch Noelle. Around my ankles, chocolate hearts were blooming out of the crabgrass. It was a beautiful day in New Jersey.

Three months had passed since the murder. It seemed greedy to talk to a widow about missing her husband, so we mostly just looked at the ground when we were reminded of him.

"I know y'all think I'm crazy. I can see it in your faces, but Eddie's still alive." In between talking Noelle kissed Angel's hands. Marco grinned at the baby, who was only an infant, but already a good-looking kid, with big green eyes like Eddie's.

Returning to the barbeque, Marco dealt out American cheese slices across the burgers. He wiped his fingers on an apron stamped "Moorings Bar and Grille."

Kurt was nearest the barbeque. With a twist he withdrew his thumb from a loop on my jeans and reached for the first plate Marco held out. "If Dottie sees you stole that apron from the Moorings she'll set you on fire while you wearin' it," he grinned.

Marco patted the apron over his stomach. "I ain't want to get no more grease on me. Last cookout ruin that red shirt that went with my Adidas suit." It was the outfit he knew he looked best in, white with red stripes, and he glanced at Noelle to see if the mention of it might have triggered some little bit of attention. She was blowing raspberries on Angel's cheeks, laughing and paying Marco no mind. The next burger, dripping with plastic cheese, he pointed at her.

"Thank you Marco. I do love a cheeseburger. My daddy made the best in the whole state."

Marco's shoulders drooped.

Noelle gave him a little sympathetic frown. "Well, he *was* my daddy." She put Angel in his bouncy seat and then reached for her plate. "But these are the second best. You can't ask for a higher complement from me. You should see all the stuff I can't ever tell another man he's the best at, first from Daddy dying and then because of Eddie being away." Her chin quivered and she clamped her lips shut before forcing a smile.

Marco took a quick glance at the rest of us and then stared off into the distance while Kurt and I looked down at the chocolate hearts that had melted into the grass. Bobby Joe rubbed his forehead, studied his Nikes. Things weren't the same. Kurt and I weren't the same. We had run out of things to say to each other. Noelle and Eddie were about the only subject we took a mutual interest in anymore.

As if he'd read my thoughts, Kurt squeezed my hand. The boys thought we ought to get Noelle to a shrink or a priest. As they saw it, apart from pretending her husband wasn't dead, Noelle was good people. She was great with Angel. He was the cleanest baby for miles, big and strong for his three months. He had those birthmarks that made him look just like Eddie; like he was covered in tiny tattoos. Most mothers would have been upset about that, but Noelle took it right in stride. It took some explaining whenever Angel saw a new doctor; a baby with congenital tattoos. But Noelle only gazed in fascination at the angel that appeared just after his birth, the eagle that spread its wings across his back when he first crawled, and most recently, a thorny cross that came through on his father's birthday.

What bothered me was everyone wanting to pull Noelle out of a fantasy where she clearly needed to be. I told Kurt that people don't build their own little world for no reason anymore than they'd build their own house for no reason. "She got a house," he said. I gave up there.

Noelle pondered our distant faces. "Believe what y'all want but nobody ever let me see the body, did they?" An Eskimo kiss joined her nose with her son's. "I paid for the funeral. I packed away his stuff. I even went and said in the mirror over and over, *Eddie is dead. You're all alone now.* Tried for a long time, but...nothing."

Marco stopped mid-bite. "But nothin' what?"

"But it hasn't sunk in. I know Eddie can hear me somewhere. He comes to me in my dreams. I can see him clear as if he was right here with me. And he does the same with Angel, I'm sure. Sometimes Angel wakes up howling in his crib, and just before I get to him he goes all quiet and starts looking up in the air above his bed, smiling and laughing just like he does whenever somebody's playing with him. A couple of times his mobile even started up, spinning round and playing music."

They say never to wake a sleepwalker and I thought the same counted for Noelle. It was a shame to shake a sufferer out of a sweet dream. It was like knocking someone off a rainbow.

The sound of the doorbell came from the front of the house. Bobby Joe went to answer it. He had a car now, loaned to him by his Uncle Twenty when Twenty was sent to Rahway for manslaughter. It was a mint condition, matador red 1969 GTO. Since Twenty was sentenced to nine years he said Bobby Joe might as well drive it so long as he was careful. Bobby Joe liked to check on that car a couple of times an hour. Several minutes passed. Kurt was about to investigate when Noelle pointed out that he might just be polishing the chrome again.

The second set of burgers were sizzling on the grill when Bobby Joe appeared in the back doorway. His cheeks were slack and he was shaking his head, looking down at a letter in his hand. "It's for Eddie," he told us, just above a whisper, "Came postage due."

"You see! I told you!" Tiny silver stars trickled down Noelle's cheeks. She was smiling and rocking from foot to foot cuddling Angel in a way that made me get a lump in my throat.

Marco cracked his knuckles. "Girl, we all wish we have Eddie back. He used to look out for us all when we was growin' up." He flashed a desperate glance at Kurt. "He's the one got Officer Thompkin on suspension for not goin' in to help after Kurt's mom hung herself. Fact, he was ready to go toe-to-toe that time Thompkin take me by the neck and try chokin' me."

Bobby Joe doubled up with laughter and slapped hands with Marco. "Thompkin ain't shake nothin' but his arm though, skinny m'fucker. And Eddie just wound up laughin' his ass off. Thompkin ain't like that much neither."

I ate the heart off my candy necklace. After a long silence Kurt scratched his forehead. "We got to open the letter. Or you do, Noelle. We can be right here or we can split, s'up to you."

The letter was pressed against Noelle's chest between her and the baby. "Somebody hold Angel."

I sat with the baby as Noelle kissed the letter up to God and tore open the envelope. Inside was a piece of paper with the heading *100 Canal Street*. Below was a handwritten message:

> *Dr. J. Bongiovi, Neurologist, is now located at the above address.*

Marco held out a thick palm, "See, girl, it was just a regular reminder. Nothing special."

But Noelle was studying the back of the letter. She held it up to the light and then passed it around. It had the watermark of an angel. It was an angel I recognized, the dark outline I had first seen on Rooster's shoulder.

"Coincidence?" Marco tried.

Kurt stood up. "Except that Eddie ain't never been to no *nor-ogist* doctor never, whatever the hell that is."

"Wouldn't he have seen a neurologist when he had that metal plate put in his head from the train accident?" I asked

"I never believed that story," Noelle insisted. "Eddie and me were open with each other, but there were some things he just wouldn't tell me. And he wouldn't bring me around his friends. I ain't seen anybody but Billy Regret that one time since your fourteenth birthday Hope. I think Eddie was into something he didn't want me to know about, for my own sake."

I thought about my birthday and the arrests. It made sense that afterwards Rooster and the rest of the bikers would have gone underground. Not given up, as I had.

Bobby Joe stood at Kurt's side and crossed his arms. "Maybe so but that don't give nobody the right to stick a fork in him." He grabbed the letter from me. "And where the fuck it 100 Canal Street?"

I looked at the angel, the outline of my mother glowing as the sun passed through Bobby Joe's hands. "The barrel factory." I said.

A big smile spread across Noelle's face. "And I bet you dollars-to-donuts there ain't a neurologist in the state with the name of my favourite singer. I used to dance to Bon Jovi for Eddie all the time."

My conscience spoke up before I could argue with it. "Look guys, Rooster told me never to go down to that part of the canal. LoboChem dumps chemicals down there."

"And LoboChem's got big trespassin' signs up, some of 'em on public property." Bobby Joe asserted. "So, we gonna listen'?"

I was the first to smile.

Potential news from the dead seemed a good enough reason to send Bobby Joe and me next door to buy a case of beer off Noelle's neighbour. Noelle told us she ran a small liquor shop on Ohio Avenue and kept some overstock in her garage. When the door opened and Ivka Repinka greeted us in a pink housedress and curlers I quickly looked at Bobby Joe. No one else had ever been able to see her before. He paid her and took the beer. When he turned to go down the steps she winked at me. "What are you doing here?" I whispered.

"Where you think guardian angel supposed to be with you cooking crazy plans? You don't cut yourself today, ok? You be careful. No bleed."

I trotted down the steps and caught Bobby Joe at the Noelle's gate. I was curious about him seeing Ivka. "She looks so young to own a liquor store." I said.

110

"What are you high? She's gotta be sixty years old. Tell you what though," he hefted the case, "she's strong for a pudgy little granny."

I held the gate open. Bobby Joe saw someone, but not my Ivka. I wasn't sure what to make of it, but I decided I would be doubly careful in the yard.

We downed the beer while we planned, or really the boys downed the beer. I had one and Noelle passed. Next thing I knew Marco was standing in the living room, barking out ideas while the rest of us ran to the basement and attic, filling a crate with the necessary paraphernalia. Somehow extra items found their way in: first aid kit, hot water bottle, a box of Pop Tarts, mace, a compass.

"What the Pop Tarts for?" Kurt laughed.

"Might be there for a long time. Somebody might get hungry," Noelle called out as she and Bobby Joe passed in the kitchen doorway.

"Fool, we only goin' a mile! What we need a map for?" Bobby Joe yelled toward Marco as he tossed some rope into the crate.

Marco waved his arm and I removed the map. "Ditch the compass too?" I asked.

"Nah, that might come in handy," Noelle called from the kitchen. "Always was something funny about Eddie and metal." She looked at the doubtful faces of the boys. "I said I wasn't buying that plate-in-his-head story, just bring it."

After seeing Angel into the hands of Madam Ivka Repinka, who still looked like an old lady to everyone else going by Noelle's comment about her arthritis, Noelle piled into the GTO with the rest of us. In addition to the tools, we had armed ourselves with baseball bats, a large Swiss army knife, a billy club and a fishing net. Bobby Joe turned the ignition key and a wavering guitar note twisted out of the speakers. "Goddamn it, I love Rock FM!" Noelle shouted to the ghost of Steppenwolf, who was sitting on the hood, bending the antennae. The music was too loud for anyone to hear her though and I gave up trying to read lips and joined the others in a head thrash as we sped off toward the barrel factory on a magic carpet ride.

Down on Canal Street the pavement ended. All the windows were open as we rolled to a stop in a cloud of dust.

"Funny how everyone still calls it the barrel factory." Noelle slit her eyes at the drums stacked behind the weed-choked cyclone fence. "Can't imagine what the hell LoboChem wanted it for. They built the factory way down the road."

Kurt looked at the fence, at the tires piled against the inside, twenty feet high. "Used to think it was a scrap yard when I was a kid. Then them big drums started stackin' up. Then tires to hide the drums"

"They leakin' too. Come out under the fence and run off into the canal. Sometime rusty-like. Sometime green or blue like when antifreeze spill." Marco put his arm over the back of the seat behind Noelle. "You mind?" he asked, when she glanced at his hand dangling beside her shoulder. She shook her head no, but kept her arms crossed in front of her.

I gazed into the water, engrossed in the memory of dumping my father's old tools. The canal looked more polluted than it had, as if it had grown murky with secrets. I could see the bobbing shapes of skeletons between the reeds.

Bobby Joe turned around. "Stinks here."

"My dad told me he'd take a belt to me if he heard I was down here again." Kurt gritted his teeth so that his cheek pulsed.

I thought of my headaches.

112

Marco jumped back in. "We ain't listen to him though did we? And after that we start seein' all kind of deform stuff. Shrimpy leg rats and no eye ducks, turtles with orange patches on they shells. Dead eels. And them cats in there ain't right at all."

"What?" Noelle shrieked, making Marco jump. "I can't abide a cat getting hurt! We always had a cat while I was growing up."

And that settled it. We were sorting a plan when a groan rose from the yard. The creaking tune of the barrel song whined around us in the wind, making our teeth chatter.

The fence was fifteen feet high and there was a brief dispute about leaving Noelle and me in the car. While Kurt and Bobby Joe argued, Marco wandered over to examine the padlocked gate. High gage wire bound the cyclone web to the support poles, all of it corroded. I thought about Ivka's warning but decided I'd just have to be careful. Marco looked down at the white nylon of his tracksuit. Then he looked at Noelle.

Marco and Kurt fixed the tow to the gates.

"If that chain rips my bumper off..." Bobby Joe warned, "We all gonna rob and steal 'til we get the money to fix it."

The GTO growled, spitting gravel. The gate strained, then with a loud ping the lock gave way. Our cheer was cut short when the rusted hinges popped and the gate panels flew off and crashed down on the roof, spiderwebbing the rear window.

Bobby Joe held his forehead while Marco and Kurt dragged the gate panels into the scrub grass. He was still shaking his head as we rolled up the drive between four derelict buildings. We armed ourselves and stepped out of the car. The buildings watched us like cornered rats. Anywhere that was not boarded over, cracked windows reflected bits of blue sky at disagreeing angles. Metal struts bled rust, leaving the broken windows looking like they were crying blood down the fractured white walls.

Something furry disappeared into a pile of corroding machinery. Noelle and I reached for each others' hands. There was another flick of fur. "That was a cat," I announced.

"Too big to be a cat," Bobby Joe snapped.

Before anybody could ask the disturbing question of what the animal was if not a cat, Kurt waved his bat toward a single intact window. "If some motherfucker got my uncle up in this bitch I'm gonna smash his head like a melon."

Energized by the suggestion of violence, we divvied up the buildings, throwing the doors open. Marco's door was waterlogged, swollen in the frame. He was still shouldering it when the rest of us reconvened near the car. Finally he kicked it so hard it screeched as it flew open. The smell inside was so rank we went in together with our shirts pulled up over our mouths and noses. Inside, sunlight raked over a concrete pit through the holes in the high filthy windows. A row of winches stood along the side wall, empty barrels perched in the seesaw mechanisms. We edged over to the pit and peered in at the electric green liquid below, keeping one foot back for balance. "Jesus Christ!" Marco choked. My eyes began to stream and that old pain – the feeling of a claw wrapping around my skull – came back again. Coughing, we piled back out into the bright day, wiping our eyes.

"See the markers up the side. That shit is 40 feet deep." Kurt wheezed.

Bobby Joe threw up in the dirt and stood back up, wiping his mouth. "Fuck, man that must be where they drainin' it, down that pipe and into the canal. Then right into the Delaware."

"They laid that pipe right at the edge of the park." I was furious. Horrified. LoboChem was the kind of company that made you feel betrayed by the legal system. Fuckers. Fuck them and what they were doing to Trenton. To New Jersey. To America. To the whole fucking world. "I found Rooster's old office." I said, getting back to our investigation of the site. "It was burned out, ransacked."

Inside the building I'd entered, papers and files lie in ashes. I'd found some in a file drawer that looked important and jammed them into the pocket of my jeans; reverting to my childhood inclination to collect evidence. A picture of Rooster, Dutchman, Billy Regret and my mom still hung charred and crooked on the wall. I tried to concentrate on the night Rooster was arrested. Had the bikers set the fire? I could see Freak Eddie at the foot of the driveway, his green eyes glowing in the dark.

I ran over and came back with two old metal signs. One read *Bantam Barrels* above the familiar angel logo. The other one said *LC Disposals*, with the yellow wolf I knew from my father's uniforms, and the coveralls of the werewolf who broke into the motel.

"There's a kennel over there," Noelle pointed. "Full of busted open cat cages. Ones that ain't busted have dead cats in them, dried like mummies. And surgery tables with drawers full of medical stuff." Her eyes teared, her voice full of rage. "They just left them here to die."

A loud meow made her jump. It was a deep cry, soon joined by several others. We turned, scanning the corners, squinting in the sunlight. Furry shapes began to slink out into the drive. I thought for a moment I was looking at panthers but as they neared I saw that they were housecats. They began to surround us, some hissing, others rubbing against our legs.

"God, they're enormous!" I stared in wonder at an arched back that was sliding against my thigh. The cat raised up on its back legs a few inches to meet my hand, scrubbing its cheek against my palm. Noelle was reaching for the heads of two tabbies.

"Look, they all got green eyes," Bobby Joe gawked.

Noelle was stroking as many felines as she could get her hands on. As she pet them, more arrived, slinking out from tires and mounds of scrap. "We've got to get them out of here!"

Marco, who was eyeing a Siamese who looked to weigh about forty pounds, stood straight. "Get 'em out how? The gate's already open."

"We've got one more building to check and then we're getting these cats out of here." Noelle marched toward the steel door that Kurt had been unable to open. Though the boys worked up a sweat trying, no amount of kicking could get it to budge. "Might have to use the GTO again," Kurt smirked.

"Fuck you, brother." Bobby Joe said.

Something was wrong. "Where are the cats?" I asked, looking around to find the courtyard cleared. Kurt and Marco lunged for their baseball bats as two snarling pit bulls raced towards us, their jaws wet with rage.

"Where did they come from?" I shrieked. The dogs' muscles rippled as they scrambled at the boys.

Bobby Joe got around the dogs and sprinted for the GTO. Gravel spit from the tires as he floored the car backwards. "Hope! Noelle! Get in!" He shouted. He'd flung the door open before the emergency break was even on.

"Get the cats! Get the cats!" Noelle screamed, but most of them had scattered. I saw one lurking by the tire wall near the cattery and shooed it into the back of the car but it darted straight out the other side. The dogs were rushing Kurt and Marco, snarling. Marco connected with the shoulder of one dog, driving it back.

"Get in the goddamn car!" Bobby Joe hollered. He forced a fluffy grey monster-sized feline into my arms and then pushed me into the backseat. Noelle clutched a white Persian around its chest. With its front paws locked over her arms, its body hung down like a small snow leopard. When we were inside Bobby Joe ran between Marco and Kurt, squirting mace at the dogs. They hunched to the ground and whimpered, pawing at their snouts.

Marco was the last to the car when the larger of the dogs recovered enough to lunge. All the weapons were gone from the crate so I grabbed the box of Pop Tarts. As Marco jumped into the car I threw two pastries out the open door into the dog's face. He snapped them in midair, then stopped, licking his chops. Bobby Joe fishtailed away as the other dog rose and chased the bumper. I tore open the rest of the pastries and chucked them out the window. We peeled away, both dogs skirmishing in the dirt for frosted crumbs.

We splayed out on the lawn of Noelle's backyard with another case of Silver Bullet. Our sentences became rushing water, forming rapids, heading for a waterfall.

"You think they was testing the chemicals on the cats?" Marco asked.

"LC Disposals is what it said on the coveralls of that maniac who stabbed me with the fork."

"Think LC's short for LoboChem? Billy said Eddie was supposedly killed back there behind the factory."

"You gonna name these fat bastards?"

"That one's Fork, and the other one's Saint Christopher."

"You can't name a cat 'Fork'. And you sure can't name one 'Saint Christopher'."

"Why the hell not?" Noelle demanded. "Those cats are about Eddie. About having faith."

We sat silent for a long time then, lifting silver cans to our lips. When the beer hit me I took the leash off the question I wanted answered. "What's up with all these wolves?"

The baby started to fuss and Noelle rolled over and reached for the diaper bag.

Marco picked up the conversation as if I hadn't said anything. "And what's up with these monster cats?!" The one named Saint Christopher stepped on his lap, blocking his face from view. "Ain't no housecats."

Noelle was leaning over Angel, unsnapping his onesie. "And what's up with this?" she asked quietly.

We gathered around and looked at the patch on the baby's leg where she was gently rubbing her finger. A fourth tattoo was forming, and when Noelle moved her hand we stared, stunned, as the thin inky lines of a cat darkened, and its eyes began to fill in with bright spring green.

The Howl & Pussycat

Some mornings in early summer the heat spiked so soon that the dew would bypass the grass and shimmer straight off the earth and up into heaven. On those days, when the asphalt melted to my shoes before noon, I would sometimes spy low-cloud angels cooling their feet in the rising mist.

Too hot to sleep under the exhaust fans when the bread ovens kicked on, Kurt was sitting, awake but groggy, in the doorway behind the Acme as we pulled up. He climbed in and I handed him an overnight bag while we drove up the street to the gas station.

There was no key for the men's room door so I stood near it while Kurt washed in the sink and changed into the clothes I'd laundered for him.

"My mom caught me folding those." I told him as he came out.

He kissed me with his toothpasty mouth and shrugged. "What am I supposed to do if she don't like me?"

"I'm just saying, I may not be able to help you out with your clothes anymore."

Bobby Joe was waiting with the trunk of his father's LeMans open. Kurt chucked his bag of dirty clothes on top of the spare tire and shook his hand. "Didn't think she was around enough to notice whose laundry you were doin'." He said over his shoulder to me.

When the five of us were back in the car Bobby Joe pulled onto Brunswick Avenue.

"Right girls, what you gonna do?"

Noelle and I rolled our eyes.

"If you don't come out in fifteen minutes, or if an alarm goes off, or if there's any sign of trouble, we haul ass. But slowly." Noelle mocked. "Honestly, you're just going to borrow some money. Do you really think the guy's gonna get that upset?"

The boys were all looking straight ahead. Kurt tightened his arm around me. "You just leave if you think they's trouble. This dude owes us some money for a job we done for him a while back and he's known for callin' the cops if somebody knocks on the door he ain't expectin'. We just walk back to Trenton if you ain't there."

"I still don't understand why you couldn't drive yourselves," Noelle commented.

Bobby Joe's eyes flicked from Noelle to Kurt in the rear view mirror. "Told you. If they's trouble I can't have my Pop's car on the scene. He'll kick me out and I'll be sleepin' with Kurt behind the Acme."

"Yeah, thanks man." Kurt looked out the window. I squeezed his leg. He moved it away and I took my hand back and looked out the other window, growing tired of confirming the little hurts with my silences.

We passed a strip mall and a few car dealers before Bobby Joe pulled into the Appliance Parade lot and backed up to the goods entrance where the car wouldn't be seen from the road. Marco had worked in the store warehouse the summer before so he knew it opened early for tradesmen and anyone else the owner wanted in his good books. Lots of jeans and work shirts were already walking around the showroom.

When I slid behind the wheel, Bobby Joe had his granny finger out. "Don't romp on the gas too hard or you'll take off like a shot. And the power steering ain't tight like new cars. You got to get the feel of it before you take any sharp curves."

"She ain't gonna have to drive it," Kurt reached down and pulled the seat lever. "We be out in a minute." On cue Noelle and I hung onto the dashboard and rocked the seat back and forth until we could slide it up to where my feet touched the pedals.

"Good luck, not that you'll need it," Noelle called out as the boys walked around to the store entrance.

120

No sooner had they disappeared than a blue Monarch pulled into the loading zone and a rake-thin man got out and opened the passenger door for a heavy woman in a green shorts set. Apart from my gliding the gear shift into drive with measured quiet, Noelle and I didn't move. As soon as Officer Thompkin and his wife were inside the store I rolled out of the lot and drove to Noelle's house.

"You know, they may be part wolverine." Noelle was holding up the front half of Fork while his back end dented her thighs. His shoulders wrinkled in her grip and he closed his eyes, relaxed with his front legs jutting out like a mummy in a Hammer horror film. "You ever seen a wolverine?" She turned the cat by his armpits to face me. Despite the jostling he stayed scrunch-faced and sleepy.

    We'd been waiting in Noelle's backyard since we left the boys at the Appliance Parade. At first, thinking they would be walking home, we weren't too concerned. Then, too many hours went by and we found ourselves waiting in the shade of the patio umbrella, held hostage by an absence of information.

    I put down the book I was trying to read with the hand that wasn't supporting a cat. "Just on T.V." I answered, glad for the distraction. "They're mean though. Can't imagine you could cross-breed one and just get the size out of it. These two must weigh more than Angel." Once I moved, it took two arms to contain Saint Christopher. He was purring loud as a weed-whacker while he rubbed his forehead against the underside of my chin.

    "Saint Christopher is thirty-eight pounds now, up four since we took 'em from the barrel yard. Ain't fat, neither." She ruffled Fork's fur. "Real solid for cats. Maybe they're part mountain lion."

    I'd had nightmares about the abandoned cattery in the barrel yard. Test tubes, exam tables. I couldn't stop thinking about all those blood tests I had in the LoboChem clinic as a kid. "I think they've been specially bred."

Toffee came up and knocked my arm with her head. I was staying at Noelle's for a few days while my mother's new boyfriend was at our apartment. Toffee and the cats did not seem to mind each other at all, except that she liked to shepherd them if the doorbell rang, or any other bell for that matter, which none of us understood. I scratched the tip of her ear and she closed her eyes.

Noelle hefted Fork around to face her. "I worried about taking them to the vet – that he'd ask a lot of questions – but in the end I didn't want them around Angel without their shots. Even splurged on the groomer. You know giving a cat a bath is no way to make friends."

"Vet say anything about their size?"

"Only that he thinks they might not be done growing. He wanted to measure them and take pictures but I wasn't having it. I'll take 'em to a new vet next time. Got enough practice hiding from doctors with Angel's birthmarks. Last place I went I had to have words with the nurse. Miss Normality got all nosy like she never seen a baby with congenital tattoos before."

I nodded. "I can't say that I have either, but people could be a little more open-minded, especially in the medical profession."

Through the kitchen window we heard the phone ring. Noelle put Fork down and went to answer it.

By that point I was already pretty sure there had been something going on at the Appliance Parade that Noelle and I weren't told. When we saw Thompkin heading into the store we took off like we were supposed to, but that didn't mean it felt good. In a panic we drove home trying to figure out what to tell the cops if we got caught. We even left the car parked over by the petting zoo at Halo Farms and walked back home through the alleys just in case anyone was following us.

122

I sighed, but the sound was lost in cat fur. Saint Christopher adjusted himself so that he was sitting straight up in my lap and I had to lean to the side to see the kitchen window around his big fluffy head. The back door flew open and Noelle ran down the steps. "They're in the goddamn Detention Center!"

"All of them?"

"No honey," she perched on the edge of her chair and put her hands on my knees. Just Marco and Bobby Joe. They said Kurt got away. Thought he'd be here. But don't you worry. I bet he's somewhere safe. He's got friends over that way…"

I cut her off. "There's nothing over that way but the Comet Motel. And his only 'friend' around there is Maxine." My temper felt like lava, broiling ever closer to the surface. "I wonder if that's why they were so laid back about telling us to drive off."

Noelle didn't correct me and I knew she either suspected or knew it was true.

Kurt and I argued a lot, but that was nothing new. We always had. And I'd suspected him of cheating. There was never any proof, just the way he disappeared sometimes. He'd be vague about where he'd stayed and I guess I told myself that if I was on the street and someone offered me a place to stay, I'd take it too. But there in the backyard I knew that wasn't true at all. If I was in his situation, I'd get a goddamn job.

Noelle flopped back in her chair. "Well, all I can tell you is those sons-of-bitches tried to keep up that story they told us beforehand, but after we hung up I called back the Detention Center and found out they're being held for attempted armed robbery"

"Armed? With what?"

"I don't know what it was, but what the hell good would it do to try to rob a store full of people with a billy club? Musta been a gun. Those assholes had us drivin' around with an illegal gun in the car. You know if this shit finds its way back to us I could lose my son!"

Noelle was trying not to shout. Out of the corner of my eye I saw a face in the window of the house next door: Ivka Repinka with a pink kerchief over her hair, hanging out at the edge of our conversation. The sight of her reminded me of all that I'd been through. Her face was like a lightning rod into a core of cold sense. "Well, this is it for me. I'm tired of worrying if Kurt's dead or in jail. College is getting close and I'm…learning stuff, stuff I'm starting to care about. I try to talk to Kurt about it but he doesn't understand what I'm saying half the time. Maybe it's best he's just gone."

Noelle gave me a sad smile. "You ain't gonna be in school forever." She took my hands in hers.

"I will be for four more years after high school, and after that, I'm getting a bike and getting out of here."

The clouds overhead were forming into great wide-winged condors in the blue sky. More than anything I wanted to reach up and grab hold of one and sail off to some kind of elsewhere where Trenton was just a story people told to scare each other around the campfire. "This isn't my life Noelle. I don't belong here."

She went quiet. I didn't want to meet her eyes. Angel took hold of the hem of her jeans and she reached down and scooped him up. "You mean you don't belong with us."

The condors sailed off in the direction of the ocean, and I tried to work out just exactly what I did mean. Toffee and Saint Christopher were spread out at my feet, nose to nose, their breath ruffling each other's hair. Toffee moved her chin to rest on the top of my foot. "I mean I can see something more than a factory job at $350 a week, and spending my nights and weekends playing pool at the Moorings. I love Kurt. Loved him. I really did." I picked up my paperback copy of *Wuthering Heights*, sandwiched it in

124

my hands. "You know my algebra teacher gave me this book, because I told her how much I used to read. She bought it with her own money, and I'm having trouble understanding it. It's work. Work that's different from standing behind a cash register for eight hours or shovelling snow or stocking shelves or serving burgers. I don't understand it and I want to understand it more than anything in the world. Every time I pick up this book I feel like a prisoner in some jail cell whose been taken over to a window for a look out at the whole free world. And it's like every chapter chips a brick out of the wall."

"Bad example," Noelle sang out, and laughed. Then her smile dropped like a yellowed leaf. "Look, sitting here isn't getting my husband back and it's not finding Kurt. I want to check that last building in the barrel yard."

Just then Toffee yawned and her tongue hit the arch of my foot. I jumped, envisioning a slug, and spilled my ice water on Saint Christopher. He meowed and shot several feet away where he hunched on guard next to the fence.

"Ah, poor thing," I cooed, going over to him with a dish towel. Reaching down to dry the white fur that was plastered to his skin I saw something through the soggy hair. "Noelle, look at this."

We stared at the cat. Across the skin of his back was some blue lettering. Peering at it I could see the letters *BO CH.* Noelle parted the fur on either side. *LO* and *EM* appeared.

"LoboChem," I said.

We studied the cat a while before Noelle pronounced, "We're gonna need some assistance."

In the parking lot of the Howl & Pussycat I felt too bare in my shorts and T shirt. I had never been inside a go-go bar and the rectangular, windowless structure of the place looked forbidding.

"Eddie kept all his phone numbers in his head," Noelle said, seeming to read my thoughts, "So I can't think of another way to find help."

We slipped between rows of pickup trucks and motorcycles and through the curtained door. Inside, hot pink walls separated a black floor and ceiling. Seven-foot cartoon cat-women in fifties style strip clothes strutted around the walls. Chilled smoky air stung my nose. The stage highlighted several dancers and one woman hanging upside down from a pole. I was amazed at the way she held on, with just her thighs, and then it sort of clicked that she was nearly naked and I felt embarrassed as if I had walked in on someone changing. I shook my head and looked away just as a heavy man with strained shirt buttons stapled Noelle in a bear hug and started talking faster than a sports reporter. "How's that little baby coming along? Best dancer we ever had. Anytime you want to come back, just let me know."

"Thanks Jedediah." Noelle stroked my arm. "This is my friend Hope. We just came along to see some friendly faces."

"You a dancer?" he asked, looking me up and down. I said no but felt my ears flush red. He shrugged, "Come back for a tryout if you want. Noelle's family, so y'all drink free for the night as long as you stay on sodas. No alcohol, I'll lose my licence for that. I'll send over some wings too."

Noelle and I sat at a small table with cherry cokes. My hand ran over my bag, tracing the outline of my book. There must have been about a hundred men in the room, some of them feeding out tips, others stretched back in chairs while floor workers straddled them, a few hollering at the girls to *Come on!* and *Go baby!* Before we left Rooster's, my mother would sometimes come and talk to me in my room. In between advice about birth control and drugs she used to warn me that not all bikers were like Rooster. As I looked around I understood. I drank my coke too fast, fiddled with the straw and jiggled my leg under the table wondering if it was safe to go to the bathroom without Noelle. Dancers came and went and I saw Noelle watched them much as you would anyone else up on a stage and I tried to relax a little and watch them too. Good dancers they were, some of them, real acrobats. A few were all boob, and just sort of wound around and wiggled a little in their stilettos, but for the most part they seemed pretty talented. Finally, after my third coke, I motioned to the ladies room, hoping Noelle would come along but she just smiled and nodded.

Waiting in line I helped untangle the earring of a tattooed dancer who had done a back flip to *American Girl*, and fastened a buckle on a platform shoe for one of the boob girls, who could not reach by herself while standing. The line was taking a while so I pulled out my book and started to read. After my turn, wanting to finish the chapter, I put my foot up behind me and leaned on the wall between a Betty Page Tabby and a Brigitte Bardot Blue Manx.

I was lost on a Yorkshire moor when a pair of boots stepped into my vision.

"What are you doin' in here, kid?"

His face was a little older, his hair a few strands greyer, but other than that, he was the same man who brought Toffee and me hotdogs in Bryant Park.

"Rooster!!" I dropped my book and jumped into his open arms. My feet dangled while he hugged me. He smelled like Irish Spring soap and fabric softener, like always. Like home. There were tears in my eyes when he put me down.

"Now, don't start that," he chided, looking away and wiping his nose with the back of his wrist. "Come on," his arm cinched around me, strong as a wrench. "I don't guess your mother knows you're here." He folded me into his side and kissed the top of my head. "Got half a mind to call her myself. You ain't thinkin' about workin' here?" He stopped abruptly at the thought, turned me to face him. His expression was so grave I think I would have changed my mind even if I'd been considering it.

"No, I'm here with Noelle. We're trying to find Freak Eddie."

Rooster studied me. "You come over and sit down and tell me what's on your mind. We still got our deal right?"

I nodded. The deal was still sealed in my heart. I could tell him anything.

We headed around to the far side of the stage. A group shout went up when I stepped into view. Sitting around the table were Coker and Dutchman, Joey Donuts and Dynamite Bob, Little Pete, Ralph Mexico, Mayor, a few men I didn't recognize but who nodded at me, and at the far end of the table, Billy Regret, who stood up and shouted that I better get myself over there and say hello.

"Enough of that," Rooster said when a tear trickled down my cheek. "You'll have everybody bawlin' with you. Can't have a table full of bikers cryin' at a strip club."

Dutchman had just released me from a crushing hug when a man with long black hair took a seat by Billy. The muscles of his back and shoulders stretched his *Trenton Harley* shirt. There was a book in his hands. He flipped the cover open and started to read. It was the copy of *Wuthering Heights* I dropped by the bathroom. I opened my mouth to speak when he happened to look up. His jaw slackened and the book lowered gently to his lap. I stood, shocked, trying to figure out if I really was looking at the slightly older face of Rick Rayetayah and how it was possible that one of the preppie jocks from my high school had come to be one of Rooster's acquaintances.

Rooster, who never missed a trick, caught Billy's attention. I got out of the way so they could talk.

"This has got to be yours," Rick said, passing me my book as I took the empty chair.

128

"It is actually," I smiled.

"You were always reading. Every time I saw you," he looked down and a strand of hair brushed his cheek. "Probably don't even know how many times I saw you. You sure never saw me." He pulled a comic frown and then smiled. "I thought you were going to be the girl who made me spend the rest of my life thinking, why didn't I ever try to talk to her?"

"Why didn't you?" As I spoke to Rick eagles flew up his arms and disappeared under his shirtsleeves. I looked up at the stage where five women with perfect bodies were dancing in G strings. "Thanks for returning my book," I said, darting a glance back at him.

Rick sat back hard in his chair then leaned forward again. "You reading this for honours English?"

"I think English is my best chance at a good school."

"Rutgers?"

When I nodded he said, "That's where I am. On spring break now. Figured coming back here was as good as goin' to Daytona. Plus I like to help out Rooster whenever I can, on account of all he's done."

"You know we used to live with him, me and my Mom? I didn't even know you knew him."

"Believe me, he talks about you still. But I didn't know him when you did. My dad was a lawyer for LoboChem. He found out about some illegal dumping they were doing. He knew about Rooster from some of the work he did with the union and got in touch. Company found out and he lost his job. He had a stroke just after that. Dad was older than my mom, by nearly twenty years. LoboChem complicated his insurance and pension up with a bogus lawsuit. We'll get the money eventually, but I would've had to wait years to go to college. My mom's even renting out the house for a while to cover her bills."

"I'm so sorry." I really wanted to touch his arm in consolation but I was afraid sparks might come out of my fingers.

He shrugged and his eyes fell on the spot I was contemplating, as if he had felt the thought. "You read Jane Eyre yet?"

A waitress was collecting orders at the far end of the table. I glanced up and saw with a twist of my guts that it was Maxine. The cold certainty that I should ask her if she had seen Kurt crept through me and I clenched my hands to warm them. I knew all in one moment that I hadn't come to the bar to find Kurt, but to help Noelle and to see Rooster.

"Let me get you a drink. Rum and Coke?" he guessed.

"Just Coke please."

I bent down as if to tie my shoe as Maxine's glance swept like a searchlight down to the far end of the table and away again.

While we waited for our drinks Rick leaned in to be heard over *R.O.C.K. in the U.S.A.* "Maybe I can take you up to Rutgers? Have a look around the campus?" His breath near my ear sent a shiver down my neck.

"I have a boyfriend," I confessed. Sitting with Rick, and given the circumstances of our meeting, lying just didn't seem possible, or necessary, or wise.

He sat back a few inches and looked down at my book again before his mouth twisted into a smile. "And now you're in love with me and you don't know how to tell him. You want me to break the news?"

"No! No!" I laughed "And anyway, tell him what? I haven't done anything wrong."

Rick swiped his hair back. "Except for agreeing to marry me. That you shouldn't have done."

My mouth fell open and I laughed again in astonishment. "I never said that!"

He placed his hand over his heart. "You can't break up with me now. You've made every other woman in the world disappear. I haven't looked up at that stage once since you came and sat down now, have I?"

I shook my head.

"So you'll have to go through with it. A year after you finish college. It'll be a biker wedding. I bet Rooster could get a quarter mile of bikes in a double row for you to walk down. We'll have to dance to Elvis, *Can't Help Falling in Love*. And for our honeymoon we'll go wherever you want, so long as we can get there on the bike. Only one thing, I'd like to take you to Cherokee, North Carolina, to meet my family. We'll make it a road trip."

Something in me spun like a top. I laughed, but I didn't want him to stop.

A sharp whistle startled me and Rick and I looked up to see the whole table was standing and waiting. Noelle was beside Rooster. He nodded at me. "I guess we know who you're riding with."

Spare helmets were passed to Noelle and me. I tried not to crowd Rick as his Sportster rumbled to the curb and then dipped into staggered formation with the rest of the bikes. The breeze caught his hair and tossed the tickling ends of it against my neck. On the sidewalk kids pointed as we rode past, flexing their wrists to get the riders to rev their engines and cheering when they did. Women in cars looked longingly at the empty seats behind the solo riders. Men in trucks held up their fists in solidarity.

We left Trenton on Route 29, flying north along the Delaware River on a ribbon of road carved out of the steep climbing hills. The water sparkled like mica under the sun.

Rooster dipped forward and back alongside us, accelerating and coasting so that the two bikes became a pair of dolphins leaping in a dark river. Noelle grinned at us behind her goggles. The helmet she had been given was red with flaming skulls all over it. As we rode, pockets of cold and hot air enveloped us, just like the sea with its warm and chill spots. It was what I loved about riding, that only a foot from the pavement there was something about the air that most people never knew, and it only took a certain amount of speed to find it.

Rick's hand appeared on my knee for a moment. The bikes were slowing for bumpy road. We rolled onto a driveway shaded by willow trees. A stand of tall pines rose on the right and beyond them, a large log cabin stood with the open sky behind.

"You girls have a look around. There's a dock where you can see up and down the river. Someone'll be out for you in a minute."

"Hey, where's your Barracuda?" I asked. The absence of the car was like showing up at your grandparents and finding the dog missing.

"Stolen." Rooster said, like that old dog had died. He and the others climbed the porch steps and went in the back door. Rick waved to me as he followed them. It was a shame about the car. But I hoped maybe Rooster was happier with an excuse to ride all the time.

We walked around to the backyard. It was large with a fenced garden off to one side and a patio with a built-in barbeque on the other. There were a few lawn chairs around, and a couple of hammocks. We went to the edge of the dock and sat watching the water rushing by twenty feet below.

"I don't like being out here while they're talking. It's my husband who's missing goddamnit." Noelle stripped the seeds from a foxtail stem and dropped them in the water.

I glanced back at the house. "That's the way it is with Rooster." I thought of the old place in Trenton and a pang hit me that if things had been different my mom and I might have lived here in the country by the river. "Crazy thing about that restraining order is my mom had to prove

132

he was a danger to me without implying she'd been in on any of his misdealings. And he helped her do it by keeping us in the dark. When we told the police we didn't know much, it was the truth." We looked at each other. "Let's go," I said.

Rooster stopped talking when we stepped into the doorway of his new office. I had an argument prepared and held my shoulders back. He considered us a minute, then nodded toward a leather sofa. "Have a seat then." His desk sat in a bay window that overlooked the river. "Noelle, there are things Eddie didn't tell you. Things he maybe would have one day, but as he didn't, I can't be the one to let you in just now. For my part, I don't believe he's dead. Never have." Noelle clasped my hand as he continued. "Thing is, you wouldn't be here now except for what you said in the bar about the cats. I didn't want to sell to LoboChem because I knew every plant they'd opened had caused a mess of problems in the surrounding areas, birth defects, ground pollution, you name it. And despite the promises of a pile of politicians they've done exactly the same in Trenton. Gordon Lobo's idea of processing is dumping his waste into the canal. Those cats were bred for testing, from stray cats, believe it or not, because of some similarities they between cats' eyes and humans'. That's why their eyes have gone that same bright green. We thought the cats were dead but nobody's been able to check. LoboChem own every politician in Trenton…. Why we've come out here."

Noelle sat forward. "Well, Eddie has those green eyes and now I see the cats got tattoos on them too. And maybe LoboChem tattooed them for ID, or maybe they got tattoos that show up all on their own. Like my son."

I sat forward and Rooster's eyes lighted on me for a moment. The room was still as he looked from Noelle to me, assessing us. Then a change in his face let me know the

Daddy gloves were off. With that expression, his face showed the miles.

"About fifteen years ago LoboChem developed a magnetic metallic particle that could be blood-borne. They meant to sell it to the military as a means of locating special ops personnel. Once injected, the product became traceable so that the carrier was distinguishable from any other body around him. You would always know where your man was and who he was, even stark naked. You could even find pieces of him. You could find out if he'd been involved in an explosion. Thing was, LoboChem knew it would never pass by the F.D.A. and my guess is they meant to either sell it to foreign or unofficial military forces or that they already had a client who wanted it and didn't care about the details."

"So they shot this shit into Eddie?" Noelle jumped up.

"They shot it into a few guys. Eddie lived."

"Why would Eddie let anyone do that?" I broke in.

Rooster's eyes were angry but his voice soft. "Because he was a teenage kid and his dad died and LoboChem offered him $40,000. Paid for his mother's house."

"And the tattoos?" Noelle put her hands on her hips.

Rooster looked out the window and took his time answering. "I think the injection, like that old saying, either kills you or makes you stronger. I think maybe Eddie incorporated it somehow. Maybe why that bastard was so goddamn sturdy. I'm guessing now, but I suppose the metal in his blood responds to emotional situations, just like your blood pressure might rise or your skin go red when you're embarrassed." He winked at me. "The metal in Eddie's blood forms shapes that maybe have some meaning to him. The thing is," and here he leaned forward with his elbows on the desk, his fingers pressed together at the tips, and looked at Noelle. "Somehow, your son has inherited this without the injection."

"What the hell does that mean? Are you saying my son might die?" Noelle went white.

"If it didn't kill Eddie, there must be something in him that bests it. The others who received the injection died within a month. Angel is…"

"Coming up to four months," Noelle said, sitting down and holding her hand to her heart.

"Now, after Eddie broke into the barrel yard on the night of Hope's birthday," Rooster looked at me and I gave him a small smile of forgiveness, "the LoboChem lawyers didn't have much on us but they were willing to push for conviction unless we backed off. When we heard they'd set the old place alight we guessed that any evidence was torched and that the best thing would be to stay away and try to work the system on them. Then Eddie disappeared. We searched for him and found his clothes torn up by those dogs out back of LoboChem. We poked around some more and the best we got was some kid sayin' he'd come across a dead man with a fork in his eye. We never saw a body."

"But you…" Noelle turned to Billy Regret. "You told me Eddie'd been found."

Billy shrugged and spoke in his slow deep drawl. "We'd been to private investigators, lawyers, everywhere. He was gone and all the evidence said they'd got him."

"So what makes you think he's alive?" I asked.

Rooster winked. "Because what Eddie did get from his break-in was the remote tracker that could find him. He hid it the night we were arrested. It's still forwarding a signal, which made me believe Eddie was alive until your son showed the same tattoos. It's one or the other of them that the signals are coming from, but without the tracker we can only receive a signal, not locate the source."

"If they're both alive, wouldn't there be two signals?" Noelle wanted to know.

But something didn't add up and I cut in before anyone could answer, "Isn't the metal in Eddie traceable even if he…isn't alive?" I saw Noelle shrink at my question, but it seemed important and I could tell by Rooster's smile that he was impressed.

Dutchman stepped in, "Might be that Angel is sending it and his Daddy isn't, or that Eddie is sending it and Angel doesn't. The signal varies with motion, so if someone is running, or rolling over in bed, or even breathing, it sends a different signal than inanimate tissue."

"Where's the tracker then?" I asked.

Rooster got up and leaned against the front of his desk. "Eddie wouldn't tell me. Known him since he was a kid but I guess if I knew such a thing existed I wouldn't want anyone else having it either. I can only think it was in the house somewhere. Might be why LoboChem wanted me to move so bad. But I never found it. It was small so he could have slipped it between the floorboards or under a corner of wallpaper for all I know, maybe he stashed it in something that wasn't there a few days later when I got out of lockup and started searching. So, Noelle, I think Eddie may be alive. I feel it and I know you do too. My big concern," he paused there, and crossed his arms, "is whether your break-in might have convinced somebody to move Eddie if that was where they were holding him."

Prickling heat crept up my neck at the realization Rooster knew what we'd done, and worse, that we might have put Eddie in further jeopardy. Noelle's face was pure despair.

"But," Dutchman cut in again, "Going by your tactics, no one who saw what happened would have thought anyone professional was involved. It would look just like a bunch of kids out doing mischief."

Billy Regret put down a glass he was holding. "Next time, we have to get it right. We need to check every

136

building, search for any basements that mighta been dug, any space large enough to fit a man."

"The letter!" Noelle exclaimed. "Dr. Bongiovi. Hope, you remember."

The paper with the angel watermark. But there was no time to react. At the mention of the name, the room sprang to life. I looked at Rooster while the others headed for the door but all he said was, "You ride with Rick again."

Back on the bike, I kept going back to Rooster's remark about what might have been in the house on the night of the arrest that wasn't there a few days later. I knew the answer. We were. My mom and me, our things, Toffee. Toffee with her special new collar that I thought was just another gift.

138

The Pit Bull Pendulum

Fear was something I knew plenty about. But running toward danger for a good reason arms you with something you don't get when running away from danger caused by a bad reason. One by one, the bikes began to spread their wings, until the flock of them lifted up over the Delaware, soaring into Trenton with purpose.

Down near Canal Street two riders peeled off and cruised around to the front of the barrel factory to keep watch. The rest of us headed toward the waterway. Gravel splattered my legs as we crawled along the towpath, making me grateful for the pair of boots Rooster chucked to me as we were leaving. They were Janie's, he'd said.

The gates on the back entrance had been replaced, the cyclone fencing battened with wire and shining new support poles. Razor wire spiralled the top. I tried to take the repairs as a good sign that Eddie might still be inside but as I walked away from the dust churned up from the bikes something dark in the pale dirt made me stop. A trail of blood led away from the gate and down the road. I pointed it out to Rooster, but he said they'd keep on with their plans.

Right on the other side of the barrel yard, just over the tops of the piled tires and tall trees, was the house where I grew up. The mutant cats, the dead fish, the five-legged frogs and the singing barrels had all been the result of chemical waste. I wondered how long it would be until cancer crept near me, or my eyes turned bright green. In the future, when I had a kid, would I degenerate into a werewolf too? Rooster said the others who were tested like Eddie died, but what about the guys who manufactured it? I guessed I knew who'd been assigned to handling the material, thinking of my father and the others in his crew. Daddy had bragged for weeks about the extra fifty cents per hour he got for working in the "development" unit.

Billy Regret pulled a set of bolt cutters from his saddlebag.

"Be done in a sec, bro," Coker said from the far corner of the fence where he was bent down in some weeds. There were a few snips from his wire cutters and he called out, "Clear!"

"Guess what man?" Billy twisted the lock with his hand. "Ain't fastened."

I sensed something by my shoulder and turned to find Rick standing behind me. The gravity in his face raised a sense of trust in me. I've always been uneasy with people who didn't recognize a bad situation. "There's meant to be a sign when you electrify a fence," he said quietly. "Whoever did this isn't too concerned with the law, especially with the place sitting right next to a park. There's a playground over there. Kids."

"Yeah, I used to be one of them," I said.

He put his hands on my shoulders. My back rested against his chest. I was glad he was there.

Dutchman and Billy Regret pushed the gate open. "Stick near the bikes," Rooster ordered Noelle and me, "Billy'll stay with you."

The men fanned out toward the four buildings in the barrel yard. I felt secretly proud to see Rick walk with them. Billy remained where he was but as he crossed his arms I noticed the bulges at his ribcage. I'd never known him to carry guns before.

I took a few steps toward the gate and looked at the rust-scarred buildings, the barricaded windows, the Frankenstein-cattery with its air vents. "The door is shut," I noticed.

Noelle looked over to the building that she'd investigated. "Well, somebody's been here, that we know. Do you think the cats are in there? There ain't any running around yet. Poor things. We should try to shoo them out.

140

People will take them in, especially if they're as sweet as Fork and Saint Christopher."

Billy Regret was watching the others and the canal road, not really listening to us. "Girls," he grumbled, "I'm gonna take a look round the side over there, make sure security ain't taken notice of us. I'll be right 'round the corner of this fence, not twenty feet. Won't be a minute."

I watched Billy saunter off. Noelle's eyes were pleading. "It's just right over there," she begged. "All we have to do is yank the door open. If they're in there they'll just swarm out like last time."

"Rooster isn't going to like this," I said, looking at the decrepit building. "But, I hate LoboChem." And with that we ran through the gate. On the count of three we threw our weight against the cattery door. It flew open, cutting the darkness with a yellow triangle of sunshine. I saw the cat cages, their doors shut. Furry bodies leaned against the mesh, some staring, others sleeping. A toppled chair and a few coiled ropes lay on the floor before us. My eyes followed the line of the chair into the shadows. Something long and heavy hung from the ceiling, swinging gently. The shape began to make sense, a man's body, wearing ragged underwear and socks, hanging from some kind of noose. In the same breath Noelle and I screamed. Then a low gurgling snarl came from the corner.

I pulled the door shut but it wouldn't catch. Shrieking, Noelle and I took off toward the nearest fence. The wall of tires blocked the view beyond. We threw ourselves up them, climbing through vines of poison ivy. At the top, I cut my leg, and looked down to see that the tires were stacked around metal girders which were chained to the fence. We looked down at the snarling pit bull. We were about fifteen feet up. The dog leapt, enraged, his powerful hindquarters bringing him within a few feet of us. Down the far side of the fence stacks of rusted machine parts were bound in thorny overgrowth and more poison ivy. We might as well throw ourselves onto rusty knives.

We crawled along the wobbling tires toward the towers of chemical drums that loomed. Billy Regret began to shout from somewhere on the drive.

"That guy was dead. He was dead, right?" Noelle asked from behind.

"I never saw anyone hang before but I guess he would have been thrashing around if there was any life left in him."

"You think we could have done anything?"

"I think if he brought a pit bull along to a suicide he must not've wanted any kind of intervention. Besides, it's not like that dog was going to sit by while we figured out how to cut him down." I stopped as my shirt snagged on the fence

"You think he was dead long?"

With a tug I freed my shirt. "He didn't smell yet. How long does it take a body to smell?"

"That's a point. I don't know. Alls I know is he wasn't Eddie."

"How could you tell?" I didn't like to say, but frankly, that was exactly what was on my mind.

"Wasn't Eddie's knees. Eddie's got nice knees, not all wrinkled like that."

We could hear the men shouting to each other. Noelle opened her mouth to shout back but I held my finger to my lips. Each time we stopped, the dog doubled his efforts to run up the side of the tires. We crouched closer to the fence. Our arms and legs were so streaked with soot it looked like the tires had run over us rather than the other way around.

"You think there's someone else here?"

"Maybe. I took some documents last time, accounting stuff. Didn't make much sense so I went to the library and had a look at the microfiche. I found an old aerial shot of this place from when it used to be Bantam Barrels. There was a door at the top of the building we couldn't get into. The boys couldn't get through those iron shutters down below, so if Rooster and the others can't either, then maybe there's a way in from the top."

Noelle's face lit up. "We'll go look then." We crawled a few more feet. "You think we should tell Rooster where we're going?"

"Nah," I said over my shoulder. "None of them are small enough to climb up here and get onto the roof this way. We're here now. Might as well help."

"Damn straight!" she agreed.

The tires were piled higher near the front of the enclosure, probably to block the view of the yard from the houses across the street. We climbed up to the ones in front of the building. One wobbled alarmingly when I put my weight on it and I saw with a pang of fear that the top tires were stacked higher than the girders. I was balanced on four tires that weren't fastened to anything.

Noelle and I were side by side. It was a five foot jump to the roof. I tried to get my balance and stand, thinking I must look like someone riding a pretend surfboard at one of those photo stalls down the shore. Noelle got to her feet, bent her knees and with a sudden leap flew off the tire, cleared the edge of the roof and landed on the black tar paper beyond. I stared after her as she stood up and grinned. "Your turn!"

I looked down at the pit bull, pacing below, his jaws turned up to us. "Oh hell no!"

"I just did it sweetie, it's not that hard."

"Well, I'm not the one used to swinging around a pole all evening."

"You're strong. Come on. It's just like the standing long jump.

I looked Noelle in the eyes. I was smack in the middle of something I'd created in a way that a lifetime of

143

imagining couldn't compare with. With a deep breath, I bent and leapt and saw myself clear the edge. My palms burned where I scraped them on the tar paper.

Noelle threw her arms around my neck as I stood.

Something behind her caught my eye. A mound of blue cloth was wadded up near one of the ventilation ducts. I took the collar in my fingertips. It was a jumpsuit. A yellow wolf glared out from the pocket. "The guy in the Comet Motel had one of these."

Noelle put her hands on her hips, "So did the guy who stabbed me with the fork."

"Well at least I know the guy in the motel is dead."

Noelle's eyes hardened. "You thought he was dead, but do you really know?"

I let my face tell her I didn't. A chill rushed across my skin. "Noelle, what if the other guys who were tested like Eddie didn't die?"

"Well, let's just not think about that right now."

She was right. We were in this, for better or worse. We gripped each other's hands and then got on with our search.

As the microfiche showed, there was a door in the corner near where we'd jumped onto the roof. We tried the doorknob but it wouldn't turn. I remembered seeing a small window below a winch on the front of the building when we broke into the yard. We lay on our stomachs on the edge of the roof to have a look over. The window was several feet below.

"We need a rope," I said, scanning the roof. "That jumpsuit looks like it might split at the thought of holding someone up."

"And it smells." Noelle wrinkled her nose and then touched her waist. "No belts," she said, exasperated as she looked at my empty jean loops. Then a light came into her eyes as she trailed upward, stopping at my chest.

"No, that's not gonna work," I insisted.

144

"We gotta try something. My Nana once caught her bra on the banister falling down the stairs and stayed suspended like that for three hours until my mother found her." Quick as that, she unhooked her bra and pulled the straps out of the arms of her T shirt.

I rolled my eyes but followed suit. Because Noelle was the better gymnast it came to her to shimmy out onto the winch, loop the bra over the support pole and crawl back so we would be able to attach the two bras together and get one of them around her so she could hang off the winch and see through the window.

When she was back on the roof I started to fasten the elastic end of her yellow daisy-patterned bra to my blue one. We got the bras together in a slipknot and after pulling on every strap to make sure nothing would come apart, Noelle put the armhole over her head and under her shoulders.

There was a squeal of rusty hinges. We turned to see the roof door fall open. My wrists were wound in the elastic under Noelle's armpits when the pit bull charged, its mouth spraying saliva as he hurtled toward us.

The dog leapt in the air. I twisted away and he clamped his jaw on the join in the two bras. The force of his weight knocked Noelle off balance, which in turn toppled me and in a second the three of us tumbled with a scream off the edge of the roof. The elastic held and Noelle and I and the dog bobbed from the winch like three beans on a vine.

"There they are!" Billy started to shout about a tarp in his saddle bag and there was a pounding of boots in the dust. "Hang on girls! We'll get you down in a minute."

I knew Rooster was going to be as mad as I had ever seen him when we got down but at that moment I only wanted to get away from the dog. He was hanging by his teeth, trying to get purchase with his paws, but I think he knew if he tried to bite anyone it would be the last thing he did. His coat was greasy and he stank like no animal I'd ever been near. "You think he's got fleas?" I shouted down to Noelle. There was a bounce as she knocked his hind feet away and then all of a sudden she screamed, "That's him! Eddie! Baby it's me! Oh my god he's here! He's here everybody!"

The dog kicked again and I twirled to get away from his feet. Looking over as we twisted in the air I could see a shape through the window, but whether it was a man, I wasn't sure. It wasn't moving and I hoped beyond anything that the fork man, or the motel man, or whoever had hung himself in the cattery, didn't consider the murder of a hostage his last bit of business.

Noelle began to kick her legs like a gymnast on the uneven bars, swinging us closer to the window.

"Don't do that!" Rooster shouted from below. I was looking at a festering tick on the dog's head and began to kick in time with Noelle. Her foot thumped the window, and someone shouted "Together!" It was Rick's voice. We sailed into another back swing, tucking our buts back so that our legs jutted out at the same angle, and next time, going forward, we let out a war whoop and thumped the window with our feet.

There was a huge crash and glass flew, pieces tumbling down the building wall and into the dirt. Something hit me in the head. "Look out!" I screamed. There was movement inside as the body on the bed lifted his head.

"Eddie! Eddie!" Noelle shrieked. We swayed back and forth, Noelle bobbing, spinning and crying as she reached for the window. The pit bull let out something between a whine and a growl but held on by his locked jaw.

There were footsteps on the roof and I looked up to see Rick smiling down at me. "Rooster's fierce as a hornet, but you did good. Just hang on another second." In a minute there was a commotion in the room and Billy Regret and

146

Rooster leaned out and took hold of us while Rick shimmied out onto the winch and cut the bra free. Billy kept the dog out the window, holding it by its back legs, and then leaned down and dropped it into the tarp where the bikers caught it. I watched as it staggered off the canvas and slunk away toward the cattery with its tail between its legs.

Even a pit bull can have a hard day.

It was only the promise of getting Eddie immediate medical attention that made Noelle let go of him long enough to get him strapped to the back of Coker's bike. He was weak and thin, and worst of all, he was missing an eye, making me think that kid really had seen Eddie in the field, only Eddie hadn't been dead. I was standing beside Rick's bike when someone picked me up under the shoulders and put me on the back of it. Rooster then walked away. He hadn't spoken to me since we came through the window.

Rick and I rode beside Coker and Noelle. She was crying and looking toward Eddie. Sometimes it takes seeing someone really in love to know you aren't. Looking at Noelle I knew I didn't love Kurt, that it was possible I never loved him. I wondered how I'd even put up with him.

When we rolled onto pavement and Rick put his hand on my knee, I laced my fingers in his. Thinking we were heading for Helene Fuld hospital, I was confused when we rode in the opposite direction. A few minutes later we pulled into the Comet Motel.

Rooster stopped in the office while the rest of us parked in the strip of spaces near the back building where Maxine lived. Dutchman went to a door at the opposite end of the building from hers and took a key from his pocket. Eddie was carried inside. Rick put his arm around my shoulders and walked alongside me into the room.

Coker headed for the bathroom and began running water into the tub. "You ain't got to do this," he told

Noelle. "I was in the service with Eddie. Ain't nothin' to me if either one of us stinkin' or naked."

"I'd be grateful if you could help with the lifting, but I don't expect anybody to smell like roses when they've only just come back from the dead." She said. Every once in a while you could see a primness in Noelle; the ballerina that might have been, if she'd grown up somewhere else.

Eddie was undressed and lowered into the tub. As Noelle kneeled on the floor and held his hand Eddie looked at her with recognition but still didn't speak. She had just started working with a washcloth and soap when Rooster came back. "Brought the doctor," he said.

A small Latina stepped around him, a yellow flowered suitcase in her grip.

"Immaculata?" I gasped.

The motel manager glanced at me for the briefest moment. Hearing the sound of the bath she glared at Rooster and scurried toward the open door, sputtering, "In the bathtub! Did anyone at least check him for cuts first?"

"I did ma'am," Coker answered.

Immaculata put her bag on the floor and leaned over the tub. In a moment Noelle cried out "No!" and Coker carried her, struggling and swearing, out of the bathroom. He took her to a chair in the corner of the room and kept her gripped in a bear hug on his lap while talking quietly in her ear. Finally she stopped struggling and sunk into him. Against his greying beard and hair she looked like a disappointed kid complaining to Santa Claus, except for the reddening leg of her jeans, wet with blood from where the window gashed her.

When Rooster still wouldn't look at me I went outside and stared out over the low buildings toward the sound of cars rushing by on Route 1. I was core tired. My city was using me like its attic, storing up every old, broken thing it couldn't get rid of in my head. I didn't live in Trenton, I was wearing it. Like a yoke.

148

With everything in me I wanted a Harley of my own. The idea of being able to take off and go anywhere was almost too much to bear. In the chrome of the bike nearest me I saw the miniature reflection of someone approach me from behind. Rooster turned me around. I started to say something but he ran his hands down my shoulders, turning my arms, then down my back and legs and I realized he was looking for injuries. At the tear in my shorts, he peeled aside the fabric where the scratch was scabbing. Then he stood and slid his fingers through my scalp. When he took them away they were streaked with blood.

"Back inside," he ordered. "Lay there." I sat on the edge of one of the beds. Sheets had been tacked up around it to provide a curtain. White towels covered the bedspread and pillows. Immaculata had her flowered suitcase open. Inside, medical supplies were tucked into the elastic loops meant for cosmetics. A suture kit was ready. "Don't usually have female patients," she nodded at the drapery. "Did you touch any of the leaking barrels or any other liquid while you was in the factory?" I said I couldn't remember. Her normal curtness had an edge of concern that I'd never heard from her before. It calmed me while I watched her load a syringe. While I slipped into unconsciousness she brushed my hair from my face and I heard Rooster say, "You make sure she's OK Immaculata. That's my daughter."

When the anaesthesia wore off, I told Noelle that I would go with Rick to pick up Angel from Ivka Repinka. I didn't want to pull a helmet over my bandage and Rick agreed to take a chance, riding slowly along the back roads.

At the house, he stood over me a minute, inspecting the wound. "She didn't even shave any of your hair off. Just a little bit of tape. You know she used to be a surgeon in Sancti Spiritus? How are you feeling anyway?"

I smiled and he stroked my cheek.

We turned toward the house to find two faces pointed at us. Marco and Bobby Joe had come out of the back yard and were leaning on the fence, the gate clanging shut beside them. I stopped short and Rick stood at my side, his gaze level on Marco.

Marco looked at us with disgust. "Where the hell you been girl?" He pushed himself off the fence and grabbed the shoulder of my jacket.

Rick flicked Marco's hand away. My heart was beating hard and I felt light-headed, still not over the anaesthesia. I wasn't up for a fight, not even watching one.

"Who the fuck are you man, tellin' me not to touch my boy's woman?" Marco pointed a wedge of fingers at Rick's chest.

I started to explain but Rick interrupted me. "She's hurt man, just had stitches. I have no argument with you, unless you hurt her more. She's just helped us out. She's one of the people. Maybe the question is who the fuck are you?"

"People?" Marco looked at Rick's clothes, seeming to put it all together for the first time. He nodded at Rick's motorcycle. "You ride. You knew Eddie?"

"We better go inside," I said. "There's news. We have to find Kurt."

Marco's face snarled in rage. "Kurt's found, girl. S'what we came here waitin' on you for. He's up in Helene Fuld with fifty-three stitches in his leg and two broken bones in his arm. My boy nearly died and Bobby Joe and me couldn't find you nowheres. Old lady said she'll watch the kid a couple more hours." I looked up and saw Ivka Repinka, young and beautiful, standing in her window with Angel in her arm. She had him wrapped in a pink blanket. She nodded at me.

Of course I was expecting the boys to be stunned, to want an explanation. But when Kurt thumped the bed with his

150

working arm, shouting "Son of a bitch!" and Bobby Joe and Marco swore about how fucked up everything was, I was confused. Rick, who was leaning against the doorframe only shook his head.

"What's wrong?" I asked Kurt.

His upper lip curled against his teeth as he spoke. "Just me and you." He said.

Marco punched Bobby Joe in the arm. "We go and leave them alone. All of us."

Rick didn't move. He wasn't scared of them and it strengthened my feelings of wanting to leave with him and forget I'd ever met them. But Kurt was a mountain of injuries. His leg was in suspension, his arm in a cast, cuts and bruises slashed his body. I could see that he was hurt, frightened even, and that his pride was kicked to the ground over not being involved in his cousin's rescue.

"Just me and you," he said again.

I met Rick's eyes one more time, hoping he would understand. "Rick – everybody - just go."

When Rick walked out of the room the sun fell out of the sky. I started to get up when Kurt said simply, "I gotta tell this story or I'm 'a lose my mind. *Please.*" There was that word. The word that used to send my father into a rage and drown my mother in a swamp of ambivalence. In the years I had known him, Kurt had never said please, not for anything. I sat stiffly on the edge of the chair, waiting.

Then he told me what happened to him.

What Was You Lookin' For?

Kurt and Marco and Bobby Joe walked around to the front
of Appliance Parade. Kurt threw the door open a little too
hard and it snapped back loudly as the boys walked across
the floor of the showroom. They had never used the gun
before. It was only a freak thing that they even had it.
Marco found it out by Donnelly Homes. None of them had
ever shot it, not wanting to take the chance at being caught
with an unlicensed firearm. It stood to reason the gun was
dirty or it would not have been thrown away. They had
nearly chucked it in the river right then and there, but had
decided to hold on to it, in case there was an emergency.
Bobby Joe's uncle getting paroled while his car was still
smashed in counted as an emergency, especially
considering the nature of Bobby Joe's uncle.

They flipped to see who would hold the gun. The
deal was, whoever carried it would run first while the other
two created a diversion.

Bobby Joe strode up to the counter.

"Can I help you?" said a man in a safety-yellow
jumpsuit.

"Yeah, I own an apartment building on Mulberry
Street and I need some new washing machines" Bobby Joe
answered.

The guy behind the counter summed the three of
them up with a glance, "Uh, yeah," he said. The way he
said it made Kurt sweat, knowing Bobby Joe didn't look
old enough to own an apartment, let alone a building. He
started thinking Bobby Joe should have just said he'd come
on behalf of his boss. But then, they might have insisted
that the boss come back instead of him, and the three would
have had no more reason to be standing there.

The clock on the wall ticked loudly onto nine. Three
women in Appliance Parade polo shirts walked behind the
credit counter, said good morning to the man who was

talking to Bobby Joe, and headed into a back room. In a moment they returned carrying cash drawers. That was it. Kurt reached into his jacket and pulled out the gun. He was supposed to say, "Hold it, this is a robbery," and then give instructions but one of the women screamed and dropped her cash tray. It crashed against the concrete floor so loudly it made Bobby Joe knock over a display of cleaning products.

"Hold it, this is a robbery!" Marco shouted. He shouted it just out of time with Bobby Joe so they echoed like they were on a long distance phone. Bobby Joe and Marco frowned at each other. Kurt felt his hand go sweaty around the gun.

Marco stormed over and snatched a drawer from one of the women who was still holding hers. Bobby Joe followed suit. Kurt bent down to pick up the one on the floor while keeping the gun pointed at the man behind the counter who was standing calmly with his hands raised. When Kurt stood up his heart went dead cold. Officer Thompkin was in the middle of the showroom floor with his arm around a heavy bleached blonde woman, looking at a side-by-side fridge.

"Five-O, man!" Bobby Joe croaked from his dry throat.

Kurt shoved the gun back in his pocket.

"Run," Marco barked, throwing his cash box to the floor where it broke open and splashed bills and coins across the linoleum.

Kurt bolted for the emergency exit. Slamming into it set off the alarm. On the way out, he tripped and the box he was carrying clattered into a dumpster and spewed open on the tarmac.

"Haul ass!" Bobby Joe shouted from the door. Kurt ran, thinking the other two were behind him. He sprinted around the back of the building, not sure if he should hope the car was still there, but it was gone.

154

The traffic on Route 1 was thick. He couldn't dodge four lanes of cars going fifty-five miles an hour and more. There was a creek that ran between the store and Baker's Basin. He had only been in the Basin a few times, and then always in a car. But for lack of another option he ran over the bridge and down the shoulder on Baker's Basin Road. A siren rose up from the lot of Appliance Parade. The cops got there fast, but then, they would with Thompkin caught in the middle of it.

A quick glance told Kurt that Bobby Joe and Marco were not behind him and he scrambled off the road into the undergrowth at the back of someone's farm, figuring the other two must have run another way.

Waist-high grass whipped his clothes as he ran until his lungs burned. The sole was coming away from his sneaker and it folded under him and tripped him twice before he had to tear it off. From the road sirens screamed through the trees and over the fields. Ahead were woods and he sprinted toward them. The gun was in his back pocket, dragging his jeans down. Low branches cut his face as he plunged into the trees.

Kurt ran through woods, backyards and strung up sections of no-man's land until he thought he must have crossed out of Lawrence and back into Trenton. When his lungs felt they would tear and his heart ached, he stumbled and then fell onto his knees in an overgrown field. Gasping, he tried to rise again, but his chest was heaving and his legs wobbled when he tried to stand. He sprawled on the ground, sweat stinging his eyes.

Thirst made his throat feel like it was sticking to itself when he tried to breathe. If he could find a main road he might be able to get some water. He struggled to his haunches, feeling the weight of the gun in his back pocket. Marco might be pissed off, but Kurt knew it would be best to get rid of it. Standing, he shaded his eyes. He could hear the highway off to the left, somewhere beyond the trees.

And then he saw a spiral of purple smoke twisting up on the horizon and knew the cars would be old Route 1, and the canal would be right beside it. The gun could be dumped there, flung far into the middle where it would sink deep.

Taking his best guess at where the canal would be, he began to wade through high weeds. Bent grasses and twigs stabbed at the bottom of his foot where the sole was torn away.

He thought he was hallucinating in the heat when thirty yards away the grass seed began to part as if a spirit were gliding toward him. There was only a quick rustle in the nearby weeds before the dogs leapt at him. He yelled in surprise and threw his arms over his face just as he felt the punch of their feet against his chest and stomach. When they had him down, they lowered their heads and let out rolling wet growls. Pit bulls. Kurt recognized their clipped ears and hard brown shoulders. Panic went through him as he realized he must be closer to LoboChem than he thought. He was near the barrel yard, where they said Eddie's body was found.

Kurt was sprawled on his back, the gun denting his backside. He lowered his right arm to try to reach it. With a snarl the dogs flashed their teeth and he froze once more. There was nothing to do but wait. Eventually the dogs would sit back, or wander off, and he'd be able to get the gun.

A shrill whistle came from the direction of the highway, where Kurt knew the canal would be, and the dogs began to bark and pace around him. A man was coming through the field. A blue hat and uniform covered him almost completely except for his scraggly dark hair.

"Yo man, these your dogs? You mind callin' 'em off? I know I was trespassin' but I'll leave if…"

The man stopped, looked at Kurt, reached in his breast pocket and fished out a pack of Lucky Strikes. He lit one off a match. On the pocket of his uniform was the faded logo of a wolf with *LC Disposals* written above it. His hair was greasy and he stank of sweat and unwashed clothes.

When his cigarette was lit, the man shook out the match and tossed it on Kurt. He crammed his other hand in his mouth and whistled. The dogs trotted to his feet and sat.

"You see," he said, taking his time, "we used to keep bigger dogs down here for security. This whole field was fenced and they had the run of it. Had some wolf-dogs specially bred in Minnesota. They had a way of turnin', so we lost a couple that way to animal control, but then the rest of 'em started gettin' sick. Ask me, I think some neighbour poisoned 'em, 'fraid their kids was gonna get ate. We was down to one last pup and somebody stole her. But that was gone ten years now." The man lifted his cap, scratched his forehead where dirt had collected in rivulets on his brow. "I did have an affection for that pup though. Meant to be mine out of that litter. Anyway, owner likes wolves. He's a hunting enthusiast."

Kurt felt his stomach turn when the man opened his mouth and picked his teeth, stumps of black teetering in shrivelled gums.

Lowering his hands, Kurt sat up. The dogs watched him but didn't move. "I'm sorry about that but I was only a kid then. I don't know anything about no wolf-dogs but I could certainly keep an eye out for one."

"You ain't goin' nowhere thief."

Kurt frowned. "How you…?"

"Think I ain't got a police radio? Think I ain't got no connection to the outside world? I'm employed you worthless son of a bitch. I got prospects. I get money for the hours I do. Now you take that gun outta your back and toss it over here or these two'll eat you and save me cuttin' up their dinner."

"All right man." Kurt reached behind him, flicked off the safety, drew the gun out and fired. One dog dropped but before Kurt could fire again the other leapt toward the gun, closing its jaws around his arm. The flesh tore and Kurt screamed and dropped the weapon. The dog leaned its body back, throwing its head right and left. Kurt kicked at its flanks, and punched it in the head with his free hand, but it wouldn't let go. He felt the arm wrench painfully at the shoulder.

"Lie still," the man said. "Lie still or he'll take that arm out of the socket."

Kurt lay back as best he could, the dog easing its fight as he did. "Please get him off man. Don't let him take my arm. I ain't mean to shoot that other one. The gun just went off."

Another whistle and the dog released. "You ain't fire by mistake, you 'an your buddies ain't break into the chemical disposal unit by mistake, you ain't take my cats by mistake. You might be here by mistake, but that's just shit luck for you."

With the gun and the dog, the man ordered Kurt to his feet and followed him through the grass. Kurt stumbled along, clutching his bleeding arm to his chest. All he could think about was Eddie, and how they'd never been allowed to see a body.

The man made Kurt stand with his face against the gate of the barrel yard. Once the padlock was unlocked and they were inside a feeling of dread came over Kurt so strong that he felt he would pass out. Worried about what might happen if he lost consciousness, he forced himself forward, through the repaired door of the cattery. The man left the dog to guard him as Kurt looked with revulsion at the dozen carcasses left to decompose in the cages.

Carrying a chair and a coil of rope, the man came back into the small room. Kurt thought about fighting but his arm was throbbing and blood was running down his clothes. He felt weak and sat in the chair when he was told.

"You know, I don't never leave here 'cept to patrol the old field. I watched everything you did that day. You all want me to lose my job. You want me to be lowlife like you but I was doin' my job. I was doin' the most important job they give me. I had my job right in that building you couldn't get into. I was laughin' like you was the wolf and I was the pig in the stone house. 'Cept I'm the wolf now. I always been the wolf."

Kurt watched as the man tied his ankles to the chair, pulled his good arm and then his bad behind him. Moving the hurt arm sent a pain through him that made him gasp for air.

"Before they put me in charge, these cats was left for dead. Couple-few was still breathin' and I nurse 'em back, let 'em out of the cages for exercise. One day the boss see and say I done a good job savin' 'em 'cause he might need 'em sometime. Told me to keep on doin' a good job. See, all this is mine. The wolf-dogs, the cats, the dogs. But you killed one of my dogs now so you gonna pay for that."

The man left for a minute, returned with a crumpled bag in his hand. On the table, he dumped out a bulb of garlic and started to break it open. Kurt was thinking he was truly crazy as he peeled the papery skin away with a razor, but when he began to draw the blade back and forth through the garlic, Kurt began to shake.

"This is for my dog," the man said, tearing the collar of Kurt's shirt. He drew the blade along Kurt's chest, opening up a stinging wound. Kurt thrashed against his bonds. "Now that ain't gonna close no time soon," he said, tossing the razor on the table.

A stream of blood darkened Kurt's stomach. "What do you want from me man?"

"Want to know why you came in here. You wasn't just some kids out for mischief. Not with the effort it took to rip my gate down. I thought the government was come. I got ready. Then I see it's just a pack of kids. And what the hell you give my dogs? They had the shits for three days."

"Pop Tarts, man."

159

"Thought you poisoned 'em, like the wolves."

"Just Pop Tarts. And some pepper spray. But they was attackin' us."

"Seem to me if I saw two dogs like these I'd keep my derelict ass out of a place. Unless you was after somethin' in here. Somethin' like burned up papers. Some kind of evidence to make me lose my job."

"We ain't see the dogs 'til we was inside."

"Shoulda run then."

"Couldn't."

"Why, what was you lookin' for?"

Kurt looked up at the ceiling.

"OK then. You ain't want to tell me, let's see how long you can keep a secret."

The man grabbed his razor blade and went for Kurt's leg. The razor tore Kurt's jeans and the man yanked the torn leg down below Kurt's knee. From his other pocket he took a length of wire with two wooden knobs at the ends and wrapped it around the exposed thigh, crossing the ends and pulling tight. Kurt squirmed but that made the wire tourniquet tighter. "What the fuck you doin' man?!"

"This is cheese wire like they use in them fine gor-may stores. We use it for somethin' else here. See, this wire gonna cut right down to your bone. So you gonna tell me what I want to know or I'm gonna turn your leg into a spiral cut ham. And it ain't even Christmas time."

Kurt pushed back in the chair but the wall was only a few inches behind him. His struggle made a line of blood appear on his leg. "What you wanna know? You want the cats back?"

"They ain't no use to me now, probably gone domestic. Besides, when they done growin' they'll be payback enough to whoever took 'em. Them cats was raised on meat, not Fancy Feast." The man tightened his grip and Kurt watched with nausea as his skin gave way

160

and the wire burrowed into his flesh. "One more time. What was you lookin' for?"

The wire dug further. The pain was indescribable. Kurt panicked as he imagined it cutting through to the bone. He thought he could lose his leg, that he might already have lost his arm. "My uncle!" he shouted. "We want to see if you got my uncle Eddie in here!"

"With a start the man loosened his grip. He looked Kurt hard in the face. Now that they were out of the bright sun, Kurt could see that the man's eyes were the bright green of pond algae. With his rotted mouth fallen open the man put Kurt in mind of a night crawler. Quickly, the man let go of the wire. Then he untied Kurt and slipped out the door with the pit bull.

Knowing he had to take his chance, Kurt clenched his teeth and pulled the wire from his leg and got to his feet. His right arm and his left leg were nearly useless but he made it out the door, blood running to the sagging denim leg bunched around his ankle.

The man was nowhere in sight and Kurt held onto the side of the building and hobbled back to the gate, remembering the man hadn't stopped to padlock it on their way in. Out the gate he went, limping wildly down the canal path. The gravel lane was not long but every step felt like someone had driven a spear up his thigh where the bone should be. He knew there was no chance but to keep going. Soon he would be past the LoboChem factory and out on the paved road. He lurched along the canal, dripping blood into the dirt. Dizziness and thirst made him desperate enough to want to drink from the canal but he knew he had to keep going.

At the road he could try to get someone's attention. There were houses just a couple of blocks away. He forced himself forward. Just behind the factory he tripped a few times and pulled himself over near a fence where he could hold on for support. His injured leg buckled and he wondered if crawling would be easier.

Just then a rustling in the reeds made him stop, his heart thrashing in his chest. It was too big a sound for rats and he was afraid the dog was after him. He knew LoboChem employees went back to the canal path to smoke joints on their breaks. He'd sold them eighths himself. What he did not know now was whether they might turn him in. Of course they might be Eddie's friends, but there was no way of knowing.

Waiting, clinging to the fence, Kurt watched, fighting to stay conscious. There was someone down in the reeds by the water. He watched with terror as a blue shirt moved, bent and searching, in the rushes. He readied himself to fight. They could shoot him or even drown him in the canal; he wasn't going back to that psycho in the yard.

A head popped up between the cattails, and then another. Kids. Two boys, maybe twelve or thirteen. One of them held up a big bullfrog for the other to see. "Five legs man, I told you!"

Kurt lost his balance and staggered against the fence and the two boys dropped the frog, who hopped back to the water along a curve, owing to the extra strength on one side.

Together it Spells Mother

I held Kurt's hand in both of mine. My cheek was resting on the sheet beside his leg, the bleached cotton freckled with my tears. He watched me cry the way you would watch yourself cry in a dream and for a long time there was nothing to say. And then, drowsily, he reached for something that was no longer in my thoughts. "I love you."

It seemed like I should answer in kind, and I argued with myself about whether I had to tell him right that very moment, given the circumstances, that for me it was over. I was sad for Kurt but optimistic about my chance to start a new life. I sat up slowly and looked toward the door Rick went through half an hour earlier.

Kurt was a lot of things, but he was not a fool. I felt his eyes burn like the midsummer sun on my profile.

"Looks like maybe you should just lef' with him." He observed.

A red flush covered my face and neck. It was a familiar feeling and in an instant, flashed me back to childhood, which made me angry when I realized how often Kurt took hold of old feelings and yanked me around by them. I drew my hands away. "I just met him. We went to school together."

"So, seein' as you fell for him in a single day of us bein' apart, which part of that suppose to make me feel better?"

"None of it. I mean, well, what do you care, really?"

He reached for my hand again. His skin was clammy but I let him take hold of my fingers. I knew I didn't want the relationship anymore. But I also felt like it wasn't possible to look at his broken body without promising him everything was going to be ok; that we would close LoboChem and stop them poisoning people into monsters. Stop them giving our parents cancer.

"They got me on some serious drugs. Painkillers. But I can still see you not the same as you was this mornin'. You fell for that dude."

I looked down at his hand. "I think I did."

His fingers gripped a little tighter. "Good thing I'm so high or I might have to get up and kick his ass." He flicked his hand, lifting mine, and I looked at him. "You worth at least that. And I ain't a great boyfriend, I know."

"You aren't mad?"

"I think I be mad later when I ain't so high. Right now I just think you ain't the type to go whorin' around. Plus, I ain't wanna say it, but what the chances us stayin' together when you go off to college?"

We sat for a while more. I was thinking about all that had happened in the barrel yard that day. When I was a kid, I swore there was a man in the barrels. It seems there was. "I guess when that guy heard that someone knew Eddie was there he locked away the animals, went up on the roof for a last look around, then went and killed himself." I offered, trying to work things out. "He must have been pretty scared of the people he works for. Anyway, thanks for telling me what happened. You never forget the person you've told your worst story to."

"Thought I was gonna die, girl," he stroked my fingers with his thumb. "Can't tell my dad 'cause he just have a heart attack listenin'. Can't tell Marco 'cause he just sit around talkin' 'bout the revenge he gonna get which ain't gonna help none with the dude who done it bein' dead. I lost 'lotta blood. Afraid if I ain't tell someone I'll wind up thinkin' I imagine it. And that ain't right. Somebody got to be responsible. And I ain't know why, but I think you got the best chance of doin' somethin'. Goin' to college and all."

My tears ran in spirals down my cheeks. Why did it take breaking up for Kurt to finally say the kinds of things I'd needed to hear since I met him? He had just wiped away

164

a twisting drop when a shadow filled the doorway. Kurt and I looked up, then tightened our grip on each other. Officer Thompkin was standing in the door.

"Kurt Thomas Reynolds?"

"Yo," Kurt answered.

Thompkin moseyed over to the bed with a walk that made me think he probably spent Saturday nights at Oakley's, or some other hotel lounge/country western bar with a clientele of suburban cowboys. He hitched up to the bed rail and fixed us with a tin star glare. "You're under arrest for the attempted armed robbery of Appliance Circus, trespassing on private property, discharging a firearm within township limits, possession of an illegal weapon and resisting arrest."

Kurt and I looked at each other like Thompkin had just told us he was the Wizard of Oz. "How the hell am I gonna be resistin' arrest from a hospital bed?" Kurt slurred.

A smile that made me want to slap him in the mouth spread across Thompkin's face. "That was just a joke. But I notice you didn't argue with the rest of the charges. Good as a confession to me. We got your butt-buddies out in the waiting room. The three of you better stick together in Trenton State, nice tasty white meat like yourselves."

Of course LoboChem had to strike back at us eventually but seeing the satisfaction in Thompkin's face made me feel as if the hospital room with its blinking equipment and striped curtains had begun to spin. There was a roller coaster drop in my stomach as I saw Kurt and myself slide down a rabbit hole. "Does his doctor know you're in here?" I asked, but my teenage voice lacked the necessary authority.

Thompkin had the kind of nose that made you think God hated him before he was born and he took a country minute to look down it at me. "The doctor knows just fine Miss High 'n Mighty." He sneered. "Yeah, I've seen the way you swan around. Now I know you were involved with the break-in at LoboChem, and I don't mind lettin' anyone else know if it helps things go my way. But we can discuss that when your mother gets here."

That shocked me out of my daze. "You called my mother?"

He let off that smug smile again. His lips flickered and snapped like a cheap bulb with too much wattage running through. "Looks like the little princess of North Trenton is scared of something after all. We have a deal waiting for your parents. They'll take it, and you'll go." He rattled off Kurt's rights and then said, "I'll leave the cuffs off, but don't fuck with me. If you even get out of this bed without permission I'll chain your good arm. You'll have to call the nurse to take a piss."

With that he strutted out of the room. Once he was gone Kurt asked, "Do he think I can piss without the nurse now?"

It was partly due to hysteria, but we laughed until we had to cover our mouths to stifle the noise. Before I left the room Kurt showed me the tear he'd taken from my cheek. It had turned into a Lucky Charms blue marshmallow diamond.

A female social worker brought me to a small room with a table and chairs and a water cooler. When she returned a few minutes later with Officer Thompkin and my mother I quickly glanced away. My mother was in a suit. They must have called her out of work. Her eyes were like lasers in her head.

"Now Mrs. Esposito…"

"Ms.," my mother snapped. A ray of hope went through me seeing she was as aggravated with Thompkin and the social worker as she was with me. "Esposito is my maiden name."

"Not married." Thompkin said.

"Not anymore."

166

"So then, Hope Esposito," the social worker tried to confirm, attending to the top line of a form on her clipboard.

"Hope has her father's name. Esposito is my father's name."

Thompkin folded his hands on the table top. "Is Mr…" he trailed off when neither of us filled in the blank. "…available?"

"No," my mother retorted. "And I'm pretty sure the point of my divorce is that that's the last question I'm going to answer about him. We are here to talk about my daughter, I believe."

"I just need to fill out these forms before we…"

My mother's gaze sliced through all the metal in the room on the way to the social worker. "What you need is to tell me right now why you have my daughter in pseudo custody in a hospital. You need to tell it to me so fast that I know inside of sixty seconds why I shouldn't leave with her and let you meet me at our home with our lawyer."

What lawyer? I thought. Thompkin looked shocked. It seemed clear he was counting on another sort of mother.

"Ms. Esposito…is it Angela? May I call you Angela? We've all got Hope's best interests at heart."

"You may call me Ms. Esposito until we become friends, which is selectively unlikely. And as for Hope's best interests, I believe I already know what those are and they do not include having any acquaintance with you whatsoever."

"A fishing net with your daughter's fingerprints was found at the site of the break-in." Thompkin muscled in. I could tell it was his big piece of evidence, and that his nervousness made him shoot too soon.

My mother was cool. "Hope does not own a fishing net. She is in fact appalled by the idea of catching a fish. She's seen too many dead ones floating in that canal you patrol." It was her reminder to him that she was once a member of the accounting staff at LoboChem. She knew who got paid for what.

"Ms. Esposito, if you continue to be hostile…"

"Officer Thompkin, if you continue to be patronizing…"

"Perhaps we can start fresh," the social worker interjected, "Ms. Esposito, it seems your daughter is implicated in a crime. The severity of the crime and her involvement are still under investigation. However it seems there is proof that she was trespassing on LoboChem property and that she may have been connected to an attempted armed robbery that occurred this morning."

I thought my mother was going to give birth to a goat when she heard armed robbery but her sharp tone was directed right back at the counsellor. "What part of LoboChem?"

"A chemical store located on the canal."

"Has she seen a doctor?"

"No ma'am, there was no reason to suggest medical attention was necessary."

"Get a doctor."

"All in due time."

My mother leaned forward and planted her index finger on the table. "You get her a doctor right this fucking second or I will bring a lawsuit on your heads that will have you crying into your beers for the rest of your lives."

Within minutes I was wearing a blue hospital gown, my feet swinging high above the floor on the gurney where I sat. "Mom, I…"

"You what? You're sorry? You're worried that maybe you've thrown your life down the toilet for a bunch of juvenile delinquents?" Her face was marble. "You were in the barrel yard?"

I nodded.

She turned her marble face to the ceiling, pressed her hands together, and for the first time since my childhood, crossed herself. Her desperation frightened me. "Mom?"

When she looked back at me there were tears in her eyes. "I don't even know if these doctors will have what you need. I don't know if I can even get it for you."

"Mommy? What is it?"

A doctor flipped the curtain aside and stepped in. He was wearing a gown and hat as well as a mask, and as he approached me he pulled on a second set of latex gloves. Behind him a nurse carried a tray loaded with vials. On each one there was a special sticker that read *Biohazard*. She put a tube with a large hollow needle in my arm and began to insert the rubber capped vials one at a time, draining blood while the doctor recorded our interview on a chart. "Have you got a headache?" He flashed a light in my eyes the way the LoboChem doctor did when I was little.

"A little bit."

"Taken any drugs?"

"No."

His back was to my mother and he raised an eyebrow at me. I knew it was important to tell the truth and I did not feel completely clear in my head but I could not bring myself to implicate Rooster. If my mother even heard his name at that moment I was pretty sure she would go buy a gun.

We were nearly through the exam when the doctor suddenly ran his fingers through my hair, feeling my scalp. He brushed my stitches and I flinched. "These are new," he observed, parting my hair.

My mother had a look. "What the hell is that? Mary, Mother of God, Hope please tell me you didn't cut yourself in the barrel yard."

"Who did these sutures?" the doctor asked, picking up my chart. "Why isn't this recorded?" He confirmed with my mother that he was holding the proper chart.

"Hope, who did these stitches?"

Under their joined fire I suddenly felt so tired I thought I might faint.

"I'm going to find out what's going on here," the doctor said, striding out of the examining area.

Thick lines creased my mother's brow and I realized that somehow without my noticing she'd gotten older. I wanted to see the face that looked at me when I was little. I had a headache, which had been growing slowly and steadily since I'd left the yard. Just like always. My mother took my hands in hers, kissed my fingers. Then she held my face and kissed my temple. "Honey, I know things haven't been the best but I love you more than my own life and I'm begging you, please, tell me everything that happened today and I swear neither you nor anyone else will be in trouble. It's amnesty day, ok?"

Her worry more than her words crashed through the layer of ice that had grown between us since she took me away from Rooster. I still thought she would flip when she heard Rooster's name but strangely it had the opposite effect. When I told her Immaculata sutured the wound and gave me several injections it looked like someone had turned a lamp on inside her. She threw her arms around me, "Thank God, oh baby, thank you God."

She released me and we wiped away tears. The sudden relief of not fighting made it feel like all the love I had been holding back had poured into the room. Mom was laughing and dabbing my face with a tissue when she stopped dead. "Oh Jesus, Hope, the doctor took blood."

I nodded, "Didn't you want them to?"

"Oh honey, I did. I did when I thought there was no antidote. I thought they might be able to do something to slow…." She took in a sharp breath, squared her shoulders

170

and for a minute I thought my childhood mother had disappeared again. "OK, listen Hope," she spoke quickly and quietly, but with an air of collusion, "we're going to have to tell a few lies. If we don't they will put together a record on you, like they did with Eddie Reynolds."

Shocked as I was that my mother spoke so familiarly about Freak Eddie's situation, there was no time to ask questions. When the doctor and the social worker and Officer Thompkin met with us I said exactly what my mother told me to: I had no idea about the robbery. I went into the barrel yard as a prank and saw nothing but old barrels and tyres. I refused to implicate anyone else who was involved without my lawyer present for the sake of my own safety. I confessed to recreational drug use of known and unknown substances on an occasional basis.

Thompkin looked whipped. Somehow my mother got my Vice Principal on the phone to tell the social worker what a promising student I was, a veritable miracle given the trauma of my early upbringing. Thompkin avoided my mother's eyes when the social worker made her proposal. "Well Hope," she said, "I think perhaps we can arrange something that would be more beneficial than sending you to juvenile detention. I think you and your mother will agree that Mercer County Chemical Dependency Treatment Center will be just the place to start a new phase of your life."

While I was relieved to have the threat of jail removed, a flood of depression broke open like a capsule between my teeth at hearing her twist that idea of change, so freshly my own, into something so confining.

The building, a sand-coloured brick rectangle, loomed like a big-shouldered cartoon of itself. Its walls beaded brown sweat under the strain of standing and trembled every so often as people walked around past the windows inside. Mom and I looked at each other. We had talked about our doubts on the drive over and a few times I thought she was going to turn around and head home, but there we were, looking at the converted reform school that still read *Baptist Correctional School for Boys* in the masonry.

In reception, my suitcase was taken and we were shown into a brown room. A woman in a fluttering skirt came in. "Hope, Mrs. Esposito."

"Ms."

Guided by a stack of paperwork we reviewed medical questions, family history. When asked if anyone in the family had a drinking problem Mom answered, "Not really."

"Can I ask what you mean by that?"

Mom shrugged. "I just don't think anyone really considered it a problem. My father stopped at the bar on the way home. All the men did."

"Every night?"

"More or less, yeah."

"And yourself?"

"I have a drink occasionally."

"How many times per week?

There was a wrinkle in Mom's brow as she counted. "I don't know, ten maybe. Maybe fourteen."

"So you have two drinks per day."

"Sometimes."

The counsellor continued with her questionnaire. After several more pages, during which I found out that my great grandmother used to take laudanum, that my grandpa was on prescription painkillers for ten years and that my mother and father smoked their fair share of marijuana back in the good old days, the woman disappeared with her clipboard.

In her absence my mother whispered, "We came in here with no alcoholics and we're leaving with five."

We were still giggling when our interviewer came back and informed us I 'qualified' for round two. She left with my mother and a skinny, skinny woman came in and shook my hand with her skeletal fingers.

"I want you to say yes to as many of these drugs as you have taken. If you do not recognize the name of the drug hold up your hand and I will read to you various street names by which it is known…Alcohol."

"That's a drug?"

"It is."

I had given three *yeses* and seven *nos* and we were into a section of the list comprised of groups of letters. When she got to one of the later compounds and I said no she stopped. "This is a program of honesty," she informed me. "We have your blood tests here."

Then I remembered that Immaculata had shot me full of several solutions. "To tell you the truth, I took a couple of things without knowing what they were."

Next, I was told that my mother had left. It surprised me that she had not said goodbye and the skinny counsellor told me they recommended to parents that they leave after the second interview phase as emotional goodbyes could sometimes be used by inducted children to manipulate parents into withdrawing them from the facility. The skinny counsellor and a young woman who didn't look much older than me then took me into a communal restroom and shower and walked me over to a stall.

"Take off all your clothes and place them over the door. When you've handed over everything I'll open the door, then you turn around in a full circle so we can see you haven't smuggled anything in." The skinny one said.

I'd never stood naked in front of a woman before and the contrast between my situation and the girls in the Howl & Pussycat was twisted enough to make me choke back a laugh. I turned around on the cold tile floor, held my arms above my head, squatted down, opened my mouth for prying latex fingers. The rubber caught my hair as the young one felt along my scalp.

"Careful," the skinny one warned, "She's got a wound back there."

Clothed, I was taken immediately to the community room where I suddenly knew how a pinball felt, rolling up a lonely corridor in that quiet moment before the game started. At a table of girls, the skinny counsellor, whose name turned out to be Bertie, gave me over to a big buddy. Her name was Natalie. She hugged me. I was then introduced to and hugged by eleven girls and twenty nine boys. Back at the table the nurse gave me one of the packs of cigarettes my mother bought. My direction was "regular Marlboros. Not lights. Not 100's." She bought me Marlboro Lights 100's. And in all the long day, that was the thing that made me cry.

Up against the length of a whole life, eight weeks does not sound a lot, but it felt like a season in hell. Rules. Two girls could sit with one boy. Two boys could sit with one girl. One boy and one girl could not sit together alone. That was construed as relationship forming. Three boys could not sit with one girl and three girls could not sit with one boy; that situation was known as "getting your self-esteem off the opposite sex". Three and two was permissible, but only for a short period of time. Anything more than five was a gang. Not allowed.

We could not drink or do drugs, clearly, obviously and agreeably. However, this overall guideline extended to monitoring that no cigarettes went into the dormitories, to prevent anyone smearing toothpaste on them, which, purportedly, could get you high when smoked. Intentional hyperventilating was also not allowed.

Apart from Crest flavoured tobacco, smoking was unlimited, based on the slogan *First Things First*, which was on the wall above us with a collection of other slogans

174

covered in yellow tar. Counsellors kept hold of the only
lighters as a precaution against self-harm, assault and arson.

I was assigned to a tough little day counsellor
named Carmella. We had group twice a day. It was where
we were meant to talk about our "deep issues".

"Tell us about your father Hope."

"Why?"

"Because we are only as sick as the secrets we
keep."

"My father's not a secret. Everybody who knew him
tried to forget him. Nobody who doesn't know him would
want to meet him if they knew what was good for them."

I thought I was being as honest as directed but
Carmella's brain doubled as an X ray machine. "You're
good at acting tough, Hope. But as long as you keep that up
you'll keep pushing people away. Everybody in here
shares, and if you don't, it's like saying your private stuff is
more sacred than theirs. Is that right? Is that how everybody
feels?"

My group members all nodded.

"My father beat us." I said, and then I just sat. I sat
and they hugged me. Four sessions later I said I hated him.
Ten sessions later I said I missed him sometimes while I
was growing up. Thirteen sessions later I wondered where
he was. That was when I began to worry if it was still me
inside of all that hugging.

The woman in the fluttering clothes turned out to be our
family counsellor. Once a week she had a session with my
mother and me for an hour. "Angela, what sort of man was
Hope's father?"

"A bastard."

"Always?"

My mother looked out the window, crossed her
arms over her abdomen. In that position it was like I was
looking at myself. People always said we looked alike but I

never saw it before. "No," she said softly. "Once he was charming. He was fun. He was handsome."

"And what happened?"

"He…" her eyes filled with tears. Her jaw opened and I could see her tongue crossing the cavity of her mouth, pressing against the top teeth. "Grown up life got to him: bills, responsibility. Then he started working in a chemical factory." Her teeth gritted so that we could hear them. "And then he disappeared."

The following week my mother and I were sitting beside each other, holding hands, visiting the time before my memory. "And then what, Angela?"

"Then he held me, and said, 'I can't wait 'til this baby's born."

"Do you believe he loved her?"

Mom nodded as she shredded a crumpled tissue. She let go of my hand to look for a dry spot. "He loved her."

"Hope, do you remember that love?"

"I remember him singing *Let Me Be There*. I remember him trying to teach me to play guitar. I remember him taking me to the swings when I was really small."

"Do you believe he loved you?"

"I believe that love is what you do, not what you feel."

"You sound pretty angry."

"That's probably right." And I thought of LoboChem, and whether my father lay at the bottom of the canal, staring at a heaven he could not get to, out of dead green eyes that would never decompose. What's the half-life of radioactive damnation?

The family sessions with Mom were twice weekly. Another hot Thursday afternoon we strayed from the popular topic of my missing father.

176

"And do you think that a responsible adult would take a minor, or indeed anyone they cared about, into a dangerous chemical dump?"

"He didn't take me in there. In fact he had Billy guard us to make sure we didn't go in. He was so mad afterward he wouldn't talk. Everybody knows LoboChem is poisoning us. Why won't anyone listen?"

"Hope, if you had a little seven year old, a little girl like you were, and you knew what was inside that barrel yard, would you bring her in there?"

"Well, no, but I'm not seven…"

"Angela, Hope's seventeen now, not seven. As a mother, can you tell us, is she still your little girl? Has anything changed in your desire to protect her, to see she's safe?"

My mother looked at me through red-rimmed eyes. "It's worse," she said. Not sure of her meaning I worried that we were about to launch into what a rotten kid I had been but what she said was, "It's worse because I've known her longer, so now I love her more."

Then we cried again, and my attempt to clear Rooster was rained under a wash of tears.

In bed at night I often heard motorcycles on the road. We were not allowed to look out the windows, so I would lay and listen to the familiar sounds and try to guess who was who. Sometimes I would pretend I could hear the hot cam shaft on Dutchman's bike even though the rumble was not deep enough or that a Sportster that went by was Eddie's high performance engine even though he probably wasn't well enough to ride. I knew they would be there if they could, and somehow, that had become the same thing as believing it was really them.

I needed the thought of them because rehab was working on me, drug problem or not. There was a new room in my mind, an open room where my father sat blameless on a white sofa as a man who was sick rather than mean. There were other chairs in the room, calm-white and waiting, ready to be filled with other thoughts, each of which had the capacity, and in fact, the imperative, to change me.

Rehab was the longest I had been out of Trenton in my life.

Breakfast was cereal, toast, decaf coffee, sugar. Lunch was macaroni and cheese, vanilla pudding with ready whip, milk, decaf and sugar. Dinner was breaded cod, tater tots, vegetable medley, giant oatmeal cookies, decaf and sugar. Night time snack was a juice drink container and a packet of cookies, chocolate chip. One morning at breakfast, the four of us at the girls' table realized we had used three-quarters of a diner sized sugar dispenser, at that meal.

We went upstairs and smoked until our next activity.

Five A.M. rise. Six A.M. breakfast. Seven A.M. community meeting. Eight A.M. group counselling. Nine A.M. community room. Ten A.M. lecture. Eleven A.M. community room. Twelve o'clock lunch. One P.M. community room. Two P.M. recreation. Three P.M. school. Four P.M. hug line. Five P.M. dinner. Six P.M. community room. Seven P.M. AA meeting. Eight P.M. study hour. Nine P.M. meditation. Ten P.M. bed. On the weekend we watched a movie on Saturday and Sunday evenings, ones without reference to drugs or alcohol. Or sex. Or life, I guess.

I thought about Rick. I made myself stop thinking about him because it cheered me up and this was considered 'using on a thought'. Anything we did to get away from the present moment was categorized as an attempt to get high. We were never alone, never unattended. We slept with the door open, flashlights in our faces on the hour, checking we were still there, still breathing. Only in the shower were we given brief privacy.

178

For those ten minutes, I would think of Rick, and then tuck him away where no one could call him a drug.

Caught staring out the window I confessed to daydreaming. I was told again that daydreaming was a means of escape, of changing reality. And again I was told that anything I did to escape reality was tantamount to getting high. So was I getting high when I was little and my daydreams took me away from my father's abuse? Carmella hesitated. While it was good for me to share those old stories from my childhood I also needed to be aware that sometimes I used them to manipulate staff into giving me the answer I wanted to hear. The sober answer, the good answer, was to stay in today. No one was beating me today so there was no need to try to get out of myself. I should stay with my feelings right there and then. I was asked to get my composition book and write fifty times *My imagination is my drug of choice and I want to live in the world today.*

When Carmella walked away I took my composition book from my locker and drew a picture of Ivka Repinka, wondering if anyone would see her but me. On the facing page I began my assignment but when Carmella came back she looked over my shoulder and said nothing. I looked back at my notebook and Ivka was gone.

The composition notebooks were for assignments and journaling. There were no calendars on the walls and we were not supposed to draw them in our books. Inside the cover of the books was a multiplication table. It listed numbers up to 100. Each block represented a day and we crossed them off or filled them in with designs to mark the time. One each day. We were not supposed to, but we did.

One day at a time.

Three, seven, eight, twelve, twenty, twenty-two, twenty-seven, twenty-eight, thirty-four, thirty-nine, forty-three, fifty-nine.

Somebody confessed in community that we were all keeping calendars and the counsellors made us open up our lockers, and sit in our smoking chairs while they ripped the covers off and threw them away.

Wipe Out

One hot afternoon during family counselling, Mom told me the whole story. In the close attic office she seemed to grow younger as she unpacked the past. Her face became her teenage face, with wide lingering smiles and light-filled eyes that wandered the windows and walls. It was the most open she had ever been with me and I stayed still and silent, drinking in every word, not wanting to break the spell.

"I was nineteen when I was hired as a junior administrator by Bantam Barrels. It was the summer of '69, my first job after high school and I wanted to gain some experience while I attended secretarial college in the evenings. Apart from me, the only people who worked in the office were a bookkeeper and a typist, who each came in one day a week. And the boss, of course." She raised her eyebrows with a grin. "Everyone else was in the factory.

"When your grandfather found out I was working in a business with so many men, he threw his hands up and grumbled for the rest of the evening. '*Just remember nobody's gonna buy a cow when they can get the milk for free, huh?*' She mimicked the grandfather I'd never met, the one who died too early to know me. "He was still peppering me with warnings when I left for work the next day. '*A man who respects you gives you a ring first, eh?*'"

"They were so old fashioned!" She shook her head and laughed, "You would've thought free love was a form of communism to see the way your granddad changed the TV channel when any mention of sex came on. Miniskirts, The Beatles, birth control, everything sent him ranting around the house waving his arms in the air and commanding me to remain ignorant of it all. Of course, he drew so much attention to it that he only made me more curious.

"The guys at Bantam laughed when I told them about my dad's tirades. They were hippies, most of them,

long-haired, bearded and bell-bottomed. They went to
protests. They smoked grass. They had girlfriends who
came and went by the week, and then came back again,
with bumper stickers on their knapsacks, from Nashville,
from L.A., from everywhere else. Girls with long hair and
love beads and names like Mooncat and Lorelia. Everyone
said *Heeey* when they came in the door. Cream and
Steppenwolf and the Stones were always playing from a
transistor radio on the windowsill. Twice a year the factory
shut down for a week and the men all disappeared off on
their motorcycles. I asked where they usually went and was
told, 'Somewhere'. I didn't know what to make of that but
then I realized they weren't meaning to be secretive, it was
just that they liked to wander.

"It was funny how it happened with Rooster. That
was the name he went by with everyone. I didn't know his
real name for the first month I was employed. I came across
it on a bill I was filing one day. Pete Stumpenauer. As soon
as I read it I said in my head, *Angela Stumpenauer.* That
was when I faced up to myself that I had a crush on him.
You should've seen him then, such a handsome man,
although I guess he hasn't changed all too much. I found
myself making eyes at him, even though I tried not to. And
I started listening when the guys talked to see if I could
catch any clue that he was taken.

"But then I started figuring, he'd been in the army,
ran his own company, what if he was older than he looked?
I knew I couldn't ask anyone without them figuring out
why I was interested, so I took a chance." Her hand flew to
her chest. "When he caught me leafing through his
personnel file I thought I would lose my job but he only
smiled and leaned against the door he had come in, those
brown eyes of his sparkling. You know that calm way he
talks – 'If you want to send me a Christmas card,' he said,
'I'll tell you the address.'

182

"Well, I went bright red, wished I could run right out of the room or come up with a good story to explain myself. Only he was standing in the way of the door and I'd spent my whole life in Catholic school. I couldn't lie to him. I told him I was checking how old he was. I was so embarrassed I thought I would just ignite, but all I could do was look at the floor.

"He came over and tapped the chart. 'You know why this isn't locked up?' He asked me. 'Because we got something around here called trust.' I nodded, and he waited for me to look up at him. 'You think you can trust me?' he asked.

"I realized right then that I did trust him and I apologized for being a sneak.

"Rooster was quiet a minute, and then sat on the edge of his desk, so that he was looking at me eye-level. He asked why I wanted to know his age.

"I didn't know how to tell him and I just said I was sorry again and ran out of the room. It was still an hour until my shift was done though, so after a quick walk around the dusty yard I returned to the office and just blurted out the truth.

"'I wanted to know if you were too old for me', I blurted out. Rooster was sitting with his feet on his desk, flipping through a parts catalogue. 'So, am I?' he asked in the same quiet voice as before." Mom drew her breath in sharply, reliving the moment. "No, eight years, just like my parents. I told him. I was waiting for rejection but then he just said, "Glad to hear it."

"I walked back to my desk feeling very self-conscious. You know how when you know someone is watching you walk it's as if you've forgotten how to? I made it across the room somehow, but for the next hour we sat, moving papers around silently. No one else came in. I worried that I would leave and nothing more would be said. All I could think was that I would go home and sit in the presence of my father and the thought would grow larger with every moment that I had thrown myself at a man, one that maybe didn't even want me.

"At 4:49 he cleared his throat. *"Do you like steak? He asked.*

"'Yeah, yeah, I like steak', I told him.

I guess he was nervous too. I could barely hear him when he started to tell me about a place down the 'burg, and asked if I would go with him.

"When Rooster picked me up in his brand new Plymouth Barracuda my father said the color was a bit racy, but he nodded and held the door open and asked Rooster about the engine. That was approval, from him.

"The restaurant we went to was small, lit with little candles under crimson lampshades. The maître d' wore a bowtie and an apron that went nearly down to his feet. He shook Rooster's hand, and took us to a table that was tucked between the velvet drapes in the front window.

"Rooster held my chair out, and when we were alone, let out a breath.

"What? I asked. I checked the shoulders of my dress to make sure my bra straps weren't peeking out. I'd worn a sleeveless sweater dress with a white bodice and a striped skirt and I had my daisy pin fastened to the skirt, just at the top of my right thigh. Nana didn't think sleeveless was appropriate for a first date and apart from pinning my bra straps to the inside of the dress, she made me carry along a cardigan, which I'd left it in the car."

"He told me I looked beautiful. Said it was nice to see me in a dress. We all worked in jeans, you see. Of course I blushed. You get that from me," she winked at me. "But I relaxed a little. I'd panicked before the date and left my mother in my room re-hanging nearly everything in the closet. 'I thought you liked girls in jeans?' I asked him.

"Rooster shook his head. 'Nothing wrong with jeans. You look nice in your jeans too.'" Mom was really

184

good at mimicking the men in her life. I could hear Rooster in her voice.

"I felt my face going red so I just looked at my lap. Rooster held out his open hand on the table. I put my fingers in his palm and he stroked the backs of them with his thumb. 'I can't figure you out,' he said. I thought I'd messed up the date already and asked what he meant.

"And he said, 'Well, one minute you're confident, laughing, this little spitfire, and the next minute you close up. I just never realized you're so shy'. The waiter came back just then and showed Rooster the label on a bottle of wine. Rooster nodded and our glasses were filled, the bottle placed on the table. It was a nicer restaurant than any I'd ever gone to growing up and something about the way Rooster seemed so comfortable with it all made me worry again about the difference in our ages. I told him I was Catholic, hoping he would understand.

"'I know,' he said, squeezing my hand, 'I know what you're trying to say.'

"I smiled, and then laughed at myself in relief. I'd only ever had dates with boys at school, ice cream sodas at Stewarts, a kiss behind the bandstand. Sitting across from Rooster, seeing him in a suit, his comfort with the wine... had made me realize again that he was a grown man.

" 'OK?' he checked, wiggling my hand.

"OK, I answered.

" 'Now, you promised me you were gonna eat a steak,' he said, opening this big cloth-covered menu. When he began to read and I looked at his face again, I took hold of the top of his menu and told him I thought he was handsome and that it was nice to see him in something besides jeans too.

"He looked up over the menu. 'Your name's not Angela for no reason. You got my head right into the clouds.'

"I'm not saying that to brag," she caught my eyes and the counsellor's for a moment, "It's just that my parents weren't people to give a compliment, and the nuns and the priests thought nice remarks about others just fed into vanity. When Rooster said that it felt like I'd won a prize and I sat back and turned it around and around in my head. When the waiter came back I had to ask Rooster to order for me as I hadn't been able to concentrate on the menu.

"On the way home, we passed a club that had a band and dancing. Rooster caught me looking at it and hung his head a little, 'Afraid you wouldn't want to see me dance,' he said. Then he let me in on a secret. Most people thought his nickname was given to him by the people he rode with, but it was actually something he picked up in high school when he'd tried to do the hand jive at a dance. He bobbed his head and lifted one of his feet and apparently it was the funniest looking move you could imagine. I'd never seen someone with a negative sense of rhythm before and when he asked if I liked dancing I made very little of it. I didn't want to hurt his feelings. I was three time champion at the greater Trenton area under 20's dance contest," she told the counsellor, who nodded, impressed.

My mother glinted like a sequin the memory, then returned to Rooster. "Anyway, I thought maybe he would improve with some practice. I tried a few times in a playful way, just to get him moving to music. It was funny because he was a strong man, and graceful in his way, but it was as if he was having kind of a fit to the tempo of a song that only he could hear. He head-butted me once and we didn't try after that."

In the chair by the window in the counsellor's office, my mother took a sip of her water and paused a moment, checking with a quick smile that we were still interested.

"And?" I said.

My mother's smile was devilishly inclusive. "It was hard to tell when people at work noticed, because no one seemed to mind. Rooster and I worked comfortably together. He wanted to take me for a ride on his motorcycle soon after our first date but I knew your grandmother would sit in the window with her rosary fretting until she saw us come home again. But over time, seeing the guys at Bantam come and go, their girls on the backs of their bikes, my desire overtook caution and I told him I wanted to go for a ride.

"It was a beautiful Sunday, late spring with every little flower box in Trenton blooming. We met at the barrel factory to save my mother the sight of me climbing onto a Harley-Davidson. Rooster lived closer to my house than the factory was to either of us, but I couldn't meet him at his place. Someone might have seen me and gotten the wrong idea. Your reputation was everything then." Her face went a bit more serious and she looked at me, "I guess we've always talked about the biological side of sex and not so much the social side. Frankly, I'm glad you're growing up in a freer generation. You have to understand that this whole idea of girls - of nice girls - choosing to have whatever they wanted in a relationship was revolutionary. Not the having sex, but the idea that you could do it and walk away, and still have a normal life and kids one day, and be respectable, like a man could...well, that was an idea that was setting fires all over the neighbourhood. All over the country. I had your grandfather to contend with and no matter how open Rooster's friends might be, my family was another matter. It put a strain on me, wanting to go further but not feeling ready for marriage. Then wanting Rooster to propose because I was taught to believe that was the only sure sign he loved me. I think the way I grew up forced a lot of people into premature marriages, just so they could have sex."

She avoided looking at the counsellor: uninterested in anyone else's point of view. What she was doing, this storytelling, was a risk against her upbringing. It suddenly was clear why she'd always been so cocky. Why she'd had to go for the big guns for even the tiniest act of rebellion. Listening to her there I realized how much strength it had taken for her to disagree with my father, her bosses, even Rooster.

"In the barrel yard, Rooster was tinkering with his bike, revving the motor. When he saw me he checked his hands for grease and then came over to greet me. He kissed me and then wrapped me in a quick hug. More and more, whenever I was close to him I found it hard to pull away. I remember wondering that day if he could tell. As he released me he held on to my shoulders a minute, like he didn't want to let go either. He took my hand and led me over to the bike.

"I was wearing my favourite jeans, flowered hip huggers with a wide green belt and Rooster warned me not to burn my ankles on the pipes, *The pipes are always hot*, he said." And she winked at me, both of us remembering the first time he put me on his bike. "They're not, by the way," she told me, "but that's Rooster. He'd rather you think the world is always dangerous than to see you get hurt even once. That was why it was so hard to believe him about LoboChem..." a crease appeared in her brow and I was afraid she'd broken the recollection, but she turned back to me and I smiled and she laughed and then I did, and she asked where she was in the story.

"I had no idea how intimate it would feel to be sitting on a bike with Rooster, wrapped around him like that. I thought I should sit further away but that was impossible and it wouldn't have been safe not to hold on to him.

"Riding was the most thrilling experience I'd ever had. Once we got out of the city I felt like I'd been given wings. Sure I was scared, but it made me feel like I was really awake for the first time in my life. And I liked holding Rooster when he couldn't see me and read my thoughts the way he always did.

"We rode along the Delaware River past Bowman's Hill Tower. We'd ridden about forty minutes when he pulled into a field lined with willow and elm trees and shut off the engine.

"It took me a minute to find my feet when I got off the bike, and Rooster unclipped my helmet and hung it on the handlebar. He took my hand and started across the field. I had never really trespassed and it made me nervous. I asked if the owner wouldn't mind. 'Don't think so', he said, 'the owner's me'. I didn't know what to say. I just walked along on that magic thought. It was a new way of looking at things for me; the idea that you could buy yourself acres of land like that. It was like a park he owned all to himself. I could hear the river. We came to a small cliff and I leaned over to have a better look at the rushing water below. Rooster took hold of my waist and eased me back from the edge. He said land up in that area was going for a song when he got out of the army. He fell in love with the place, and decided to grab it while he could.

"We sat on the cliff's edge and he showed me where he wanted to build a house behind us where the pines ended. And build a dock right where we were sitting. He didn't want his children growing up in the city. Near the river they could run and climb trees and fish. Then he...he ran his thumb and forefinger around my ring finger. He told me his ideas about the barrel factory, ways to expand away from the wineries and into other areas of manufacturing. He had designs for containers to make chemical disposal safer. And then he looked at me closely and told me that actually I never said anything about what I might want to do, where I wanted to get to in life. I stopped and thought. It was the most wonderful question, just because no one had ever

asked me before. I told him I'd like to have my own
business. I'd been paying attention at work and running a
business didn't seem as hard as it was made out to be.

"Rooster laughed and said that was probably the
truth but it might be best if I didn't let the secret out. He
didn't know anything when he started. Running a business
was all about having forward motion. You just had to
believe in what you wanted and then convince other people
you could do it. And then you worked seventy hours a week
for a decade or so." She laughed. "It was some of the best
business advice I've ever heard."

Mom looked sadly at the back of her hands for a
moment, stroking them thoughtfully, aware that she was
mocking herself. Then matter-of-factly, she picked up
where she'd left off. "While we were on the subject, I told
him I wanted to move out of Trenton. I liked the idea of
travelling a little. I wanted a car, and maybe even a
motorcycle." Her chin quivered and she mashed her lips
together. "We lay back on the grass and watched the
clouds. I was in his arms and he stroked my hair back and
kissed me again. 'I love you Angela'. He told me. 'It's
nothing I say lightly. I want to spend my life with you if
you'll have me.'

When tears trickled down her cheeks the counsellor
was quick on the draw with a box of tissues. I moved
forward but my mother shook her head. "Wait honey," she
said, "Or I'll never get it all out.

"Next door to the barrel yard there was an empty lot
where neighbourhood kids hung out. Though they weren't
exactly kids. Some of them had been to my high school and
were probably older than I was. Most of the time I ignored
them but one day as I was walking to work I heard music.
Someone had run an extension cord from a house across the
street and a group of them had a record player going. There
were a couple of girls there, mixed in with the usual pack of
boys and a few of them were dancing. It was wild music,

like no other I had heard before and the kids were waving their arms as if they were swimming while the girls wiggled their hips and shook their hair. I wanted to stand somewhere and watch them but I was totally exposed, walking down the side of the lot to the yard entrance. I was trying to hear what the record was so I could buy it.

"Then a boy was at my side. He was out of breath and I realized he had run across the lot to catch up with me. He looked to be near my age and he was as handsome as anyone I'd ever seen, handsome like a movie star."

"'I just came over to ask you a crazy question', he said, 'I could see your head moving, and I want to know if you want to dance.'

"Well, I was flattered. 'You came all the way over here to ask me to dance?' I asked, and he held his hand out to me.

"We ran back across the lot and I tossed my handbag down with the others. Introductions flashed around and then the record started again. He told me that we'd gone to school together, that his name was Lee.

Her mind back in 1969, Mom whispered, "*EE ee ee ee ee Wipe out!*"

"I danced and danced and when I got to work a half hour late, and Rooster asked if I was ok, I lied and told him I'd overslept, that it wouldn't happen again.

The counsellor's office was quiet for a while. By the look on her face, I could see pain rise up in my mother like a wave cresting far off shore. I had that same feeling of awe that the ocean always gave me. The instinctive, gambling sense that this was the big one.

"There was no explanation for what happened." The girlish timbre of Mom's story voice was overcast with the serious, mahogany tone of our everyday, "I started joining the group of kids on my way home from work if they were around. And when Billy Regret saw me and casually mentioned it to Rooster, I said only that I'd gone to school with them. I got an attitude about it, telling him I wanted to have fun, that I wasn't done being a kid yet...just because he was.

"It wasn't that I didn't want a house and kids, I did, and I wanted them with him, just…not yet. My parents approved of him, his friends liked me, and it was like I was rolling downhill on skates into another phase of my life and I wasn't ready." She took a breath so deep it made me inhale reflexively. "I saw myself turning into my mother and it made me feel my life had been condensed to something so much shorter than I wanted it to be.

"But I loved Rooster. He encouraged me to learn, to try, to think about how things might be done differently. I came into work and found brochures for two local colleges, with a note saying maybe I should think about something more than secretarial school. And he was so patient. I'd told him it was important to me to wait for sex until I was married, and it was." Tears began to roll down her cheeks. "But, I guess, when I was dancing with Lee, I wanted someone to not be so patient."

Her black eyes shone. "I'm your mother and maybe I shouldn't say this, but I wanted someone to push things where I was too good a girl to go. They were terrible thoughts, I felt then, and I shoved them away. I loved my dates with Rooster, riding and walking in the woods, planning the house near the pines. We became regulars at Marino's; the maître d' started ribbing Rooster that he'd better pop the question there, where they could provide the Champagne on the house.

"One Friday I was on my way to meet Rooster. He'd left work early to pick up some motorcycle parts and I was supposed to wait for him in the park and we would go riding. I was walking, and then suddenly Lee was walking next to me. And then Lee had his arm around me, and he kissed me and I was kissing him back. And only then did I hear the motorcycle. I heard it in the background, slowing

192

down, standing still, its engine revving. I pulled myself away, looked at Lee, the hunger in his face, looked to the road where I knew Rooster would be. And he was. I won't forget that look in his eyes – like when hurt is drowning in disbelief, but not quite fast enough. He shook his head, and rode away."

We had a short break while the counsellor went and told the receptionist we would be running over the hour. But you can't stop a cresting wave. She was barely back in the door when Mom started crying openly. "All the way through it I felt like I'd left my own body. Some concoction of joy and hate and music and wanting to be free came over me and I just went with Lee in a car. When it was over, I went home and cried."

I left my chair and sat on the floor beside my Mom, and put my head on her knee. She stroked my hair while she finished what she had to say.

"Rooster didn't give me a hard time at work. He tried to talk to me at first, but I felt too dirty. I felt too dirty to dance with the kids in the lot anymore. I avoided everyone. So much so that your grandmother even showed up at the barrel factory on my day off. When Rooster couldn't give her an answer she only said to him, 'We had hoped'. He told me the next day and I wanted more than anything to fall into his arms and tell him the terrible thing I'd done. And I think he just might have been strong enough to forgive me, but weeks had gone by, many weeks. So many I knew...something...

"Your father did the honourable thing. I should have been grateful, your grandmother told me so as she altered her own wedding dress. There was no time to shop for a new one, no time for a big reception. Not before I started to show.

"All the way down the aisle I wanted to turn and run. I wanted to tear across Trenton and find Rooster and see if there was any way we could have our life still, the

193

one we talked about by the river. But it was too late. I was terrified I would lose Lee in the process and if Rooster wouldn't have me, and I couldn't figure out why he should, I would have been disgraced. Your grandfather was so upset he might have put me in a home."

She turned my face to her. "So when you were born, with your father's blue eyes, I made up my mind to pour all the love I had into you. I wanted to make the world perfect for you, to make sure you grew up smart and strong and able to have as many choices as possible."

The air was still and the three of us let the stillness shape us. And a belief stapled down on me right then; that my mother had woven her whole adult life as a kind of ladder for me, and that the worst thing I could do to her – the worst thing I could do with my free life - was not try to climb it to someplace higher.

Now Wouldn'tcha Barracuda

Doubting your perception in Trenton is like doubting your karate punch when your fist is heading for a cinder block. You can believe in the Holy Trinity, lottery tickets, or that Bruce Springsteen really remembers you because he said hello, but *believe* you must, or something inside you breaks.

When I saw a Vitamin C orange Plymouth Barracuda parked on the corner of Parkway Avenue I wondered about reality in a way I never had before. Transfixed by the *For Sale* sign, I stood in the lot of a small garage trying to figure out whether the car I was looking at could really be there. Rehab had been like a kind of mangle where every ounce of anger that was wrung out of me drained with it an ounce of imagination. Without that filter, I just didn't know what was what, and it scared me.

The mechanic, a quiet, thin man, came and stood beside me, wiping grease from his fingers into a blue rag. My voice wavered, "How much?" I was hoping the money my mother had given me for graduation would be enough to cover the cost of the car, a 1970 classic identical to the one Rooster drove to take her on their first date.

The dashboard was cracked, there were a few rust spots and the seat was locked so that I nearly had to lie down to reach the pedals. I handed the money over. Before I could drive away, I rolled up my coat and tucked it behind my back so that I could see over the steering wheel. When the engine turned over the car shivered into a throaty purr. There was a lot of play in the steering wheel and out on the road it felt like I was hanging on rather than controlling things. Being in the front was not so much different than riding in Rooster's Barracuda as a child. "I wonder if you *are* Rooster's Barracuda," I asked the car, patting the dashboard.

At home I honked until Mom came out of the apartment. I hadn't seen her hair in a ponytail for years. She ran her hand along the bright orange paint. "So long as it watches over my little girl," she said with a wink as I stepped out.

A few days later when the trunk was filled with my clothes, books, music and a tiny fridge, I gave Toffee a good long scratch and then opened the driver's side door.

"You sure you don't want me to come with you honey? I could follow in the Toyota." Mom said, stroking Toffee's greying muzzle.

"I'll be all right," I said, hugging her. I knew Toffee probably wasn't up to the chaos of drop-off day at college and that my mother probably wasn't really up to the drive. Mom had been tired a lot lately and looked too thin. Despite it, there was a smile on her face that had been there for most of the summer. After all those years, part of her was getting to go to college too. Seeing her expression was the payoff for my agreement in rehab to stay clear of the fight against LoboChem. Officer Thompkin had threatened to slap Rooster with an endangerment charge. Due to the restraining order, which my mother found out she couldn't remove while I was still a minor, I was a liability, a risk to what he was trying to achieve. After a while it made sense that I would be better off getting a degree and working for the EPA or Greenpeace or becoming a lawyer if I wanted to make a difference. It was only a couple of months until I would turn eighteen. I could stay away from Rooster and the bikers until Thompkin found someone else to harass.

With a smile I headed for College Avenue. Mom waved until I was out of sight.

Where fitting in during high school had been an ordeal, college was exactly the opposite situation. Everyone was new, so no one was. And rather than rejecting differences,

196

people showed up hoping to find them. My Harley shirts were coveted, my motorcycle boots pronounced sexy and every little thing I said about Trenton was fascinating to kids from Florida or Nevada or Iowa. Fall turned cold and I barely noticed. My classes were challenging and it took a lot of work to keep up. One Saturday while I was sweating blood over my statistics textbook my roommate Kirin came bounding through the door, followed by Becka and Rob. "Come on, you ready?"

"Let me finish this page," I grumbled, turning back to my notes.

Kirin lay her head and shoulder on the desk so that her face was smiling up from where my tables used to be. I laughed and Becka and Rob pulled me to my feet. They rifled through my closet, yanked a sweatshirt over me and stuffed a hat on my head. Rob did the honors of holding up my leather jacket, which got a soft oooo of appreciation out of the group.

"Ok, ok!" I grabbed my keys and student ID and we piled out the door, ran up the parking deck and jumped in the Barracuda.

There was traffic on the bridge into Piscataway but the music was on and Becka kept patting my shoulder excitedly. "Tailgate party! It's so cool you have a car!" Neon flyers ruffled on telephone poles and fences as we approached the Raritan River. It was Halloween, and the day of our Homecoming. There would be parties everywhere that night.

We were just off the bridge, going about thirty-five in a line of traffic when the car stalled. I glanced down at the ignition as it slowed going up the hill to the stadium.

"Look out!" Rob shouted, just as a deer darted down a wooded hill and straight across the road, missing my bumper by inches.

"He would have run right into us if you'd been going normal speed," Kirin said, wide-eyed. "Good car," she affirmed, stroking the dashboard. There was a line of cars waiting to turn into the stadium and I was able to put the car in park and start it again.

There was a cold crackle in the air and the sound of the band warming up through the barren trees. We made our way through a red and white crowd armed with stocking hats and thermoses and found a place to park at the edge of the lot.

I had never been much of a sports fan but it was infectious being in the middle of a crowd that was so pumped up. Still though, I found myself searching the faces around me for Rick Rayetayah. He was a year ahead of me and an engineering major, which meant we were unlikely to be in any of the same classes. And in a school of 50,000 students, I knew that scanning crowds for him was like trying to locate a particular gull at Seaside. Still, I let myself look sometimes, knowing he had to be somewhere; on a bus, in the dining hall, waiting for a gyro at the grease trucks. Somewhere.

At halftime we were ahead by a few points and I joined in with the crowd singing *R-U Rah Rah! R-U Rah Rah! Hoo-Rah! Hoo-Rah! Rutgers Rah!* The marching band came on and someone's arms wrapped around me from behind and lifted me in the air. When he put me down I saw that it was Jacob, a boy from my dorm. "Thought you needed a lift," he said.

Becca pointed at him with a giant foam #1 hand. "You coming to the frats?"

"I'm going if Hope's going as a Playboy bunny for my birthday."

"I'm not getting you anything for your birthday," I said. "And I am damn well not running around in October in a bikini."

Jacob made a mock tragic face. "What are you wearing then?"

198

The team ran onto the field again and the cheering drowned out my need to answer. It was cold and the second half of the game was so close no one sat. We stomped out hands and feet, huddled together, wrapped our cold fingers around a shared thermos. Rutgers was behind. Fans were shouting and air horns went off. The school chant reverberated around us and the band whipped up and demanded victory. And there, right in the last few seconds of the game, the ball was caught in the end zone and we won.

The great scarlet wave of us, unleashed, stormed down the bleachers and out onto the pitch. We moved in a body of thousands, hats and pom-pons and cups and streamers flying into the air. The football team, the cheerleaders and even the band were lifted high above heads and carried like trophies around the field. We hugged and hugged each other until it seemed like we had won a war rather than a game.

The crowd ran out of athletes and everywhere girls were being hoisted into the air. A man lifted me onto his shoulders. I didn't know who he was. All I could see was a red and white pompom hat. He held my knees and I hung on under his chin. Over the crowd I could see Kirin on the shoulders of another stranger. We waved, shouted, but the noise was so great we resorted to pointing wildly in the direction of the car. I laughed and then I could not stop laughing. It was the first day in a very long time that my spirit felt free. I threw my arms out and found the little girl who'd learned to fly on the back of a Harley.

I was set down in the parking lot where nearly every car on campus had been decorated with victory messages in shaving cream but the Barracuda remained clean. The stocking cap disappeared in a fanfare of scarlet.

Kirin and I threw on our Halloween costumes and headed out. From party to party we went, meeting mummies wearing rolls of toilet paper, ghosts in striped

199

sheets with their jeans poking out of the bottom, Dracula's
in capes made of the dorm draperies and everywhere,
everywhere, boys with war paint, dressed as Indians. But
none of them Rick.

Then it was time for essays and finals and goodbyes full of
promises for a great next term and it was Christmas break.
At home with cups of cocoa and our Christmas tree
decorated I asked Mom about Rooster again. We'd gotten
back from the tree farm just as an ice storm was beginning.
I'd had to carry the tree. Mom said she didn't feel up to it.
"Do you think life will sometimes forgive you for turning
away from the right guy for the wrong one?"
        She looked at me with a knowing smile. "It's not
really Rooster you want to know about, is it?" Mom had
done well working for the state and had been promoted
nearly every year since she began. There was a confidence
to her that made me proud when I thought about her
struggle from her first job as a receptionist after my father
left.
        We sat by the window, watching branches bend
under the weight of winter. I told her the secret I had kept
in rehab. I wondered if the memory was like a soap bubble,
and would pop if anyone else touched it, but after I told her,
Rick seemed more real. We made popcorn and she told me
how she used to walk past the barrel yard, hoping for a
glimpse of Rooster, too scared to go find him and make
things right. "Then the yard was sold. So that day in the
park, when you first met him, you remember?" She checked
and I nodded, "Was the first day I felt like there might be a
chance again. And I don't care how corny it sounds, but I
believe if somebody is in your heart and you're in theirs,
they always find a way back to you."
        A twist of longing took hold of me and I wondered
then if I wanted Rooster back with my mother even more
than I wanted to find Rick. And then I knew the two

200

thoughts were merely offshoots of the same wish. I missed having a family. My birthday had come and gone but I realized I had no way of contacting Rooster other than to drive up and down the Delaware River trying to find the entrance to his driveway. And apart from that, the thought crept in that he might be angry with me. After all, it was due to me that the cops were paying attention to him again. I figured it was probably best that I just stay away.

January came and with it five new classes. They were all tough. Freshman year was the proving ground before declaring a major. American Lit required the reading of a novel a week, and they were all new to me. They were all good books I didn't feel right about skimming them. The basement study lounge was filled with worn armchairs and I often fell asleep there with a book on my lap.

I made friends. And there were guys that were cute or nice or smart, but I still felt some of the separation I always had, that sense of being among people whose norms were foreign to me. Their worlds were made of cooperative parents and wall-to-wall carpets and three car garages. But as the term passed, surrounded by optimistic peers and books and the promise of a brighter future, I looked out the window one day and knew I'd become normal too.

I don't know if it was that thought that set the universe on end, but something happened to the weather just then that I'd never witnessed before. It was a week before Spring Break. My attempt at a legitimate lab report was spread across my desk when I heard thunder. There hadn't been a sign of rain. In fact, rather than dark, the sky had gone an impenetrable white. I went over to the window and looked up into a solid cap of clouds that started and ended with the edge of the earth. There was another rumble and snow began to fall. To *pelt*. Big flakes made a rushing sound as they hit the trees. The sky was coming apart.

I went back to my desk. Midterms were coming and the report was due the next day and I was only partway to understanding how to go about making the amount of food consumed by ten rats into more than three sentences. But the snow fell harder and louder, tapping tiny crystal fists against the windowpanes. I went back to the glass, to check how deep it was. An inch.

I'd sat back down, determined to concentrate, when a colossal boom from above was followed by a long low roar across the sky. I rushed back to the window in time to see that the atmosphere had torn straight down the middle. Stars and planets and every good intention in the history of humankind was falling down head over heels through the gap. A new god had been born. Some timeless time bent the air and every still thing outside the window was wearing now three inches of snow. Five inches. Eight inches.

Another sonic boom rattled the window panes.

Doors up and down the hallway began to open. Two girls ran by my door, bundled in sweaters and hats. Then more people passed, pulling on jackets and gloves. Finally I threw on my boots and coat and joined the stream of people heading for the front door.

The dorms were emptying and the courtyard filled with shrieks and flying snow. Clumps of snowflakes landed on my face, like feathers that melted and stung with cold. I caught one on my tongue. Another series of rumbles and a big rolling crash came from the sky. There is a difference between fun and frenzy and I saw in the spellbound bodies around me that I was not the only one who'd been shaken out of the modern world. The pagan dance of the girls brought the flakes down faster than gravity and drew from the building at the center of the courtyard a tall, broad shouldered boy. He appeared in the archway of a building. His low, deep voice echoed down from the top of a flight of stairs. "Snow thunder!" He bellowed.

It was a call to action.

202

Someone started to run and it got us going like a stampede, over lawns and toward the dining hall where two guys in crew coats had dragged a tray cart outside and were handing them out. The nearest park had hills running to the river and we flung ourselves down them, sliding on trays until we were caked in snow. We were devotees, so far inside the weather that we became immune to it. Snowpeople, abominable, indestructible.

Bodies collided, helped each other up, redistributed trays, latched onto each other and tromped back up the beaten snow to throw ourselves down the hills it again. And then one of the hands that latched on to mine held.

I looked down at the fingers that were wrapped around my own as a crust of pearlized snow sealed our hands together. He was a tall boy, wearing a thick wool sweater. A scarf was wrapped several times around his head, so only his brown eyes showed. He took the end of it and began to unravel as I watched.

"Rick."

"Hope," he smiled, "I've been looking all over for you."

There was one casualty that day. Coincidence died quietly under an avalanche of icicles. Whatever normal was, it wasn't for me.

Proud Buck and Laughing Doe

Just after finals I decided to surprise my mother by bringing Rick home to meet her. Rick and I took the long route, heading over into Pennsylvania, taking our helmets off as we rode along the river to Washington's Crossing. Summer break had just started. Rick and I began going out with each other the day of the snowstorm and that very night we'd scrunched into a phone booth and he rang Rooster and told him the news. We were full of plans.

I got my motorcycle permit and Rick was going to start teaching me to ride. We were going to work for Rooster for the summer, but we had a few days off first and decided to spend them on the bike. Now that I was eighteen, Mom and I agreed that I would remain in the dorm for the rest of my degree but that I could spend summers helping Rooster gain the attention necessary to make LoboChem clean up the factory and the area around it. He had targeted a list of agencies, lawyers and reporters who had dealt with class action situations of our kind and he wanted Rick and I to help him build the case. The big news was that Billy Regret had found the plans for the construction of the vats while doing some maintenance work at LoboChem, and it looked like some corners had been cut in the installation.

We pulled off the road Rick stopped the bike beside a crooked jack fence. "I'm keeping you to myself for a little while before Rooster and everybody gets sight of you and hogs you for the rest of the day." He said over his shoulder.

I hopped off and Rick pulled a knapsack out of the saddle bag and took my hand. We walked until we found a grassy glen near the river. I lay on the blanket and Rick took my boots off before he lay down. I wanted to wear sandals but he was as strict as Rooster on that front, though he didn't argue with my wearing shorts, which Rooster was always dead against.

"You like being on the football team?" I asked

"R-U Rah!" He said, stripping off his T shirt.

I laughed. "Did you play in the homecoming game?"

He stretched out on the blanket. "Yeah, it was unbelievable watching the stadium pour onto the field like that. For a minute I knew what my ancestors felt like, downhill from a sea of white men. I got tossed in the air like a kid."

"Me too. Someone put me on his shoulders. There was no fighting it, really."

"Close your eyes and think of Rutgers."

I closed my eyes and something feathery tickled my eyelids. I opened them and found a tiny daisy. Rick tucked it in my hair and then rolled on his back. His hand came to rest on the front of my thigh.

"No offence, but you seem so much different than the guys on the football team, both now and in high school." I said.

"And you're a lot different than the girls who hang out with bikers."

"Am I?"

"You know you are. I play football because the scholarship money is good. I don't have to take so much from Rooster. Anyway, I like the game. Some of the guys are all right. They wanted me to join a frat but I didn't want to do it. Too much partying. Not enough time to study. They even keep essays on file so they don't have to do as much work. That wouldn't fly with engineering."

Rick's braid lay along his shoulder and I took the tip in my fingers and watched the sun dance blue off the shiny black strands. "Do you think that when you graduate you'll find an employer that's sympathetic to your ideas?"

"Develop clean chemicals? Yeah, I think so. I mean, I believe in what Rooster is doing but let's say we get LoboChem shut down, how long do you think it will be

206

before someone else takes their place? So far as I can see the only real hope is in the market; find a responsible way to do what LoboChem does, and do it cheaper. There are giants out there in chemical manufacturing who would love to play the environmental card with the government."

I thought about that. "I still want to close LoboChem down. Maybe someone else will try to take their place but if LoboChem lose enough money it might send a small shockwave through the chemical industry."

Rick ran the back of his fingers down my cheek. His other arm slid under my waist and pulled me against his side. I waved the end of his braid with the elastic band. "Can I undo this?" He nodded and I began to unravel his hair, combing it through my fingers as I went. When it was undone I let it fall against his chest and rested my face against it.

"You know, when you play football one of the perks is supposed to be all these girls hanging around the frat parties. I didn't like many of them. They tried to impress you by knowing your stats but you could tell all they were looking for was a chance to be NFL wives. Also, when they found out I was Indian they thought being with me would be like some Lifetime channel special and I would carry them off to my tepee. I couldn't believe how many girls have Indian fantasies. Doesn't seem to take more than two beers before they want to tell you about them either." He pulled me further onto him. "You don't mind me talking about it, do you?"

"What, the fantasies?" I felt my face go red.

He looked at me. A sparkle came into his eyes. "I meant the girls."

"Oh...no, no that's the past." I could feel my blush spreading and I turned away from him.

"What was that *Oh*? Hang on, not you too?"

"Shut up." I laughed and rolled over.

He turned on his side and rested his face against mine, his chest to my back. "Well, I can see there is only one thing to do." He sprang up and then pulled me to my feet. In one swift move he threw me over his shoulder and started to carry me across the field. One of his arms was wrapped around my thighs and the other swung at his side.

"Where are you taking me?" I called out, laughing.

"I am taking you to my tribe where you will share my lodge with me. We will call you Laughing Doe and you will know great happiness in the land of the elders."

There was a historic village back near the bridge and Rick was striding that way. A row of wooden colonial structures sat on the river side of the dirt road. "I'm taking your woman!" he called out to a group over by the barn with the Durham boats in it.

"Keep her, she talks too much!" A man called back.

"Hey!" I shouted in protest. The family laughed and Rick with them and I tried to smile the best I could flopped over Rick's shoulder like I was. When we got back to the blanket Rick put me down on my feet and held me by the shoulders. "You are now Laughing Doe. You are my woman from now until our souls join the stars when we will sit in the sky side by side forever. What do you say?"

Catching my breath, I laughed. "I say, Proud Buck, that you are the only warrior for me."

"Whew," he exhaled, then stretched out on the blanket and pulled me back down on top of him. I settled into his side again and he stroked my fingers. "I have to say," he confessed after a minute, "I wish I'd thought to do that earlier. That was a lot easier than asking you out."

On the way home, the bike started stuttering and failing. Rick pulled over in a gas station. After an inspection he shook his head. "I can get you to your house but I better not chance it getting back to Rooster's.

208

Rick called Rooster, who agreed to meet us in the parking lot of my apartment complex in Billy's pickup truck so they could load up the bike and take it to his place to work on it. "Said he'll have us on the road again in no time." Rick kissed me before he got back on the bike.

When Rick cut the engine I heard Toffee barking. She still jumped around whenever she heard a Harley, thinking it was company. I felt happy knowing today her five-year vigil had paid off. A Harley was bringing friends once again.

When we walked in the door I knew something was wrong. It was 6:00 P.M. on a Friday and my mother was in her bathrobe. She'd been crying. The sight of Rick gave her pause but she recovered quickly and did her best to smile, inviting him to stay for dinner and insisting we have a seat while she made some iced tea.

"What's the matter?" I asked her, as she got the pitcher ready. Even Toffee seemed subdued. Rick asked if he should go and Mom said absolutely not. She was fixed in a brave stance, cracking ice out of trays, when Rick spotted the problem.

"Did you just find out about this?" he asked, gesturing to letter on the table, several pages thick.

"Oh, that's, oh, I...I didn't want...with Hope's finals. I wanted to wait..."

I took up the letter Rick was pointing to. "What is this?" I asked him, although the paper plainly stated at the top that it was a toxicology report.

"You used to work at LoboChem?" Rick asked.

And then I knew.

Mom busied herself with dinner preparations. Rick asked her not to bother but she said it would be therapeutic to prepare something besides seaweed soup. Apparently she had gone macrobiotic since the doctor first voiced his suspicions.

By the time the doorbell rang I'd forgotten about the arrangements we made. The house was filled with the smell of baking lasagne when I opened the door. Rooster stamped his feet on the doormat before giving me a big hug. "Thought you were going to be in the parking lot?" he asked Rick, grabbing his hand in a shake and hugging him with the other arm.

My mother had been running the blender and came out to see who was at the door. She stopped, looking like a Geisha in her bathrobe, and Rooster stopped, halfway out of his jacket, and they stared at each other until Rick coughed.

"That's just what they do," I told him, as the moment passed and they collected themselves.

"Rooster, how are you?" my mother asked.

"Ain't never seen you in your bathrobe this time of night, Ange. What's going on?"

She made some excuse and Rick stuck his hands in his pockets and looked at the floor. Rooster glanced from one to the other of them and then at me. I handed him the letter.

As he held it I couldn't help watching his hands. The pages looked smaller in his grip than in anyone else's and yet more volatile too, like they had finally found the right catalyst and might ignite at any moment.

"Lasagne?" Mom quipped, just when I thought I wouldn't be able to stand the silence any longer.

Rooster's voice was thick and burdened and he did not glance up from the letter. "I'd love some."

"Welcome to the family," my mother laughed, patting Rick's shoulder as he sat down at the table.

When we were seated and my mother was filling plates, Rick pointed to a line on the report, "It's the same combination as the others." He was as calm as I'd always remembered him.

"Others?" I asked.

210

"The others who contracted their cancers at LoboChem." My mother answered.

I turned to her in shock. She met my eyes but then switched her gaze to Rooster. "Looks like I threw my life away twice by not trusting you."

Rooster had set the letter on the sideboard and he sat with his shoulders squared and his arms resting on the table, forming an unintentional wall around his plate. "Well I've never liked easy women."

I laughed, not because I thought it was the right thing to do, but because it was something to do and I felt out of control of myself. "What's going to happen, Mom, how bad is it?"

She looked to Rooster and then to me and it reminded me of that first meeting in the park, when so much more was being said than what I picked up on. "I've had tests done every six months since I left LoboChem, so they caught it early. Chemo starts Monday. Can I interest you in some wig shopping while you're on break?" Her laugh had a hint of desperation that crackled around the room like a static shock.

My mother's hair was her pride and joy and I looked at it, pinned up in loose waves, and felt angry. I found myself gripping my fork in a kind of power-drunk wonder. It seemed a real and imminent danger that I might walk out the door and run straight to Trenton and plunge it into Gordon Lobo's eye. The real barrel man hadn't hung himself in a cattery shed. He was a businessman.

I felt Rooster's hand over mine and I relaxed my grip as he slid the fork away from me. "There are better ways," he said, and I remembered what Mom said about his reading minds. It had always been true.

I thought about my promise to stay away from LoboChem and looked at my mother. "Yes, there are." She agreed.

She dished up the lasagne and after that, the rage flew out of the room and we ate and laughed. There is a kind of abandon born of immortality and another born of mortality. Though they are of equal potency, the latter is far more focused.

Work Experience

Billy Regret, besides having discovered a few nasty secrets about the installation of the chemical vats, had also managed to collect several samples from the leaking seals. Rick had arranged access to a chemistry lab at Rutgers by garnering the sympathy of one of his professors who was interested in industrial pollution. Rooster set up a desk for me in his office. After having answered a phone call from one of the reporters Rooster had been trying to make contact with, it was discovered that I had a certain flair for rhetoric. I began to handle many of the issues having to do with the press. There was one reporter in particular who was interested in our case. His name was Michael Smiley. He worked for the New York Times and had an aunt who was recently deceased of breast cancer. She had worked at LoboChem for fifteen years.

Through Michael, I came to understand how to put together evidence that would stand up to investigation. All of Rick's work needed to be verified by Professor Aronoff at Rutgers, which Aronoff agreed to after seeing the initial results.

One morning in early July Michael called. I'd just dropped off the first results of Billy's samples. He ticked through the report, his voice fired with anger and excitement. "And this is the stuff leaking inside the factory? How many employees are exposed to this area around the vats?"

I jotted down his questions, knowing he was informing me of what needed to be clarified, rather than encouraging any sort of speculation.

"This is good, but what you need to get is samples from other areas of the factory. That will be enough to claim damages on employees. But if you want these guys punished, really punished, you need some samples that show this is leaking into the community. You said you believed this was being dumped into a canal? Get water, soil, plants, animals, everything you can. This Aronoff guy is a big name in academia, he'll know who to talk to about any testing he doesn't usually do himself. Does anybody know you're gathering evidence?"

"Not as far as we know, but we'll have to be careful getting the stuff from inside the factory."

"Well, I'm sure Aronoff is professional, but academics are sometimes open about discussing their ideas with each other. LoboChem funds a lot of work in New Jersey colleges. If I were you, I'd focus on the outdoor samples. Get them quietly and get them now, before anyone else hears about what you're doing."

I said I'd get onto it right away and call him as soon as we'd collected from the community areas.

"Hope, listen huh, be careful?"

There was no answer in the lab where I phoned Rick but he wouldn't answer if he was in the middle of testing. Rooster had gone to meet with a lawyer. I thought about what Michael said. If Aronoff had said anything to any of his colleagues it would soon be too late to take the samples we needed. The only way to call Billy or anyone at the factory was through the phone in the break room, where it was easy for others to overhear. And knowing LoboChem, it was possible the line was monitored.

Rick left a spare bag in the office for transporting specimens. I filled it with empty vials and bags, threw in a couple of pairs of gloves and a mask and got into the Barracuda. I knew right where that pipe was leaking and I looked a lot less suspicious than the bikers, I thought.

The tree of heaven was in full bloom. But where Bryant Park seemed smaller than I remembered it, the tree had also grown, and dwarfed me as it always had. The canal's way of reminding me I was still not as big as that place.

214

A mixture of feelings had swept over me as I walked across the playing fields. The banks of the area where the drainage pipe had been laid were now thick with weeds, and I had to hunt around for a while. I was wearing jeans, but as I crunched into the spiny pigweed I wished I'd worn long sleeves as creatures began to scurry in the undergrowth. Deep in tick territory I pushed aside some tall grass and began taking samples.

Gloved and masked I filled one jar with surface soil and another with some kudzu that I'd extracted to the roots. Then I made my way down along the pipe until I heard a squishing under my feet. My foot was sinking in mud when something landed on it. Before I could stop myself I let out a shriek as a rat sprung off me and hit the top of the pipe where it scurried away. Reflexively, I looked toward LoboChem, but the pipe was a ways from the boundary fence and the fence several hundred yards from the factory itself.

I filled a jar with water, and stopped to label all three before heading to the canal. Half of the containers I'd brought were filled and marked when I heard a rustle in the grass. Determined not to let another rodent spook me I crossed the canal path and found a puddle of bright green water. I bent to fill a jar.

Something knocked into me and pushed me to the ground. The jar bounced off the canal wall into the water. My rubber gloves tore as I tried to avoid hitting my face on a broken slab of concrete. The face mask muffled my scream and I wanted to yank it off but my arms were pinned under me. Someone heavy was on top of me. Hands grabbed at my breasts, squeezing them, pulling my bra out of place and pinching my nipples. I fought to get out from under him, but my hands slid on the pebbles and my knees were sunk in mud beneath the heavy legs of whoever was on top of me.

I got one hand free but when I tried to pull the mask away the attacker grabbed the side of my hair and slammed my head against the concrete.

I was groggy when he turned me over. My eyes rolled, looking out through the mask at the cloudless sky until my T shirt was yanked up, trapping my arms and covering my face. I saw only that the man had a shaved head and a smashed nose, like it had been broken many times. He grabbed my hips and bit my stomach. I jerked and he fell on top of me, his chest pinning me while he yanked open the buttons of my jeans. Garnering my strength, I pushed against the ground as hard as I could and drove my face against his head, pulling my mask aside. I screamed then, as loud as I could. His fist hit me hard in the cheekbone and my head smacked the ground again with a thump that sent me into darkness.

When I woke I was looking at the sky and it took me a minute to remember where I was. I could smell the tree of heaven and I thought Toffee should be with me. Then the pieces started to fall into place and I was afraid to move. I knew I was the subject of a story that I didn't want to know the end of.

But staying near LoboChem frightened me more.

My back was sore and I lifted myself up gingerly on bruised arms. My jeans and underwear were wrapped around one of my ankles and the sneaker from my other foot was lying a few feet away. I put my leg back in my panties and jeans and pulled them up to my thighs before I got to my knees and brushed the rocks and grass from my back. My arms were sore as if I'd been exercising heavily and it was hard to reach around behind me. I pulled my shoe on, got my clothes straight and looked around. Everything was silent except for the breeze that rustled the reeds. My head hurt and I felt the bumps, but it was more than that, there was a sparkling aura everywhere I looked.

216

Of course, after lying by the drainage pipe, the chemicals were having their effect on me. Though the landscape was wildly overgrown I began walking, instinctively, back toward the playing field. When I reached the mown grass I saw two boys tossing a football. They looked at me but I kept on, heading for that house at the top of the park, heading for my mother and home.

I was in the playground under the trees when it occurred to me that the house was the wrong color. And then I knew what happened. The pain inside my head was spreading toward the pain on the outside. He had a bald head, a smashed nose. I could not see his face clearly. I remembered only one thing that struck me as odd. His eyes were plain blue and somewhere inside I thought they should be kelly green. I sat on a swing and let it rock gently. Fuck reality. Fuck rehab. Fuck that asshole. Fuck everyone. Fuck LoboChem. Fuck Rooster. Fuck Rick. Fuck me. Fuck my mother. Fuck the dog. Fuck life.

The chain was cool against my temple. I closed my eyes.

"Little girl go to hospital."

I swung, to and fro, to and fro.

"Little girl go to hospital."

I turned toward the voice. Ivka Repinka was sitting on the swing next to me.

"I don't want to."

"Have to."

"Oh yeah? Why? So they can tell me for certain that I was raped?"

"So they can find man who did."

A deep sob started to shiver to life in my lungs. It felt as if it would choke me if I let it out. "Where the fuck were you? Huh? Where was Madam Ivka Repinka and her host of unholy angels?"

Ivka got off her swing and came over and put her arms around me. I did not have the heart to fight her and the sob broke free.

When I had cried until I ran out of tears, she took my hand and walked to my car.

The first thought on my mind when the doctor said I could go home was to get to Rooster's and call my mother. I didn't know if I could tell her but if I did I wanted him there to help in case it hit her badly. It was hard to know what stress might do to her while she was having chemotherapy.

When I pulled into the house by the river there were several cars parked on the drive. I hadn't counted on that. I'd been making a series of promises to myself since waking up, promises that had to do with getting from one step to the next. And I'd gotten myself to Rooster's on the promise that he would be there alone, and would keep the rest of the world away from me for a little while until I could figure out whether telling my mother might kill her.

Before I'd even stopped, a woman hurried over to the car, her bright red hair shining in the sun.

"Janie!" I said, letting her hug me as I got out, though her hands on my scraped up back felt like a slap on sunburn.

She leaned back, her palms on my aching shoulders, "Oh honey, now didn't you come out just as gorgeous as you could?" She was beaming proudly when her eye caught the bruise on my cheek. "Baby, what's happened?"

I began to tremble. The day felt like a volcano that was about to explode from my mouth.

But then Rick appeared around the back of the house and I felt my legs nearly give out from under me. Janie kept her hands on my arms and she was looking at me closely.

218

"You got that extra sample bag?" Rick asked, brushing my hair back. "Hey, what's that?"

My migraine had faded but even without the pain, I felt just as locked in. Like they were talking outside of me and I was talking inside of me and we could not make our words affect each other. I blinked at him.

"Baby you out there?" A man called from the back yard.

It was Rooster's voice, and just as I tried to lift my head to answer it Janie called out, "Right here!"

I looked at her. Rooster came around the corner and stopped, seeing the two of us together. He wasn't calling me 'baby'. He was calling Janie 'baby'.

Fury rose in me. It was an infantile reaction. I wanted him with my mother. I wanted our family back. I needed them and now Janie had screwed it all up. A violent tantrum gathered momentum deep in my mind like a storm brewing deep at sea, and still I could not let out a single word.

"Hope, what happened? Where have you been?" Rick spoke to the side of my head, more insistently.

In Rooster's face I could see that he knew what I'd just figured out. He was with Janie. And why shouldn't he be? He and Mom broke up a long time ago.

I turned to run but realized I couldn't and instead walked away, and went in the house, upstairs to the bathroom with the big tub that overlooked the river. I filled it up, letting the sound of the water drown out the chatter in my head.

There was a knock at the door. "Hope, you've got us worried. Will you let us in a minute?"

I knew I should say that I was already undressed, buy some time, but I still found myself unable to talk. Janie's voice joined in the plea and then Rooster's heavy knock. I thought in a minute he would threaten to get the skeleton key and open the door but then they went quiet.

The bath was full and I took off my clothes and looked in the mirror. I was covered in scrapes and bruises. There was no way to hide it from Rick for long. But I could hide for a little while. I got in the water and Ivka sat on the side of the tub. She was in a pink nurse's outfit with one of those old stiff hats on her head, the hat trimmed in rhinestones. She poured from a bottle in her hand and the tub filled with pink bubbles and the smell of roses. I closed my eyes and sat back in the warm water and let it wipe away the smell of chemicals.

I had made up my mind to tell Rick and Rooster together, and to ask Rooster if he would help me tell my mother, so when there was another knock on the door, I opened it. I had expected Rick or Janie so I was surprised to see Rooster. I was wrapped in one of his bath towels, which reached below my knees but I still felt awkward for a moment.

"I've got something to tell you kid. Get dressed and come downstairs."

"I have to tell you something too." I said. I was happy the words came out but they sounded too big when they did and I wanted to take them back.

"All right. Come out to the porch when you're dressed."

I came downstairs in a pair of Rick's shorts and one of his T shirts. A sudden violence overtook me when I approached my clothes and I threw them in the bathroom trash bin. I wanted to tell Rooster right away before I lost my nerve but when I got outside there were a dozen bikers on the porch.

"Sit down here," Rooster said, putting his arm over the back of the two-seater wicker chair that held him. I sat down carefully, feeling Janie's eyes on me again. And again, I had the great sense that something was wrong. None of the bikers had looked up when I came out. Wildly,

I thought they knew somehow. I wrapped my arms tightly around myself and squeezed my knees together.

"What's going on?" I asked. My voice was shaking.

Rooster gave me the most serious look he ever had. "Phone rang while you were in the bath. It was the infirmary at LoboChem. A centrifuge malfunctioned and sent one of the vats off its supports and into the next. It caught two men under it. One of them has been taken to St. Francis with severe burns. The other..." his lips whitened as he pressed them together, "The other ain't made it. Billy Regret died in the LoboChem infirmary twenty minutes ago."

Later that night, when I was about to drive home Rooster caught me at the foot of the porch stairs. "What'd you want to say before?"

"Nothing," I said. But I said it too quickly and walked away rather than look at him.

Battle Hymns

Rick tried to come and see me for days but it was not until Billy Regret's funeral that I saw anyone besides my mother. I said she wasn't well, used that as an excuse not to go to work or come out. I didn't think Rooster was buying it but I knew with what happened to Billy his attention was divided. Mine was too. And for as real as my grief about Billy was, it also provided cover from explaining to my mother why I'd been sitting in the house watching *The Breakfast Club* for three days straight.

I was having a battle with reality. Not as in knowing the difference between reality and fantasy, but as in wondering why reality should be allowed free reign. The doctor told me that I had not been raped, but sexually assaulted. Apparently my attacker got as far as he did and then, the doctor guessed, was scared off by something, or possibly feared that he had killed me. She asked if I would talk to the police. All I could think was that Officer Thompkin would show up or at least find out what happened, and I couldn't say for certain that I wouldn't kick him in the head if he talked to me the way he'd talked to Kurt.

Eventually I would have to tell. But every minute that I held off telling was a minute that I could deal with the part I remembered, which was bad enough, and not the part I didn't remember, or the further damage that could have been done.

Toffee hadn't left my side for days. She slept on the foot of my bed, and crept up when the nightmares came, to lay beside me in the dark. She came to know when the dreams were at their worst and several times, while I was reliving the attack in my sleep, I was called out of the scene by a low growl and would wake to find Toffee with her chin on her paws and her tail thumping softly. I guess she must have recognized the change in my breathing or the

223

fluttering of my eyes, that I now knew happened in REM sleep, but it didn't make her any less magic to me than she'd ever been.

The morning of the funeral I woke with her beside me. It was a day with a purpose and for Billy, I was determined to function. Rick was at Rooster's house and I passed through the throngs of gathered mourners and found him sitting on the edge of his bed with his face in his hands. I stood beside him and he wrapped his arms around my waist and rested his head against my stomach – right over the bite bruise. I don't know if I would have been able to allow it except that his own pain was so great. He was crying and I think the tears helped me see that he was Rick, and not anyone else, and I held him. Then I brushed and braided his hair with a lace of black suede, and he pulled on his jacket and we left.

Three hundred Harley-Davidsons rode from Lambertville to Trenton and parked along the street before the whitewashed steps of Calvary Baptist Church. Rooster was on the top step wearing a black suit and tie, standing beside a pastor, nodding at bikers as they made their way into the church.

Rick needed to wait with the other pall bearers and we stood to one side and watched people arriving. To anyone else their clothing might have looked like their everyday gear, and maybe even disrespectful for a house of worship, but I saw the changes, the marks of mourning. Mother Hubbard had taken off all her jewellery. Janie Spades had her hair pulled into a tight bun and stood off to the side of the steps in a simple black dress. Most of the women wore long sleeves, and several of the bikers had black ties on, hanging down the fronts of their Harley shirts. Coker had slicked his hair back and it looked both ridiculous and endearing. That morning I'd found the jacket I was wearing the day Billy Regret saved me from the boys of Lawrence Junior High and was wearing it over my black dress.

Rick put his arms around me. "You're shaking," he said quietly into my hair. I took hold of his hands and held onto him tight. I would be able to tell him. He was worth telling. It was worth giving him a chance to help me.

When it was time for him to take his place by the casket I went and sat in the front row as Rooster had told me to and waited while the church finished filling up. Janie slid in beside me and fixed one of the pins in my hair. She took my hand and, looking around the church, started to play absentmindedly with my fingernails the way she used to when I was a kid. Somehow knowing she was oblivious to my anger at her made me see how empty the anger was, and when I did, it was gone, and she was Janie again, and I was glad she was holding my hand. Janie always made me know there were some people you got so close to that they stopped seeing you as separate from themselves, no matter how much time had passed. I bet Janie didn't even know it was my hand she was worrying and not her own. I leaned against her shoulder to let her know she was not alone, which worked to let me know I wasn't either.

"I didn't know Billy Regret was Bapist," I whispered.

"Oh, he was a good Southern boy. Born and raised in a little Georgia town called Enigma. His mama's still down there. That's where he's going for burial. They're putting him on the Amtrak tonight. Rooster's going along to see he gets home safe." She mashed her lips together and I gripped her fingers.

The church had simple yellow walls, polished wooden pews and plain altar furniture. A modern stained glass window shone pastel light on the white flowers put out for Billy. The side door on the platform opened and the choir filed in and lined up in rows. Their robes were white with gold piping and their expressions were dignified and made me feel comforted that Billy's death was being taken seriously. The choir master entered, nodded, turned and raised his hands.

The choir began to sing slowly, bearing the words like a precious burden. *Mine eyes have seen the glory of the coming of the Lord...*

There was no preparation for the wave of feeling that the weighty fury of their words brought up in me. I had always known funerals to be sombre and sedate, full of organs and incense and a repetitive thankfulness for Christ's mercy at a time it was very hard to feel mercy was what you'd received. But as I turned to face the procession, and saw the men who meant the most to me in the world carrying on their shoulders the pale wood casket that held our Billy, I knew that the strength of the song in the throats of those singers was all that was holding me up.

Billy was placed on a stand just before the altar steps and as the choir reached the last lines and Rooster and Rick came and stood on either side of Janie and me I felt something different than I'd ever felt in church. I listened. I didn't know how 'the soul of wrong was His slave' given all that had happened to me in my life, but I supposed, if I was still standing, wrong hadn't won, and that maybe that alone was the point. If there was more bad than good in the world, there'd be no world.

An energy was rising around me and looking at the set to Rooster's jaw I realized what it was. We were not going to just let Billy Regret fade from the earth. Rooster planned this service and I knew without being told that it was he that chose to open with a battle hymn. It was an announcement, that song. We were going to war.

Reverend Wayne walked up the steps, laying his hand on Billy's casket as he went by. After the choir's last note he greeted us and spoke plainly about a Billy Regret I didn't know, a boy of eighteen from a small farm town. Wanting to see the country he'd build a motorcycle from

226

spare parts and rode it as far as it took him. The bike fell to pieces beneath him on the *Trenton Makes* Bridge. As a young assistant minister the Reverend had found Billy asleep on the meditation bench behind the church and helped him find a job and a place to live. The way he nodded at Rooster let me know exactly who had provided those.

The sermon, if it could be called that, so friendly it seemed to me, was over in fifteen minutes and the congregation was invited to speak. It was new to me, seeing everyday people take to the altar, and I watched as one after another, the bikers headed up and said their peace. Some read a few lines of poems or songs, some went up silently and raised a fist, some said only goodbye. Chipmunk kissed both her hands and laid them on top of the coffin. Dirty Mike took her place, looked down at the casket and said, "Ride the clouds buddy, skywrite us a little something so we know you ain't down below."

Without knowing what I was doing, I found myself standing before the altar, knowing I wanted witnesses for what I had to say about Billy Regret. I tried to collect my thoughts and all I could see was him hanging that little unicorn over the fence for me and leaving without a word. I looked up at the sea of bikers. "I used to think the world was always going to be a scary place, but then someone like Billy comes along and makes you realize that most of the time someone *does* come along. Before, during or after you're hurt, someone comes along. I used to think I'd lost my father, but fathering is something given to you by lots of people all through the course of your life. Billy was one of my dads. Goodbye Daddy Billy."

There was a connecting murmur from the people and as I looked up I saw someone in the back row, a woman in a beautiful suit wearing a black crinoline hat with ostrich feathers over her short hair. My mother, come to

227

pay her last respects, smiled at me. I smiled back and she raised her handkerchief as I took my place again.

The casket was then carried out to the sound of a gospel choir and three hundred bikers singing *Midnight Train to Georgia*. Sometimes singing is all the proof you need that something in the universe loves us all.

Rick and I stayed the night at Rooster's. Rick lived there most of the time since his mother moved to South Carolina to be near Cherokee. Rooster had gone on the train with Billy, and Janie had everyone back to the house. When the night was dark and nearly everyone had gone Rick asked me to go out to the dock with him. A month before, he had been approached by a recruiter on behalf of LoboChem. They'd offered him a great salary, benefits, things we knew none of the workers on the floors got. We'd laughed at the offer.

I was building up the courage to face telling him what had happened when he suddenly said, "I'm going to take it.

He didn't have to tell me what. I'd seen him talking to Freak Eddie for over an hour. "No," I said. Then I ran, off around the house and into the field that ran the long way to the road. I knew I couldn't outrun him. So did he. When I stopped and sat down in the grass he came and sat behind me, wrapping his arms around me. "Not for long," I said.

"No," he said into my hair. "Just long enough to end this."

It Takes a City

Rick knew something was on my mind. Rooster had taken to jibing me about growing up and not trusting him anymore. Janie was watching me with quiet suspicion. In front of my mother I was putting on award-worthy performances of good cheer.

I was sitting on the dock behind Rooster's when Toffee trotted purposefully across the grass, Freak Eddie at her side, his pirate patch replaced by a new glass eye. It took Rooster a while, but he finally found an ocularist who was able to match the electric green of the other, and do it without any questions. Toffee reached the end of the dock, sat down and let out a single bark.

"What are you doing here?" I started to laugh. And then I saw what Freak Eddie was carrying. The specimen bag that I'd abandoned at the canal hung from his hand, still covered in mud. I turned back to the water. I thought he might put it down or go away but this was Eddie. His heavy boots shook the dock as he walked over and sat beside me.

After all the time I spent trying to find a way to get the words together, Eddie did all the talking.

"I notice you ain't been saying nothing to no one." He said in the sure metal rattle of his voice. "Barely go near your boyfriend. Jump a mile when somebody walk up behind you. Now if you want to talk I expect there's a dozen people you might go to before me, and you ain't talkin' to any of 'em, so I ain't here to pry no confession. Fact, there's only one word you've got to say, and that's only under the condition that you feel like sayin' it. Now," he gave a little jerk to the bag in his hand, "I don't want to hear this ain't the bag you had with you. I don't want to hear you wasn't at the canal alone without tellin' a soul where you was goin'. I don't want to hear some son of a bitch security guard didn't try to rape you. I don't need to hear what you'd like to have done to him because I promise

I got worse in mind. I don't need to hear if or when you're goin' to tell Rick or Rooster. You got only one word you need to say to me. You got five minutes to say it. That word is *stop*. And unless I hear it, I'm goin' to take care of this."

So we sat, and I thought, and I waited, and I found that I did not want to say anything still, and it made me happier to know that finally my silence had turned into a good thing.

After five minutes Eddie put the specimen bag down between us. "Give that to your boyfriend for his laboratory. Tell him I'm busy takin' care of some business at the canal."

It didn't take him long to find the girls. Three seemed enough. The worst part was that each of them thought she was the only one and Eddie was sure there were more. He kept me apprised of everything, sitting down and telling the details to the river while we watched the water go by. He thought it was important that I know what was going on, that I should see justice in action.

Eddie got himself onto the visitor's list for the Detention Center and got the word out about who would be arriving inside. The more I listened the more it seemed Eddie knew everyone in Trenton. The day I was attacked, Coker had seen one of the security guards making his way along the canal path in a hurry, mud all over his knees and elbows. He'd mentioned to Eddie that the security guard had gone up to the office covered in mud. Bald guy, ruined nose. Used to be a boxer. Capper "Moonshine" Golding. Eddie's main job for the underground arm of the union was finding out who was on LoboChem's side, and who supported the workers. Golding had been hired in the middle of a hiring freeze. To Eddie this spelled out a favor owed.

Once Eddie had a name he spoke to a few friendly cops. Next it was the boxing gyms.

230

When the girls agreed to press charges, Golding got word of it and started keeping a low profile. He'd moved out of his mother's house and she was claiming he'd left the state. Eddie didn't buy it. And he knew no matter where Golding was he wouldn't be able to stay away from the ring. In a dive called *Hero's Boxing World* Eddie found what he was looking for. He waited outside. Golding had grown his hair a little but Eddie recognized him. There was no hiding that nose.

Golding had been sparring and was tired when he stepped out, still rotating his shoulders, and saw Noelle putting her lipstick on in the side view mirror of a van. "You Moonshine?" she asked.

"I'll be anybody for you," Golding said, stepping into the alley where the van was parked. Noelle crooked her finger for him to come closer. It was quick work for Eddie and Kurt to get a sack over his head and throw him into the back door of the van.

"Remember you said that darlin'," Noelle told the struggling body before she got out and ran down the street to where Dutchman was waiting for her.

Eddie admitted there was a certain satisfaction in taking the former legend down to Perry Street and opening up the back of the van. Bound at his ankles and feet and with the sack still over his head Golding shook and finally pissed himself while negotiations for his body settled on 'two hundred dollars for three days'. He struggled while Kurt and Eddie pulled him from the vehicle, knocking the sunglasses that Kurt had taken to wearing. With the help of Coker and Dirty Mike, who'd done a fine acting job as the voices of the pimps, they carried him around in a circle to make him think he was being moved and threw him back in the van. Dirty Mike jumped in the front to drive, and keeping up his act, told Golding what he would be submitting to. At one point, Kurt laughed, out of nerves, but it worked to the illusion, because Golding began to cry at

231

that point. "Don't use up all them tears," Dirty Mike said, getting back into his role after Kurt's outburst, "The kind of guys who'll be fucking you like a cry baby. Something sweet about a little cry baby, huh?"

Golding was shaking violently. Deciding he'd been suitably scared, they drove back to North Trenton and dumped him on the front lawn of a well-kept house on Pear Street. The van pulled away and the men watched from up the street as Officer McCool opened the front door of his house and ran his hand over his white blond crew cut while he looked at the bound figure that had just rolled into his birdbath. He reached inside for a radio, made a call and then went to Golding and crouched down to unfasten his ropes. Just before he took off the hood he raised his fist, only shoulder height, but Eddie received the message for what it was and drove away.

I told Eddie how touched I was that Kurt helped out. Eddie told me Kurt didn't want me to know, that all he'd said was he wanted me to feel like I didn't have to look over my shoulder for the rest of my life.

From there we just had to wait. Golding had warrants, plus the new charges from the other girls he'd attacked, so he was off to the Detention Center with a few men waiting on his arrival, then court, then prison where he would find a few more people who'd been reached by Eddie's word. Even convicts hate rapists.

On the first day of the trial Rick and I got to the courthouse early. Eddie was right, it had helped me to know about the process of justice as he helped it along. By the time the court date came I wanted to see justice stand on its own two feet. I was glad that Golding was going to face the judge. It was in all the papers. Word on the street was that no one was surprised.

"Who's that?" I asked Rick as we sat a few rows back from the prosecutor's bench.

232

Rick had taken an interest in the case alongside mine, and to his credit, no matter what he suspected, had never confronted me directly to find out the truth behind my sudden interest in the legal system.

"That," he said, "Is Delorae Donofrio, former Miss New Jersey semi-finalist and mother of Capper Moonshine Golding. She was the sweetheart of more than a few high rollers in Atlantic City, which is how she had connections to get Capper going when he started to show some skill with boxing."

I looked at the defence table, "Expensive suits," I said.

Rick lowered his voice, "Those are LoboChem lawyers. I recognize a couple of them. That one on the end I don't. They've brought in someone who specializes in criminal law to argue the case. Funny how the LoboChem lawyers were well-versed enough to prepare most of it though." Rick rarely showed much in the way of fear or anger but just then his eyes looked fierce. These were the people who undid his family. He had his own internal battle going on. "I didn't want to tell you Hope, I know how badly you want to see this guy in jail for what he did to those girls, but Delorae Donofrio never lost her taste for high rollers. She's dating Gordon Lobo. That's how her son was hired during a hiring freeze."

I took Rick's hand. After Billy's funeral I found I didn't have trouble being near Rick as long as we didn't rough house the way we used to. It had been slower coming back to that kind of horseplay than sex. I didn't associate sex with the attack, but feeling the force of a man's strength still made me feel vulnerable, though I was improving. Eddie had helped me see that my physical strength wasn't the strength that was going to protect me. What would protect me, he said, was telling the right people when I needed help, and using my brain to gather all the information I could. Freak Eddie had borrowed one of

Rick's suits. Every day of the trial, he sat in the back row wearing a pair of tinted glasses to cover his green eyes.

The trial lasted ten days. Each of the girls gave her testimony and I alternated between watching them and watching Golding. I don't know if my feelings would have softened if I'd seen any sorrow or remorse on his face, but I didn't get to find out. He looked impassive for most of the trial, and at each break, turned and smiled and shook hands with people who'd shown up and sat near him. His mother sat directly behind him, every day. She was a glamorous woman, in her late forties, who wore good Versace knockoffs and trophy jewellery.

I watched her profile when the court was shown photographs of the contusions on the bodies of the three girls. One had a bruise on her cheek just where mine was and I felt Rick's hand tighten on mine for a moment. Capper's mother also showed nothing, only the low level defensiveness I suspected she carried everywhere. She'd made a statement to the press that people had always been trying to get a piece of Capper; that she was used to it.

The trial was over quickly. The physical evidence from two of the girls who had seen a doctor immediately afterward was dismissed on a technicality, and the women discredited as witnesses for having been seen socializing in the bars Golding frequented. The strength of the third case relied on the other two since the woman had not gone to a doctor, only told her girlfriend immediately afterward. On charges of three counts of rape, Capper Moonshine Golding's conviction was lowered to assault and he was assigned 1,000 hours of community service. The judge looked disgusted and I hoped it was on behalf of the victims.

From several rows up I heard Eddie's knuckles crack. I thought it was a piece of my mind snapping loose, like a tie rod under too much pressure. I had the sense that one more bump might send me wildly out of control. There

234

was a murmur from the defence table and Delorae reached forward and put her hands on Capper's shoulders. I admit I was thinking of murder.

A tall cop came walking down the aisle and leaned over the barricade to the prosecution table. I could see his white blond hair under his hat. It was Officer McCool.

When McCool stepped back, the district attorney conferred with the three women and then addressed the judge. "Your honor, in light of the judgement may we approach?"

The courtroom went quiet again as both attorneys spoke with the judge. When they returned to their seats the judge addressed the court. His expression had changed, to one of mild satisfaction. "In light of the discrepancy between the crime the jury agrees has been committed and the sentence handed down, it is reasonable that those upon whom these crimes have been committed have a say in the manner in which the defendant will serve his sentence, within the confines of the law and the opinion of this court. Therefore, Capper Golding will serve the state of New Jersey by delivering no less than 1,000 hours of community service on the Delaware-Raritan Canal cleanup crew." He leaned toward the table of LoboChem lawyers. "He will wear exactly the standard provided uniform and he will serve his time on the section of the canal immediately behind the LoboChem factory. He will at no time be assisted by anyone in the LoboChem organization." The judge then turned to Golding, "Capper Golding, it would be in your best interest to make certain you never again darken the doorstep of a New Jersey courtroom. In the meantime, I hope you're not afraid of the water."

It turned out Golding *was* afraid of the water, and Eddie, after putting out word to the canal crew, went by once a day to see he got plenty of exposure to it. He brought me down on his Sportster once to watch for myself. Golding had been a welterweight, so, seeing they had an audience, when a few knocks didn't land Golding in the water, two members of the crew picked him up and threw him in. The guard, conveniently, was looking in the other direction.

On the way back from that canal trip, Eddie pulled in to the Colonial Diner and took a booth in the back. It was best with Eddie not to say much, and only to ask questions when you really had to, so I sat quietly and in a few minutes a young nurse came in. I recognized Ditsy Marie and we hugged for old times' sake. When I motioned to the uniform she said she had graduated from the LPN course at Mercer and now worked at the LoboChem infirmary with her mother.

Eddie waved the waitress into action and she brought us coffees.

"How's Noelle and Angel? He get that flu going around?"

"Strong as an ox. Gonna be beating me up soon. Noelle can't barely lift him. She sent pictures." Eddie passed her an envelope. She took it smoothly and in return, handed over a thick manila envelope.

Eddie opened it and took out a set of photocopies.

"I didn't even believe you when you asked me," she said, "They're not LoboChem employees, but our doctor is going and seeing them at County Corrections. What on earth are they examining the canal crew for?"

Eddie began to read, "You looked at this?"

"Didn't have time Ed, nearly got caught putting the originals back in Dr. Crag's office."

Eddie showed her the chart in his hand.

"Jesus Eddie, this is the same weird stuff the doctor checks for in the guys in Development. Blood tests for metals. Body hair counts? Iris colour changes? What do they think is happening to these guys?"

236

Eddie took off his sunglasses and she looked at his bright green eyes. "Oh God, Eddie, they're dumping it in the canal water?"

We stopped at Kinko's and made extra copies of the reports. Back at my house, Eddie pulled into a space to drop me off. My mother was standing on the lawn in her work clothes, with Toffee sitting beside her. Eddie gave her the envelope from Ditsy Marie. In exchange she handed him Toffee's collar, and my suspicions about the night when everyone was arrested were confirmed. My dog had been wearing Eddie's tracker for five years, though I guess Mom only found out recently. Eddie walked Mom to her car while I took Toffee and put her in the Barracuda. She looked naked without her collar but to me it also seemed as if she'd been freed of a heavy load. I scratched around where the band had left a dent in her coat. And then something occurred to me. I took a breath and parted the hairs between Toffee's shoulders. I searched patiently, knowing I'd find the dark blue inky letters. And there they were: LOBOCHEM. Toffee: the last wolf-cross puppy stolen from the fields behind the barrel yard.

I gave her a hug. Before he left, Eddie told me to stay at Rooster's until the evening. I drove to the train station and picked up Michael Smiley who had taken the express train from New York. In Rooster's office I gave him the health records of the cleanup crew and he asked to borrow the phone. The first number he called was the Commissioner at the Department of Corrections. The Commissioner had a loud voice and Michael grinned at me when he bellowed through the phone that he was going to get straight on to the infirmary at LoboChem. Dr. Peter Crag would be told to surrender all of his files on the cleanup crew or face losing his licence.

I spent the rest of the day manning Rooster's office, staying within earshot of the phone, and faxing papers for Michael.

One by one, people began to arrive. First was Janie who went and started up the barbeque. I helped her get the food ready and brought the radio out on the porch. Then my Mom came. She'd changed into a T shirt and jeans and sat beneath the shade of a maple tree. Noelle and Angel got there next and my mother spread out another blanket for them. Coker, Ditsy Marie, Dirty Mike, and finally Rick were all there when Eddie and Rooster's bikes rumbled up the drive.

"Dr. Crag's first reaction to the phone call was to contact the lawyers at LoboChem. You know, Dr. Crag is a nervous man, he can't keep anything quiet. As soon as he was off the phone with them he broke out into a sweat, and called his own lawyer." Ditsy Marie told us, "You should have heard him shouting. He's in there hollering *'The company lawyers are saying make sure the records are never found and you want me to hand them over to the DoC?'* I could see him, his face red as a tomato. Next thing he slammed the phone down and came out to where I was sitting with a 'new employee' who was waiting to have blood drawn." She nodded at Rick.

"Maybe he trusted me because I was in a suit," Rick said, "But all I told him was 'lose the keys'. He put them on the table beside me and walked out the door. Next thing I knew the cops were there."

Coker lit a cigarette, then, remembering himself, walked far away from my mother with it. "Old Dr. Crag kept on walking, straight past the vats, out to the loading dock and through the parking lot, still in his white coat. Everybody in the place knew something was up."

Dirty Mike laughed. "I was in the truck, waiting to load, looking straight at McCool's cruiser. McCool got out and the doc froze. When McCool passed him through the

238

gate with the subpoena, Doc pulled off his coat and threw it in a dumpster, jumped in his Lexus and split."

Michael took a glass that Janie offered. "The Commissioner at the DoH is also in." He toasted my mother with his iced tea and she nodded graciously, having executed her role as asked.

"Well, at least you can go get yourself a decent job now," Janie said to Rick. "You can hand in your notice as quick as you please."

Rooster raised his hands suddenly and we all went quiet. The radio announcer had come on with a news flash. Although we missed the beginning, Rooster quieted us in time to hear the end:

...The fire came to the attention of the police at approximately 2:30pm today. Hamilton and Lawrence Townships have sent backup response units to assist with the blaze. Given the hazardous nature of the chemicals kept in large store on the site police are now beginning the evacuation of the North Trenton area surrounding the LoboChem factory. Residents are asked to report to the non-denominational shelter that has been set up at Our Lady Queen of Angels parochial school.

Rooster met eyes with each one of us, ending with Rick. "Sounds like they've saved you the trouble," he said.

Purple Mountain Highway

The highway crosses a landscape where red earth fades into smoky purple mountains that recline around the rim of the sky. I can see the horizon for 360 degrees. The world is so much bigger than I ever knew it was.

I told Rick what happened that last day at the canal, finally. I went to see a therapist a few times and she helped me see that I didn't want any more secrets in my new life. If I was going to be in a relationship, I wanted it to be with someone who saw the same things I saw. Rick and I came up with our own kind of therapy for me, and between him and Rooster and Dutchman, I passed my motorcycle licence test in record time.

Riding alone is different than being on the back, I can see everything and I feel awake. I feel the need to be awake in a way I never did when I was a passenger and the ride was a matter of trust. Now the person to trust is me.

Billy Regret left only three things in his will. What money he had went to his mother. His tools went to Rooster. His chopper he left to me. Coker scratched his head about the modifications for a while but I think he was also struggling with the idea of tampering with Billy's bike. But then one day he announced that there was simply no way for me to ride it the way it was and a month later I got my bike.

Following the fire, Michael Smiley's story appeared in the Times. It didn't help LoboChem any that Gordon Lobo hopped a private plane to Nevada shortly after the blaze was called in, proving he knew more than anyone that North Trenton was no place to be with his factory on fire.

One of the clauses Rick's dad had included in the sale contract of Bantam Barrels was that Rooster reserved the right to buy the property back for sale cost should LoboChem ever choose to sell it. The factory was burned beyond repair but after Michael's article was syndicated,

241

the EPA swarmed to the site. This resulted in a major cleanup on a federal budget. Lobo sold and the bikers owned a piece of canal real estate again, and at 1970's prices. After the settlement, Coker and the others used their compensation money to set up a North Trenton Harley dealership, right over the spot where Rooster's office used to sit, and allowed the surrounding land to go fallow for a while, and heal itself. On their lunch breaks, the guys from Angel Harley-Davidson sit out back of the garage and watch egrets fish the canal, though they still won't fish it themselves just yet.

But not this month. I finished my degree at the same time Rick was awarded his Master's, and to celebrate, the dealership decided to go on vacation. There's a *Closed for Sturgis* sign in the window next to the new calendar which has a picture of me on Billy's chopper on the front cover.

Riding through open country I remember my first ride with Eddie and the way I used to dream of escaping the narrow streets of home. Up ahead of me a red headed woman waves for me to catch up. The sun is setting in a thousand amber swords across the dessert. Rays hit the pack of bikes on the road and cleave the chrome, which gleams across the highway like angel's wings. I look at the sidecar on my bike, at Toffee with her special dog goggles that Mom got an optician to make. A worn out atlas is fastened into a side pocket, out of the wind. I hardly need it with all the bikers around me, but I had to bring it, for old times' sake.

I start to catch up to my family just as an Indian brave with a long black braid pulls up beside me. I think about what he told me today, about his acceptance letter regarding a postdoctoral position at the University of Colorado where I am interested in an MA program. For all I've wanted to travel, I never realized how hard it is to say goodbye to home. Of course we'll go back, but visiting isn't the same as watching a place change slowly under your feet. Visitors don't get to see a pod of five-legged frogs born or egrets appear in salvaged wilderness or a tree of heaven sprout back up out of charred ground, green like it should be. But I am looking forward to mountain air. I'm looking forward to clear streams.

A neon sign draws us off the highway and into the forecourt of a fifties-style motel and diner. We decided as a group to take the very long way around. I shut off my bike and look up at the sign, *The Grand Canyonder. Spectacular Views and Good Coffee*, it boasts.

I'm the last one in, having taken Toffee to our room before joining the rest. She's an old dog now and likes her quiet when she's not riding. In the diner, the group have taken up the tables along the front window, from the cash register to the side door. Rooster is lecturing Rick about types of motor oil, telling him *he doesn't care what Rick thinks he knows now that he's going to be Dr. Rayetayah*. About motor oil and all things Harley, Rooster is always right. Mom is pulling her hair into a ponytail and trying to find something healthy on the menu. She's put some weight back on and is looking like her cocky self again, if a little softer.

Spirit in the Sky is playing from an old Wurlitzer juke box in the corner. It's been 24 years since the song was released but you wouldn't know it by the vibe in the air. Time means nothing in Magic America.

"You block aisle. Little girl need to find seat. There," the tall blonde waitress nods with her pink hairnet. I look down the table and see a seat beside Rick that I would have sworn was empty when I glanced a moment earlier. The waitress works her way down the table, filling coffee cups, and then goes outside for a smoke break.

Rick motions for me to come over but I mouth to him that I'll be back. They'll be there a while, talking about tomorrow, which are the best roads and where to stop. I have some time.

Seeing my family is happy, I go outside and sit on the curb next to Ivka Repinka. Ivka has switched to one of those smokeless smokes and her pink uniform is made of organic cotton. She scolds me for coming out to talk to her rather than sitting by Rick, but I can see she's secretly pleased. Then she goads me for a little while, making me say that she was right all along, that all along everything was going to be OK, just like she said. I have to say out loud that she is the best Ivka ever, and that I've never wanted another one. Satisfied then, she touches my biker boots with a glittering fingernail and the leather begins to spin with psychedelic pinwheels.

And Ivka is right. Everything is OK. Everything always was, just because one day it was going to be. We keep living and trying and learning and loving and hurting and bleeding and sacrificing and laughing and then one day, it's all just OK. We believe in the dark. And then one day, we know. Out under an open sky in big country, we know.

I sit back and Ivka Repinka smokes her electric cigarette while we watch the sun set in wild pink waves over America.